I0598177

The Van Gogh Deception

Michael Paulson

BooksForABuck.com
2010

Michael Paulson

The Van Gogh Deception

Copyright 2010 by Michael Paulson, all rights reserved. No portion of this novel may be duplicated, transmitted, or stored in any form without the express written permission of the publisher.

Warning: The unauthorized reproduction or distribution of this copyrighted work is illegal. Criminal copyright infringement, including infringement without monetary gain, is investigated by the FBI and is punishable by up to 5 years in federal prison and a fine of $250,000.

This is a work of fiction. All characters, events, and locations are fictitious or used fictitiously. Any resemblance to actual events or people is coincidental.

BooksForABuck.com
December 2010
ISBN: 978-1-60215-135-2

Chapter 1
An Overheard Conversation

The color of Paris is gray.

You are probably thinking how can *La Ville-Lumière*—the city of lights—be gray?

I came to that conclusion after moving into my flat, an hour ago. I reside on the first floor of a boarding house above *Cafe de Flore* at number 17172 Boulevard Saint-Germaine. The building is Haussmannian in architecture. It was built around 1860. The landlady of this not-so-luxuriant establishment, Mme. Flaubert, is a libidinous soul of seventy-some years.

There are four floors in her establishment. Each contains four apartments—except for the top one. The penthouse suite, where Mme. Flaubert resides, occupies that entire level. The dear woman needs the space. You see, she shares her expansive quarters with two young men.

I will let you think about that. But be warned. No matter how you construe it, you will be spot-on.

According to Mme. Flaubert, my rent includes the evening meal. Each dining, she assured me, would be an unforgettable experience. Unfortunately, I missed this evening's offering while reclaiming my trunk from a storage rental. This, of course, explains the unending growling from my stomach.

Bathing and bodily-function facilities are as convenient as in any Parisian boarding-house, or so Mme. Flaubert claimed. Merely a brisk jaunt to the staircase, followed by a two-floor sprinting ascension, supplanted by a leisurely lope down the third floor hall to the last door on the left. What could be more opportune in the middle of a cold night?

My name is Stuart S. Stuart. The 'S' also stands for Stuart. I was named after my uncle who, at the time of my christening, was regarded as the epitome of success—at least for my family. Why not? Uncle Stuart is educated. He is an artist of some repute. But, most importantly, my uncle is very rich. However, reputations are often misleading.

Some time after I graduated from high school, Interpol instigated allegations concerning Uncle Stuart. At the end of these, this international police agency claimed to have proof that my uncle's fortune was acquired through theft. More precisely, Uncle Stuart forged works-of-art by various masters and sold them to an unsuspecting public. As you might suspect, those who were cheated wanted my uncle's blood. Fortunately, at least for my uncle, he was able to avoid arrest by abandoning his beautiful villa at *Cote d'Azur* in France, and fleeing to a slightly smaller accommodation in Sao Paulo, Brazil.

If you are wondering why a move from France to Brazil would be expedient when Interpol is in hot pursuit, the answer is quite simple. In Brazil, extradition laws do not apply.

Naturally, my family was stunned by Interpol's claims. My mother immediately disowned Uncle Stuart. In fact, the entire Stuart Clan agreed it was the best thing to do. Except for me, of course. How could I? During my school years I spent every summer with Uncle Stuart, enjoying France and all it had to offer. Besides, what business was it of mine how my uncle earned his living? If the rest of the world had a complaint against him, so be it. But leave me out of the ruckus.

Like my disreputable uncle, I am an artist: a painter. Unlike him, I do not create forgeries. I must confess, however, to replicating the techniques of Degas, Miro, Klimt, Matisse, and Van Gogh numerous times while being tutored by Uncle Stuart. He insisted. But those paintings were merely his way of instructing me in the painter's craft.

Unfortunately, my own creations, while technically well-formed, are bereft of soul—or so goes the general critique. At first I took offense at this assessment. Could the critics not see the depth and breadth of my talents? Did I not depict all the nuances of each image in precise detail? In each work, had I not captured the breathtaking techniques of a dozen or more masters of the art? Then it slowly sank in. The critics were absolutely correct. I was mimicking life on canvas instead of capturing it.

What was I to do? Abandon my dream? An artist lives only when he creates. Anything less is mere existence.

I did, quite briefly, consider joining forces with Uncle Stuart. But when I suggested it, my mother threatened suicide. She did so with such fervor the poor dear required hospitalization. My father, of course, celebrated her invalided departure. After nearly thirty years of a marriage built upon mutual tolerance, he was looking forward to what he hoped would be her funeral.

But I am digressing from my story.

It was Uncle Stuart who suggested I go to France. There, or so he declared, I would find the creative inspiration I lacked. But how would I survive? The cost of living in Paris is unconscionably high. To my delight, Uncle Stuart offered to fund the entire venture. So I packed my bags and made the journey.

But after several months of trying to stimulate my creative juices, artistic success continued to elude me. Uncle Stuart told me I was trying too hard. He said to give it time. That, all I needed was one great adventure and it would come together.

I was willing to persevere, of course. What young artist would not enjoy living in Paris? The sights. The smells. Well, the sights, anyway.

Unfortunately, about that same time my source of funding became an issue with my mother. She vowed to hang herself if I took another nickel from Uncle Stuart. Naturally, my father told me to ignore her threats. If there was a chance of my mother stretching a rope, he wanted to explore it. I, being a loving son, immediately complied with my mother's wishes. I instructed Uncle Stuart to refrain from sending my monthly stipend.

That decision, of course, did not work out well. Within a short time, I was evicted from my hotel. A few days after that, I ran out of money entirely. In fact, I was at the point of selling my blood to purchase passage back to the United States when Uncle Stuart stepped in, again. If I could not accept his money, then he would assist by finding me employment. To that end, he arranged an internship at *Musée du Louvre*.

My work at the world's most famous museum is undemanding. I am employed by the painting-restoration department on the second floor of the Richelieu wing. It is not a glamorous job. I am a paint color-mixer, and general helper. The pay is not great. But it meets my needs. In fact, my first week's remittance allowed me to abandon the dumpster, in which I was sleeping, for this depressingly gray flat.

I have one friend in Paris. A sympathetic coworker named Maryse Rousseau. She took pity on me after hearing about my difficulties in locating reasonably priced accommodations. It was through her intervention with Mme. Flaubert that I came by this less than luminous residence. Not that I decry Maryse's assistance. Quite the contrary! Without her, I would still be studying the walls of that dumpster instead of the unending gray in this dismal flat.

Naturally, after receiving Maryse's kind assistance I extended an offer in kind. Surprisingly, she did have a small request. Maryse asked me to store a very ugly sculpture, in my flat.

I, of course, agreed. Who was I to deride a five-foot welded-construction of cast-off automobile parts supported by a massive lead base clumsily inset with chips of glass? Particularly, since the creator of that metal monstrosity was none other than Maryse Rousseau.

Considering Maryse's assistance in securing this flat for me, you are probably wondering about her relationship with the ribald Mme. Flaubert. It is the same as mine. In fact, Maryse lives next door to me. I find that quite erotic. I find everything about her quite erotic. Right now, through the thin wall separating our flats, I can hear Maryse puttering about. Naturally, I am imagining her doing so stark naked.

Stop scolding. I know it is a crude way to mentally treat my one and only friend. But you must understand. Maryse Rousseau, unlike this fetid place of repose, is breathtakingly beautiful. I and my magic-nightstick—that all-reasoning tool each man carries between his legs—are fascinated by her. In fact, whenever she comes near we both rise to the occasion.

Yes, yes. Considering my romantic history—or the successful lack thereof—getting involved with a woman is the last thing I should be considering. Unfortunately, my all-controlling nightstick operates on a level quite distinct from cognitive reasoning. As such, I am trapped within his resolve to pursue and propagate with the beautiful Maryse!

For a French woman, Maryse Rousseau is tall. She is also very slender with shining black hair. It drifts down her back like molten basalt. From behind, if one is watching her hair instead of another hypnotically moving attribute, her tresses catch the light and shimmer. It is as if the basalt is cooling into reflective crystals only to re-melt each time she moves. Her skin is tanned a caramel hue. It looks as soft as warm butter and gives off an intoxicating vanilla scent. Her eyes are large and brown with flecks of gold, and jade. One look from those and my heart melts. Her ears are tiny and delicately formed. She adorns the lobes with diminutive, gold earrings. Her lips are full. When they spread into a smile, my passions leap. When they pout, my magic-nightstick tries to beat its way out of my whiter-than-whites, in order to assuage her unhappiness. Her nose is exquisite. I have no doubt it was carved by an angel.

From the front, most men would agree that Maryse could start her own dairy. From the back, the allure is heart-thumping. From any direction, watching her stride is like seeing a moving metronome with wondrous attachments. When she bends over, it is a religious experience! I have only seen her do this once. But the vision is emblazoned upon my memory like a firebrand. Each night, before I go to sleep, I replay that scene in my head—several hundred times.

Unfortunately, Maryse is married. Although, strictly speaking, she is estranged from her husband. They are going through a divorce. I have not been told the details. But it is quite obvious she is the one who desires to be shed of him. I have never met her husband, but I imagine he is suicidal over their separation. Who would not be?

There is no need to cluck your tongue. I know, I know. Falling for someone who is married is futile. However I cannot help myself. Maryse Rousseau is my fantasy come-to-life. And from my magic-nightstick's prospective, she is a Godsend. He has been dancing ever since I first laid eyes upon her. I suppose if I were to admit it, Maryse is an addiction. But what an addiction! One visual dose of her and I am sprinting through clouds all day! Curiously, I feel as though I have known Maryse for some time. Long before this latest trip to France. But that is impossible. I would have remembered her awe-inspiring attributes.

Getting back to my hideous domicile…

My flat has one room. This is quite large and rectangular. It has a very high ceiling. But it has only one window. Consequently, trying to make my flat double as a studio will be extremely difficult. There would not be enough light. The window, itself, is a small, vertical-swinging affair. Beyond it is a view of the alley and the usual collection of garbage cans. On the other side of the alley is an abandoned warehouse. The latter lifts seven gloomy, brick stories to the sky. Its broken windows seem to stare down at me, accusingly. Probably, because of last night's dream concerning Maryse and my magic-nightstick.

My flat has three pieces of furniture: A gray velveteen davenport, which pulls out into a bed; a full-length mirror, for those occasions when a young man might dress to go out for a romantic evening; and, a makeshift table of bricks and planks. The table rests between the davenport and the window. The mirror is propped at an angle, in one corner— next to Maryse's hideous sculpture.

As mirrors go, it is not the best. In fact, it is cracked from top to bottom right down the middle. But I don't plan any outings, any time soon. Consequently, I do not anticipate a need for its reflecting qualities.

The wooden floor in my flat has been painted countless times. How could it not since first being laid in 1860? Each coat of paint varies slightly in color. However every layer of pigment is one shade of gray or another. In several places these have worn so thin I can see the wood-grain in the planks.

Curiously, the paint is nonexistent in a single spot about the size of a basketball. This anomaly is midway between the door, and the window. Upon examination, I took this to be the result of tap-dancing footfalls by countless previous residents, desperately trying to dissuade a resolute band of invading cockroaches. However that theory does not take into consideration the finger-size hole in the ceiling directly above the spot.

But once more, I have drifted.

What is the first thing you notice about a place, when entering? Its design? Its color? Its size? No. You notice its odors.

Smell is unavoidable in a building. The new ones reek of paint and resins. The old ones are fouled by the leavings of previous inhabitants. Ancient ones, like Mme. Flaubert's Boarding House, are standouts in the stench arena.

Right now, my nasal passages are in a state of torment. Try as they might, my nostrils cannot filter the overpowering essences of garlic, urine, mold, more urine, vinegar, and even more urine. Doubtlessly, the lengthy traverse to the toilet explains at least one of the prevailing odors. Be that as it may the stench makes my eyes water, my sinuses clamp shut, and my magic-nightstick hide its head. Perhaps if I open the window…

Will you look? There I am, my reflection trapped in that broken mirror. Can you believe it? I have the coiffure and beard of a Neanderthal. Not to mention those deep hollows in my cheeks, and the dark smears beneath my eyes. I am coming across like something black-haired from a Neolithic cave!

Never mind. Tonight, I shall get a good rest. Tomorrow I will not only look considerably better but I shall receive my second pay-packet. Since my rent is paid, those monies can be used for a luxury or two. Obviously, a haircut is overdue as well as a beard-trim. And, if there are a few coins left over, I shall treat my wardrobe to a trip to the nearest launderette.

Did you hear that? Out in the alley something crashed.

For those of you who have not visited France and are considering it, we Americans are hated here. Even when fluent in the language, as I am, we are openly reviled. If you are mugged in Paris, do not bother to telephone the police. They will not come to your assistance. If you are injured, the same is true for emergency medical services. You will have to manage your own surgical procedures - whereupon you will be arrested for practicing medicine without a license. Right now, I suspect a burglar is on the prowl out there. Excuse me while I check it out.

Ah, the source of the noise is quite obvious. Fortunately, members of the Parisian criminal element are not responsible. Working in unison, a dozen or so rats have toppled a garbage can. Will you look at them? They're the size of well-fed cats. In fact, every one of them is plump enough to roast. A little salmorejo sauce, a glass of burgundy, then for desert... Dear God, what am I thinking?

"Damn it, Buji, we've waited three months for that money!"

Before you start scolding, that was not me cursing. It was someone else. I do not know who. I am supposed to be alone in my flat. At least I hope I am alone. I certainly did not agree to double occupancy when Mme. Flaubert and I negotiated price—despite her hand on my thigh.

"Calm down, Bouvier. We'll talk to him. We'll get our cut."

That also was not me. It is a different male voice from the first. Triple occupancy? Mme. Flaubert will certainly hear about this—unless, of course, the other occupants are diseased figments of my imagination, or they have a picnic basket to share. A leg of chicken... Some potato salad... Maybe a garlic pickle...

"And if the dirty bastard continues to stall?"

That was definitely not my imagination. It was the first voice, again. Without a doubt, that fellow is a type 'A' personality with homicidal tendencies.

"We won't give him that option."

I have never been a believer in the supernatural. Spooks are fantasy material for novels, and movies. But the rising hairs on the nape of my neck suggest something in my little hovel is seriously not right—smells aside.

"Your frigid bitch might think otherwise. What then?"

"Leave her to me!"

If you were a fly on the wall you would see me slowly turn away from the window and dart my eyes from corner to corner. Doubtlessly, my eyes would look enormous. Not that I have enormous eyes. But they get that way when I am terrified. And what could be more terrifying than a pair of ghosts holding a conversation—in my flat?

No. My original contention of single occupancy is completely correct. There is not a living soul in sight. So, I must be hearing complaints from the dead.

"I say we cut Baudouin out, altogether!"

Baudouin? Where had I heard that name before? I think it was at work. Or had Mme. Flaubert mentioned it when she told me there was a third opening in need of filling?

I will let you think about that, too.

"You're going to get us all killed, Bouvier!"

"Not if we handle it right."

Ah, so the voices are coming from the mirror. There is, as I recall, precedence for such hauntings. I do not remember the title of the story. But it involved a beautiful young woman, a vain stepmother, a poisoned apple and seven little guys who had a diamond mine.

"Don't be ridiculous!"

"The greedy bastard's getting a third, isn't he? For what, Buji? Sitting on the diamonds for three months and then stalling on the payout? If you don't have the stomach for killing Baudouin, I'll do it!"

Wonderful! Not only does my flat stink, but it is haunted by Murder Incorporated.

"If you kill Baudouin, François Chiappe will hunt us down. I didn't steal sixty million to end up in that Mafioso's sights."

Diamonds? Sixty million? François Chiappe? Mafioso? Not only was I listening to ghosts, but rich ghosts who were acquainted with the current head of the Corsican Mafia!

"Chiappe doesn't worry me."

"Then you're a fool!"

"I say we put it to a vote, Buji."

Democracy in action among the dead? Who would have thought?

I went over to the mirror and tilted it toward me. Other than a wall fitted with a ventilation cover, there was nothing behind it. Then I heard the sound of scraping chairs. This was followed by the tap-tapping of quickly receding footfalls.

Obviously, those noises are coming through the ventilator. Well, that is better than having a pipeline to ghost-hell. But where would that conversation have originated? There is the café, directly below. Those two men could have been sitting in chairs beneath an overhead vent. But the source could also have been from somewhere else. Such as in Mme. Flaubert's Boarding House?

I set the mirror aside, shoved the sculpture away and then squatted down in front of the vent. The two mounting screws were loose as if it had been removed recently. Had some prankster placed an electronic device behind it to play the dialogue I had just heard? The French are known for their love of playing pranks on Americans.

Using my thumbnail I backed out the screws and removed the cover. But to my surprise, nothing out of the ordinary was being hidden by the cover. Well, nothing that would replay a recorded dialogue. But there was one small curiosity. Mounted next to the ventilation pipe was a brass speaking tube, its open end pointed toward the vent cover. So, had the sound come through the vent or out of the speaking tube? Was the tube connected to the restaurant? Or was it connected to another apartment? Perhaps, Madam Flaubert's?

I pushed the cover back in place, and then thumbed the screws in to hold it there. Then I stood up and put the mirror and sculpture back into their respective spots.

I know what you're thinking. I should telephone the police. But what would I tell them? Some crony of François Chiappe is going to be killed? What's new about that? Mobsters probably lose a man every month to nefarious action.

Yes, yes. I agree I have a responsibility to all of humanity. But you're not considering possibilities. Although I did not find an electronic device to replay a recording, the entire conversation still could have been a joke. Isn't it more likely that two other tenants at Mme. Flaubert's, sitting in front of the vent or speaking tube in another flat, staged the entire conversation for my benefit?

All right, all right. I agree it *could* be for real. I admit the anger in the voices sounded genuine. But you're forgetting the Parisian perception of Americans. I could possess a taped confession, a video of the forthcoming murderous event, and serve popcorn topped with slightly salted Béarnaise sauce during its viewing. And still the police would doubt my veracity.

No. I don't care what you say! I'm staying out of this.

Chapter 2
Unexpected Turns

Musée du Louvre has a grand history. Originally, it was a 12th century fortress built by King Philippe Auguste. He called it Palais du Louvre. Under Louis IX the Louvre became the home of the royal treasury. When the Bourbons took control of France in 1589, Henry IV stamped his own style onto the structure by removing remnants of the original medieval fortress. Then, in the early 1600s, Louis XIII razed the entire north wing as the start of yet another renovation. Modifications by various owners continued until the Louvre's conversion to a public museum on November 8, 1793—a direct result of the French Revolution.

If you are wondering why the French Revolution is to blame for the Louvre becoming a public museum, the answer is quite simple. What else does one do with a big fancy box after guillotining its residents?

Nearly nine million people visit Musée du Louvre, annually. World-wide, it is the busiest of all museums. This, of course, can be attributed to the 300,000 paintings and sculptures on display. Besides traditional art, the Louvre exhibits archeology, history, architecture and furniture. In fact, art at the Louvre comes in all forms—except mine.

My supervisor there is M. René D'aubigne. He is an expert painting-restorer, with nearly thirty years of experience. No one is more highly regarded by the Louvre's management, the Réunion des Musées Nationaux, than René. In fact he is the only restorer assigned his own restoration room. The others must share work accommodations.

Since starting work at the Louvre, two weeks ago, I have found René easy to get along with. But on one occasion I did notice a rise in his ire. It occurred when he was handed a painting that should have been restored years earlier. But his anger was short-lived. It has to be. We are usually quite busy. You see Musée du Louvre performs restorations for the entire world, not just for its own art. So if you have the odd Matisse lying around and it needs a little touchup… Well, now you know who to contact.

Although far from young, I would not regard René D'aubigne as old. He is about my father's age. René is plump and of middle height. He combs his gray hair forward to conceal its receding growth-line. Looking at his coiffeur from the front it is not unlike seeing sod being lifted from the ground by an invisible shovel, particularly when he walks and the mat of hair flops up and down. His face is round. His cheeks are red and pudgy. He has small dark eyes and a crooked nose. Below the latter, René grows a bushy black moustache. He chews this whenever he is nervous.

René is married. But I do not think he and his wife make a good match. On the few occasions when she has telephoned, poor René nearly defoliates his *depressor septi nasi*. And after his wife rings-off he curses her, vehemently. In fact, on more than one occasion, he vowed to kill his frigid spouse.

M. René D'aubigne has a secret. Or rather he tries to keep one. Twice, now, I have heard René on the telephone talking to someone named Fabienne. Although I hear only one side of their conversation, it usually gets quite naughty. So I suspect he and she are having a blazing affair. If so, I would not be surprised if his wife brings him to task, quite unpleasantly. Hopefully Mme. D'aubigne's retribution will not mean the loss of his head—or Fabienne's.

He has never mentioned children. So I assume there are none from René's sanctioned union. Perhaps Fabienne is to blame? After spending an evening with her, René is probably too exhausted to meet his wife's marital expectations. This, of course, must aggravate husband versus wife discord. In fact, it might even explain his spouse's antagonistic telephone calls. Poor thing. She probably feels completely abandoned. Although, this is probably not a new experience. From René's description, Mme. D'aubigne could play the ice-cold monster in any number of horror movies—sans makeup.

"I picked up our pay-packets this morning, Stuart," René remarked, as I settle at my workstation. "I put yours in your center drawer, as before."

I jerked it open and took out the brown envelope. Then, with the eagerness of a seven year old unwrapping a Christmas gift, I tore open my pay-packet and took out the fold of bills and collection of coins. Tonight I would celebrate—modestly, of course.

René tilted toward me, frowning. "Those hollows under your eyes have gotten worse, Stuart. What's wrong?"

I stuffed the money into the pockets of my jeans, and dumped the envelope back into the drawer. "I didn't sleep well, last night."

"I find drinking a bottle of Claret helps," he casually returned. "The wine mutes my wife's complaints."

There was a painting in front of him. From my brief view of the work as I entered the restoration room, I recognized it as a Degas. The canvas is still framed. But the tools on the table indicate that it will soon be shed of its wooden support-structure.

"Wine makes bad dreams worse, René," I countered.

René shrugged, resuming his examination of the Degas. "Only when a man is too thin. Put on some weight. Ten or twenty pounds, at least. Then the wine will make you sleep like the dead."

"The dead, or rather soon-to-be, is what my nightmare was about."

"You've never had a nightmare 'til you've dreamt about my wife," René snorted. He hesitated making a sour face. "I have them all the time. The trouble is the frigid bitch wakes up as soon as I get my hands around her throat."

"Last night's mental drama was about a conversation I overheard."

He batted the air with one hand. "Never believe what you hear, Stuart. Some people—especially politicians—make a living from telling lies."

"I didn't believe what I'd heard—not at first. In fact, I convinced myself it was a sick joke by my fellow inmates, at Mme. Flaubert's. But this morning... Well, I'm no longer firm in that conviction."

"There are only three truths in life, Stuart. Death, taxes, and misery in marriage. Forget what you heard."

Impatiently, I fanned the air with both hands. "René, I think a man is going to be killed."

The color drained from his face as he jerked toward me. "Where were these men when you heard this? Were names mentioned? Did you see them? Who were they going to kill? They didn't mention me, did they?"

I wagged my head. "The voices came from the café below my flat, I'm pretty sure. And, no, your name was not mentioned."

"See what you've done?" he tittered, making a nervous gesture. "You've gotten me worried about dreams!"

"Do you think I should tell the police?"

"Tell them what?" René made a disgusted face. "You heard people talking and had a bad dream? Don't be ridiculous." Then, he curled a beckoning finger. "Take a peek at this, Stuart."

I went over to where he was perched and looked across his shoulder. The painting on the table in front of René was, indeed, a Degas. But for some reason its blue rendition of the *Singer in Green*, raised the hairs on the back on my neck.

"Breathtaking, yes?" he breathed.

I nodded, my eyes scanning the canvas trying to detect what bothered me about the work. Then, like a cannon ball hitting my testicles, realization struck home. Nearly ten years ago my uncle—the one who I am named after—had me create several Degas as part of his mentoring process. One of which was a blue version of the *Singer in Green*!

"Where did you get it, René?"

If you were a cockroach crawling upon the ceiling, you would notice the sudden gray pallor in my complexion, quivering spasms in my legs and the incessant bobbing of my Adams Apple. Depending upon your angle of view, you might also notice the clenching and unclenching of my buttocks as a very nervous magic-nightstick searches for a place to hide its head, in shame.

"It's the property of a good friend of mine, M. Cesar Avoyelles," D'aubigne returned. "Cesar wants it cleaned and re-hung." One of his hands darted above the painting, going from spot to spot: pointing, but never touching. "Look at the brushwork, Stuart. Look at the composition. This Degas is exquisite!"

I moved to a position beside him, to get a closer look. Then I focused upon the canvas' unpainted edges, looking for telltale, brown staining. Marks applied by forgers intended to fool purchasers into thinking a canvas is old enough to be the work of the signatory. In actuality these phony indicators of bacterial encroachment are the result of instant coffee being sprinkled upon the cloth and then misted with water before the naked canvas is placed in an oven to 'age.' I reached out and discretely dragged a fingernail through one of the spots, and then held it to my nose. Either Degas had been careless with his espresso, or this was not one of his creations.

"How long has M. Avoyelles had it?" I asked.

"Five or six years, he said." Then René's hands splayed, covetously. "I would give my left nut to have this hanging in my house."

"I don't think your wife would appreciate such a trade, René."

"Bah! As far as she's concerned, cutting off my balls was a prerequisite to marriage." He let go a long covetous sigh, his hands once more darting back and forth above the painting. "Look at the model's eyes, Stuart. Look at the delicate lace of her gown. Look at the tilt of her bosom. It is as if Degas breathed life into this canvas!"

I leaned over the painting and carefully studied the individual brushstrokes. Almost immediately, my worst suspicions were confirmed. Not only was this a forgery, but I had painted it!

As the roach, you probably noted my abrupt upward jerk, several barely controlled spasms in my buttocks as my magic-nightstick found security in hiding, a redness going to my ears, followed by my right hand frantically gripping my belly; as if my soul was about to depart through it.

"Dear God, René," I groaned.

"I know. I know," he nodded. "I lust over it, as well."

A swarthy man with a pockmarked face entered the room. The newcomer was long and lank, with curly black hair and a ruddy, almost livid complexion. His eyebrows were black and heavy. His chin was square. He was dressed in a well-tailored brown suit. The gold jewelry on his fingers and wrists suggested he was made of money or, at least, had access to a lot of someone else's. He looked to be about forty years of age.

"M. Avoyelles!" exclaimed René, with obvious delight. D'aubigne scrambled from his stool, and hurried toward the visitor; both arms outstretched. "I was just telling my assistant about your Degas. It is magnificent!"

The fellow shook hands with René and then went over to the painting. But Instead of looking at the canvas, Avoyelles' probing eyes studied me—as if he knew the truth about the 'Degas'.

"What do you think of it?" he asked me, in a cultured voice.

From where I stood I could smell his expensive, citrusy cologne. "I think I've seen it before."

"Stuart," enjoined René D'aubigne. "This is M. Cesar Avoyelles. He owns the Galerie Avoyelles at 32 rue ste croix de la bretonnerie. It is an establishment catering to the *crème de la crème* of Parisian society."

"Nice to meet you," I muttered, unable to look Avoyelles in the face.

The gallery owner said, "Your uncle's told me a great deal about you, Stuart."

I blinked in shock. Then I slowly raised my eyes to his. "*My* uncle?"

Avoyelles nodded. "Last month I visited his lovely seaside villa in Sao Paulo. We talked at great length about you." His face broadened into a smile. "I hope you and I will form the same close friendship your uncle and I enjoy."

"Indeed?" murmured René, suddenly eyeing me as if I had just descended from the heavens.

"It was I your uncle contacted when you requested help in finding employment," our visitor continued, in a self-deprecating manner. "And through my connections here, I arranged for your appointment."

I gaped in shame. Not only had my uncle screwed this poor guy with the phony Degas, but Uncle Stuart went back to the well for another dip when I asked for help!

"You were literally a lifesaver," I softly returned. "I am very grateful."

"Are you ill, Stuart?" asked Avoyelles. "You've gone quite gray."

I nodded, not lying in the least. Obviously, Avoyelles did not know the Degas was my creation. Had he known it was a forgery he would not have assisted when Uncle Stuart made the request to find me a job. But that did little to ease my embarrassment.

René winked at Avoyelles. "I'm afraid Stuart had a terrible dream last night."

Cesar Avoyelles looked down at the painting and made an odd face. "I have been offered a small fortune for this, René. And I've accepted it. After the cleaning and remounting, I want it framed as well. I will let you choose something suitable."

The words came out of my mouth like a death cry. "Dear God, you can't sell it!"

Both men's eyes narrowed at me, in suspicious surprise.

"What I meant to say is," I hastily added, "you mustn't part with such a wonderful work of art. Why not hang onto it, M. Avoyelles?"

"Stuart has a point, Cesar," chimed René, authoritatively. "Degas *is* a master without peer. I would be hard-pressed to sell such a beautiful work."

The gallery owner gave René's shoulder a friendly pat. "You get too attached to art, my friend. Business considerations must come first."

"I do not agree, Cesar," René D'aubigne said, with a determined shake of his head. "Art is all that matters."

"You forget," cooed Avoyelles, "I have several other Degas. So why should I not give up one if the price is right?"

"Did my uncle sell those other Degas to you?" I enjoined, fearing to hear his answer.

The art gallery owner nodded and grinned. "At a price I could not resist. It was when he was leaving France for Brazil. Your uncle did not wish to take the Degas' along—probably because of the difficulty in getting them through customs."

"I – I - I." My stomach hit the floor and bounced twice, during my stammering. Then it rose up, churned and tried to turn itself inside out. If the truth about the 'Degas' ever got out I was certain Avoyelles would fold, spindle and mutilate me – with René's help! "I am so sorry, M. Avoyelles."

The gallery owner frowned in confusion. "But why do you say that, Stuart?"

"You must forgive Stuart, Cesar," René told Avoyelles, with a wink. "My young assistant is not his usual self. Last night at supper, he heard some people discussing murder."

"That would certainly give me indigestion," returned the gallery owner, tugging at his nose.

"He even dreamt about it," René added,

M. Avoyelles gave a sympathetic nod. "There is nothing worse than a bad dream."

"Except when they come true," I mumbled.

"Your uncle tells me you are a notable art-talent in your own right, Stuart," Avoyelles remarked.

"Notable?" I gulped. Then my mouth started running off so rapidly I could not stop the words. "Every artist learns to paint by copying the masters. Ask around. It's not like I'm some forger trying to screw the world!"

"Calm down, Stuart," warned René, patting my shoulder. "You are getting over-excited. If your stomach acid starts churning and your breakfast backs up on you, there's no telling what might happen."

Avoyelles said, "Perhaps I could see some of your paintings, Stuart?"

You, as a cockroach on the ceiling, would have noticed my knees buckle, my eyes bug and my tongue immediately slather with foam. This is a completely normal reaction from a new painter when someone of importance requests to see his artistic endeavors. Please ignore it.

"You—you—you want to see *my* paintings?" I spluttered.

The gallery owner nodded. "If they are as good as your uncle described, I would love to offer your work to my customers."

Again, René looked at me like I was heaven-sent. And for a brief moment, I was nearly convinced of it. Or at least, I was certain my maker had finally taken time to smile down upon me.

"I would be honored, M. Avoyelles!" I cried.

"Of course you would," gurgled René, nearly stunned by this morning's turn of events. "What artist would not be?"

"You will have to forgive us, Stuart," Cesar Avoyelles declared. "I must speak with René privately about a personal matter."

I nodded, woozy with excitement. If Avoyelles had been female, doubtlessly I would have proposed marriage. I could not believe it. He actually wanted to see my paintings! At last, my dark world was taking an unexpected turn toward the light. Then I remembered the 'Degas', and I nearly vomited. How could so much good happen in the midst of so much bad?

Cesar Avoyelles escorted René D'aubigne out of the room. The two men spoke at length in the hallway just beyond earshot. As they conversed, two other men appeared; one quite tall and powerful; the other, short and dumpy with a shaggy mane of dark hair and a thickly curled van dyke. They, too, entered into the discussions between Cesar and René. Finally, Cesar Avoyelles and the other men moved off and René returned to his worktable.

"You should have told me you were acquainted with M. Avoyelles," he gently scolded.

"I wasn't until you introduced him, René."

My eyes went back to the painting and humiliation formed a huge knot in my belly. I knew admitting to its creation would probably mean the loss of my job, and negate Avoyelles' interest in my paintings. But I could not let my representation of a Degas continue to pass as genuine.

"About the Degas, René…"

"I want you to remove the canvas from its frame," he interrupted, taking off his work apron. "I would do it myself. But I must attend the monthly meeting of the Réunion des Musées Nationaux. After that, I have some errands to run. I should be back sometime following lunch."

"But René…"

"We'll talk later, Stuart. When you get the canvas free, see what we have in the way of frames. I think something simple – perhaps plain aluminum would be best. That way the frame will not detract from the painting's aura."

"I'll do it right away," I told him.

After René left, I carefully removed the wooden structure framing the canvas. Then I laid the canvas flat on the table, face down. Written in old French, was a price using the currency of Degas' time. Below this was a signature, a business name and a date. This bit of scripting was also in line with the time the painting would have been created. The price and business name are simple things. And although not verifiable facts, they added a bit of convincing provenance to the painting.

As my uncle used to tell me, "People want to believe what they see. All it takes is a little bit of convincing to make them believe the world is flat or a piece of art is genuine." At the time he said that I thought he was simply being encouraging about my own efforts. Little did I know he meant it in the literal sense.

My uncle's familiar handwriting on the canvas added that little bit of convincing. How could he have used me in this fashion? Like an idiot, I painted the 'Degas' and later on he sold it! Or was this a mistake on his part? He could have confused it with the genuine Degas', in his collection. Or were any of them legitimate?

For the next several hours, I busied myself with cleaning the restoration room, sweeping and dusting. I had not been instructed to do so. This was more or less penance for my sinful reproduction of a Degas. Even though I had not created it with the intention of deceiving anyone, I still felt ashamed. I also felt afraid. I knew I *had* to disclose the truth. I could not let Cesar Avoyelles compound this terrible situation by selling the painting to someone else. But at the same time I was terrified to expose the work as a fraud. To do so meant giving up everything, and returning home in disgrace.

I tried to convince myself that there was no real harm in keeping quiet. More than likely, whoever made the offer for the 'Degas' would have the painting examined by an expert, before taking possession. Therefore, any disclosures concerning its validity would be the responsibility of that expert. As an outsider he would have no way of knowing who had actually created the 'Degas'. Therefore I would not be at risk. The expert would merely proclaim it a fraud and M. Avoyelles would, in turn, seek reparations from my uncle. Naturally my uncle would pay restitution to salvage his friendship with Avoyelles. Just desserts, to my thinking. So, where was the harm in my silence?

But what if the painting passed muster, so to speak? Obviously, it had done so already. Avoyelles certainly would have hired an expert on Degas' to examine it. No gallery owner in his right mind would do otherwise. But experts had been fooled before and would be again. If this was deemed a Degas, what were my options? My lowly opinion, as an apprenticed art-restorer, would hardly be taken seriously. Not, against that of an expert. Somehow I would have to convey the truth to Cesar Avoyelles, but in a fashion that would exclude my involvement as the forger.

"Aren't you a busy-bee?"

I turned toward the female voice to see Maryse Rousseau watching me sweep the floor.

"What brings you here?" I asked, my magic-nightstick starting to make its usual salute to her presence.

"It's time for lunch," she casually returned. "Would you like to join me?"

Me? Other than the brief encounter involving my need for an apartment, and her desire to have me store that hideous sculpture, Maryse and I had shared very little in the way of conversation. Admittedly, there were the usual interactions between coworkers during the course of workday activities. And, of course, there was the ride to and from work on the Métro, where she sat at one end of the car and I on the other—drooling as I stared at her. But nothing so far had suggested there would be anything personal between us.

"I'm not dressed very well for an outing," I returned.

She shrugged. "We're not going to an exhibition. Just lunch. If you've made other plans, I understand."

I wagged my head, again amazed at the turns this day was giving me. First, there was the phony Degas from my past. Then, Cesar Avoyelles wanted to see my paintings. And now, the beautiful Maryse was requesting my presence at lunch.

"But I'm on what most people would consider a tight budget," I warned.

"No problem. Coffee and rolls at Le Fumoir are reasonable. It's a quick walk from here- just off Rue de Rivoli."

You, no doubt, are on the verge of reminding me that Maryse is married. But I tell you plainly—I am not being seduced. As surprising as this request is, it could hardly be considered a romantic overture on her part. I admit my magic-nightstick is already planning for the wedding night. But he is an impulsive sort. I, on the other hand, am inclined toward the practicalities of a relationship. Like the purchase of condoms before my nightstick gets too far ahead of me in our irrepressible fantasies concerning Maryse Rousseau. Nevertheless, I shall not jump to any conclusions concerning her invite. Maryse and I will merely be two coworkers going out for lunch—and nothing more.

I leaned the broom against my work table. "You lead and I'll follow."

After making our luncheon purchases at Le Fumoir, Maryse led me onto its terrace. We selected a table out of the sun but near enough to the edge in order to enjoy the view. Then we settled down to our meal.

She was quiet at first, nibbling on her roll and sipping coffee. It was as if Maryse was not sure how to bring me into conversation.

I broke the silence with, "Do you go to the beach, often?"

"Not as often as I would like," she returned. "But I don't drive. I don't have a driving license."

"Really? It wouldn't take much to teach you."

Maryse shrugged. "I manage with public transportation." She took another bite from her roll. Then her eyes came up to mind as she sipped her coffee. Eventually she said, "Cesar tells me he hopes to sell your paintings in his gallery."

You need not say it. Obviously, her interest in me is entirely due to Avoyelles' remarks. And, yes, I am disappointed. Most of me, anyway. One of my parts sees this turn of events as a white flag being waved to mark the last lap before heading into the home stretch.

"He was just being kind," I returned.

She tilted toward me, smiling. "Don't be modest, Stuart. Cesar does not handle the art of just anyone."

"The truth is I have an in with him. You see, he and my uncle are friends. Therefore, this is merely a friend meeting an obligation to another friend. Nothing will come of it."

"Honest, too?" she teased, easing back.

I winced at her remark. "Sometimes."

Maryse nibbled at the roll, eyeing me curiously. "Where do you draw the line? At honesty, I mean?"

"I—I talk too much."

"Your uncle being Cesar's friend means nothing." She set down the roll and picked up her coffee cup, obviously not placated by my explanation. "Cesar is the consummate businessman. He would not offer your paintings if he did not think he could profit by them. Therefore he will assess your talent on its own merit before deciding. Do you have an example of your art in your flat?"

I nodded. "Several."

She reached across the table and squeezed my hand. "Why not let me see them? I know what Cesar likes. I could give you a fair assessment on what his opinion will be—if you're interested."

The touch of her hand was electrifying. I started to turn my hand over so I could grasp her fingers. But she withdrew hers too quickly.

"Cesar also said something odd," she continued.

Her continual reference to M. Avoyelles by his given name, suggested there might be something along the lines of romance, between her and him. That, also, was disappointing. To my eye, she was the most beautiful woman in the world. Also to my eye, I was nothing but a rumpled bag of bones. Therefore logic dictated that there would never be anything between us. Still, her casual referrals to him did tug at my heart.

"Odd, in what manner?" I asked

"It had to do with a Matisse."

My cheeks warmed as I imagined my uncle offering to sell one of the Matisses I had painted to M. Avoyelles. Or was there more to it? Was it possible M. Avoyelles actually knew the truth? That he was in league with my uncle? Or did he merely suspect, and this unplanned outing was his idea – for her to quiz me on the other paintings I had replicated? Was Avoyelles building a case against Uncle Stuart? Or me?

"A Matisse?" I choked.

Maryse nodded. "Cesar expects to gain possession of one that will shock the art-world."

"From whom?"

"Your uncle. He claimed it was the pride of your uncle's Matisse collection."

"Dear God, no!"

A peculiar pained expression passed over her features. "I beg your pardon?"

"What I should have said was I hope my uncle is not planning to sell anything from his collections. I know how much he loves each and every painting. Particularly, the Matisse's."

Maryse shrugged. "Sometimes money becomes an issue and things treasured must be sold." She sipped her coffee and then set down the cup. "When I was very young my mother worked for a rich man who had a villa in *Cote d'Azur*. He was tall and bearded—trimmed in a Van Dyke. He was an art forger."

The location of the villa, the reference to the beard and the description of the man as a forger, gave me an immediate flashback to my summers with Uncle Stuart. He always had a maid. But during two summers the maid was a particularly beautiful woman, not unlike Maryse. That woman had a daughter. The girl was two years younger than me, well-equipped for her age, skinny with very long dark hair. She had this habit of coming out of nowhere to watch me every time I was on the front patio, painting. It was quite unnerving. She would smile and I would get all flustered. The maid and her daughter moved on before the following summer.

"My mother was his maid for two years," she continued. "Thinking back, I also believe she must have been his lover. We had a small cottage on the grounds of his villa. I remember he had a great many paintings." She fell silent, thinking; her eyes still upon me. "He had a nephew. The boy visited the two summers we were there. I used to sit out on the patio at the table, and watch the boy paint. He was my very first sexual fantasy."

Dear God! She was her! The over-developed, skinny girl!

"I was—I mean, he was?"

She nodded. "It was quite hot, both summers. So he wore nothing but a red Speedo. At the time, I had no experience in sex. So I found it quite fascinating the way his Speedo would magically extend, not unlike a car's electric antenna, whenever I would watch him. Of course after I became acquainted with male anatomy I understood. But at the time I could not imagine how he worked such magic. You remind me of that boy—the way you walk, mostly."

"The expanding Speedo was probably because of the kid's nerves."

Maryse nodded. "He was very nervous. His uncle used to tease him for not talking to me." She laughed softly. "I didn't mind. He was such a gifted artist. It was like watching a miracle take place every time he put brush to canvas. Not to mention, the distending Speedo."

I tried to swallow. But my throat had gone as dry as desert sand. If she realized who I was she would also realize the paintings Avoyelles had purchased were forgeries! She would tell him. He would tell René. I would be arrested and, at the very least, deported!

"Red does sort of stand out," I whimpered.

Maryse laughed. "Oh, it did."

"You're a close friend of M. Avoyelles?" I asked, purposely changing the subject to give my magic-nightstick and my nerves a breather.

Maryse made a vague gesture. "Cesar is a business associate of my husband's."

"Your husband is an art dealer?"

"No," she chuckled. "Baudouin is more of a—a problem-solver."

Baudouin? Why was that name so familiar?

"I guess that means you and M. Avoyelles are dating—since you and your husband are divorcing?" I suggested.

"Of course not," she returned, with a fervent wag of her head. "I've known Cesar for several years. But our relationship is strictly from the business side of things. He sells my sculptures—well, if I am to tell the truth, he has sold two of my sculptures. But I am hopeful for the rest."

I took a bite of the pastry and offered a nervous nod. What was I going to do? I reminded her of me! My walk? That was the problem. I would have to change my walk. Maybe a limp? Or I could add a non-committal wiggle? No, that might get the attention of people who it was best to avoid.

A male voice at my back said, "I hope I am not intruding?"

I looked over one shoulder to see a tall, well-dressed man of about forty years. He was thin and well-muscled. His shoulders were broad. He wore a dark blue suit and a crimson necktie. His complexion was deeply tanned; his eyes were small, black, and bright. His hair had been black, but was now turning an iron-gray: it was very dry, wiry, and thick. His lips were thin and nearly colorless. His chin was strongly chiseled. When he reached our table, he stopped beside Maryse, bent down and kissed her cheek.

"How wonderful it is to see you, Maryse," he purred. Then the man settled into the chair next to her, ignoring my presence.

Scratch both me and my magic-nightstick from the race to her bed. The blush spreading across Maryse's cheeks indicated she had already bagged, tagged and shagged this one.

"Stuart," Maryse said, "this is another of Mme. Flaubert's tenants. Dr. Michele Molyneux."

Dr. Molyneux twisted in his chair and extended a hand.

I took his mitt with reluctance, and we shook.

Not only was he rich and handsome as well as obviously entranced by Maryse, but he lived in our building. This, of course, not only made their trysts frequent but conveniently arranged. No chilly Métro ride for him after a night of searing, unbridled sex with the breathtaking woman of my dreams. Molyneux could just turn out the lights and prepare for the inevitable rematches, before dawn sent him back to his own bed.

"Mme. Flaubert mentioned having rented to an American," Molyneux told me, in English. "How do you like Paris, so far?"

"This morning's been a bit of an adjustment," I returned, in kind.

He nodded, sympathetically. "Adjustment is something I am very familiar with. My home is in Neuilly-sur-Seine. But my office is in Paris. So, during the week I stay at Mme. Flaubert's. It's the holidays I find confusing. Then, I'm not sure where I should be." He laughed at his own wit and twisted back toward Maryse, took her hands in his and continued in French, "I am so sorry to hear of your divorce."

"It is no one's fault, Michele," she softly replied. "Life must move on."

Molyneux gave a determined shake of his head. "I should have been told about it—beforehand. Considering what Baudouin insists I do, I'm not so sure I can go through with it. You and I…"

She raised a finger to her lips, warning him that speaking French in my presence was not going to exclude me from what he was about to disclose. Molyneux gave me a nervous look. I smiled, and resumed eating my lunch.

"Everything is settled, Michele," she said. "We must do what is expected. *Finis.*"

He kissed both her hands and stood up. "If you need to talk, Maryse, you know how to reach me."

"You are a good friend, Michele."

Molyneux gave me a parting nod, and then left.

Although Maryse had made an effort to identify Dr. Molyneux as a friend, I could not help but wonder what she had stopped him from saying? Had they been lovers before she and her husband parted ways? Was he the reason for the divorce?

"You're popular, today," I remarked. "First there was Avoyelles and now Molyneux. Is he your personal physician? Or is the good doctor a member of your romantic following?"

"I have always been faithful to my husband," she replied, clearly irritated by my words. Maryse glanced at her watch. "I'm afraid we had better head back. I don't want René complaining that I kept you too long."

* * * *

When I reached the restoration room, René was at work cleaning the 'Degas'. I wanted to blurt out the entire truth. But my courage failed me. Then I decided to put a spin on my intended disclosure. I would merely suggest the 'Degas' was a forgery, and leave it at that. In so doing, I would complete my moral obligation. But at the same time I would not be condemning anyone—particularly, myself.

With quickly rehearsed words upon my lips I strode over and told him of my suspicions.

"A forgery? Nonsense!" René D'aubigne bellowed. "Your uncle sold this to M. Avoyelles."

"Which only means my uncle was—fooled, as well."

"Ridiculous! Do you think Cesar Avoyelles would pay a fortune without having it authenticated?"

"No, but…"

"Where do you come off making such a reckless suggestion? Don't you realize your careless remarks could damage M. Avoyelles' professional reputation? His gallery could be ruined!"

His angry reaction seemed excessive as if something else was behind it, something that had occurred between his leaving and my return.

"I – I - I wasn't trying to…" I protested.

"How could you possibly think *I* could be fooled?" he blustered on, thumping his chest. "Me, who has restored more than half a dozen Degas?" He thrust a finger at the canvas. "Look at the age of the canvas. Look at the paints. It is a genuine Degas, I tell you. I would stake my life on it!" Then he reached into his pocket and pulled out a slip of paper. "Here," he said, handing it to me. "This is the address."

"Address to where?" I asked, completely bewildered.

"The address to Baudouin Rousseau's home, of course. Three rue de l'Ancienne-Comédie." Then he jerked the note from my grasp, and pocketed it.

"I don't understand, René. What has…"

"Don't you?" His hands went to his hips. "Then let me enlighten you. You went to lunch with Maryse. M. Baudouin Rousseau saw the two of you—together—and took offense."

"Wait! Baudouin? Now, I remember why his name is familiar. It didn't register when Maryse and Molyneux mentioned her husband. But…"

René's arms flailed the air with exasperation. "You're going out with a gangster's wife and you're thinking about familiarities? Get your head out of your ass!"

"But, her husband is going to be…"

"Do you know who Baudouin Rousseau is?" he interrupted.

"Maryse said he's a problem-solver."

"He's a member of the *Unione Corse* – the Corsican Mafia. He is a *Sgarrista* who reports directly to François Chiappe; the *capo d tuti capi*—the boss of bosses! How's that for being a problem-solver?"

"That's him! It all fits."

René arms flailed the air, again. "Can you not focus? Baudouin wants to see you promptly at ten o'clock, tonight."

I gave my head a determined shake. "René, it's a lot more serious than you think."

"Of course it is. He is going to kill you!"

"No, you don't understand…"

"Could you not keep your hands to yourself? What in God's name possessed you to seduce his wife?"

"René, I did not seduce Maryse Rousseau!"

"Tell that to him!" He waggled a threatening finger. "But I would not count on Baudouin Rousseau believing it. That man is a shark! He's killed at least a dozen men!"

"René…"

He gave my chest a sharp jab. "You will go! You will be polite. You will apologize and promise to never see her again. And you'd damn well better be on time. Or else you are fired!"

With that, he stormed out of the room.

I slumped down on my stool. As usual, my life had come full circle—from dung heap to dung heap. I get fooled into thinking everything is going my way, and then bam! I'm dropped back into the stink—this time, right up to my chin. If only I had not gone to lunch with her… If only…

Wait. Something was not copasetic. The one and only time I have lunch with Maryse, and her husband spots us? There was a chance of that, but it was damn slim. More than likely, there has to be something else behind it. Why, for example, had Maryse invited me if her soon-to-be-ex-husband was the jealous type who murdered people over cold coffee and rolls? And why had she asked me today, of all days? I looked like a caveman reject. Regardless of what René said, her husband had not called. It had to have been someone else. But who? Avoyelles? If he knew the truth about the 'Degas' I could see him ordering her to ask me out. She would make me squirm by taking me down memory lane. Then he would telephone René with that ridiculous threat! Or was it Molyneux? No. He would not have known who I worked for.

All right, say it. Avoyelles and Maryse suckered me. My ego took the bait when Avoyelles expressed an interest in my paintings, and she trotted me down the garden path to the quicksand pool at the end, where I jumped in.

Wait. There must be still more to it. What about René? Why had he gone from envious, when Avoyelles was here, to fulminating when I got back from lunch? It was completely out of his character. Do this. Do that. Or I'm fired? Why should he care what Baudouin Rousseau thinks about me? No. He also must be involved. It was the three of them conspiring together. Whether I went as ordered, or not, I would still be fired.

Wait! I could turn this whole thing around on them. If I told Baudouin Rousseau what I had overheard last night, I would become his friend for life—albeit the acquaintance might be short-lived, considering what was discussed. Still, my forewarning could save his bacon. I'd still be out of a job and without any hope in hell for my paintings to be sold in a Paris gallery. But at least I would have had the last laugh. Brilliant!

Not so brilliant. If I tell Baudouin what I overheard, he'll kill me. After all, he was involved in that diamond heist. That, in turn, would mean a long jail-term for him if I went to the police. Gangsters were not averse to murder when it came to avoiding prison. No. I could not tell him anything about the overheard conversation.

Wait! What if Baudouin Rousseau did see us and did leave that message? The odds were against it. But it could be true. If I went, I would still have my job and Avoyelles would still consider my paintings for his gallery. Assuming M. Rousseau did not kill me.

Wait! All I have to do is explain that Maryse and I dined at her request. Further, that such an event will never be repeated. Further still, I had no sexual feelings for her whatsoever—because I was a foreign fag. Afterwards, Baudouin Rousseau would beat me within an inch of my life. But I would go home a wiser, breathing, albeit a limping man.

Chapter 3
Murder Comes to Call

For those who think crime does not pay, think again. The estimated annual income for organized criminals exceeds a thousand-billion dollars, or 3% of the world's gross national product. The lure of such vast wealth would be a powerful seducer for the average Corsican. To them, a stubby mobile home on an unkempt hillside constitutes a villa.

I spent the rest of the afternoon keeping silent. Not that silence reigned in the restoration room. René had plenty to say. He continued complaining about my remarks concerning the 'Degas', my impudence for assuming that he had been fooled by a forgery, and his suspicions about my connections in the art world. The ones he presumed I had but he did not know about and about which he should have been told. When my workday finally ended, I was actually happy to climb aboard the Métro for the crowded ride back to my foul-smelling flat.

There were three vacant seats in the last car, when I reached it. I quickly settled into the window seat of a vacant pair, and closed my eyes. With the meeting at Baudouin Rousseau's residence hanging over my head, I had much to think about. Should I pass on cremation if he kills me and go for burial? If the latter, do I really need an oak coffin or would pine serve? And what about leakage? Lead-lining a coffin is not cheap. But is it more expensive than selecting an internment location on a hill-top where the drainage was better?

"What's got you shaking, Stuart? You're trembling and muttering as if Azreael is waiting at your flat?"

I looked over to see Maryse Rousseau settling into the seat next to me.

"I can't seem to get away from you, today," I glumly responded.

She made a sad face, "What makes you say that?"

"I think you know."

"Know what?" Maryse demanded, firmly.

I batted the air with one hand. "Nothing. Forget it."

Like the invitation to lunch, her sitting next to me was a first in our budding albeit ended friendship. Normally, Maryse and I keep to different areas of this public conveyance, going to and returning from work. And during the ride we each tended our own thoughts, and fantasies. Maryse reads mystery novels. I scratched, while my magic-nightstick plotted to seduce her.

Maryse squirmed on the seat, pressing closer. Despite my belief that she, Avoyelles and René had set me up for trouble with her husband, I found her nearness enticing. The scent of her vanilla-like perfume teased my nostrils. The warmth of her flesh exhilarated my heart. As for my nightstick, it was trying to climb out of my whiter-than-whites to wink at her.

"Stuart, if I've done something to upset you I have a right to know," she whispered, pressing her right breast firmly against my left arm.

"Did you tell your husband we were going to Le Fumoir, today?" I asked.

She frowned. "Why would I do that?"

I shrugged, assuming her evasion was just another form of lying. "No reason."

"Didn't you have a good time, with me?"

"While we were having lunch, yes. Not so much fun, since. You, René and Avoyelles saw to that."

Maryse circled her arms about my left one, and pressed it even more firmly against her breast. "Me? What did I do?"

"Your husband."

"Stuart, please stop talking in riddles," she protested. "Tell me what's wrong?"

"Is your husband violent?"

Her head wagged, but eyes remained steadily on me. "Baudouin is a pussycat."

A pussycat? How can she say that? According to René, during one of his many post-lunch vitriolic outbursts, Baudouin Rousseau was penciled-in as the next leader of the Corsican Mafia. Not only that, but Baudouin Rousseau was suspected in at least a dozen murders. And if that was not enough, Baudouin Rousseau's success at gathering information through torture is allegedly unsurpassed! Pussycat, my ass!

"All right, just in case I've got it pegged wrong, René told me your husband is part of the Corsican Mafia," I told her. "You claimed he was a problem-solver. Which story is true?"

"Baudouin is a Mafioso. But he is also a problem-solver," Maryse replied, without hesitation. It was as if every upright French male formed such alliances. "My husband answers only to François Chiappe, the top man. But what has that to do with you being angry with me?"

"I, uh… Well,…"

"My husband and I are divorcing, Stuart." She playfully stroked my hair. "Baudouin has no claim on me. He certainly would not dictate what I do or who I do it with."

"But according to René, my having lunch with you was akin to attempting suicide. Or at the very least, it forces your husband to cut another notch in his pistol-grip."

"Suicide? Notch? Pistol-grip?" she frowned. "What exactly did René say to you?"

"René told me to meet with your husband tonight. I have to be there on time and politely apologize for my transgression—that being our luncheon. Look, I'm sorry about the Degas. I truly am. But it wasn't my idea for Avoyelles to buy it."

She took one of my hands and held it between hers. "Stuart, I can see you're very upset by René's remarks. But I had no part in them. Further, I have no idea how my husband, René, Avoyelles and that Degas fit together. But I promise you, my husband did not ask to see you."

I pulled my hand free. "René told me your husband telephoned while we were at lunch. René said your husband wants me to meet him tonight at ten o'clock. If I don't go, René is going to fire me."

She drew closer, sternly wagging her head. "No. That cannot be. Not tonight."

"Why would René lie about it?"

"Stuart, all I know is my husband would not have made that call. No way would he demand to see you tonight, of all nights."

"Somebody called. Obviously, it was not René's imagination. So who? Avoyelles? Or, maybe, Molyneux? It had to be someone who knows where I work and who I report to and who knew we were having lunch."

Her face went white. "I think I know."

"Who?"

"Leave it to me, Stuart. It was a just bad joke. I will make certain it does not happen, again."

"René didn't think it was funny. Neither do I! Was it Avoyelles?"

Maryse hesitated visibly, and when she spoke at last, it was as if with a conscious effort, her words chosen carefully. "Stuart, I want you to forget about tonight. I want you to stay home. I'll come to your flat and keep you company."

"I can't do that. If I don't go, I'll lose my job."

Maryse made an impatient gesture. "No. You won't lose your job. I promise."

"It was Avoyelles, wasn't it? Look, Maryse, if I could refund his money for the Degas, I would. Believe me, I would."

"Listen to me," she urged, her words coming fast. "I will handle this. There is nothing for you to worry about. There is nothing for you to do."

I wagged my head. "You weren't there when René was screaming at me. He was serious!"

Maryse let go of my arm, shifted in the seat, and leaned forward pensively; her hands clasped over her knees. After a moment she straightened, took her cell-phone from her purse, turned it on and dialed. As she lifted the phone to listen, her face seemed to stiffen into white chalk. A few seconds later she began speaking to someone on the other end of the connection, in Corsican. I don't speak that Romance language. But I caught two words she uttered in French: 'Bastard' and 'fall-guy'. When Maryse rang off, tears were streaming down her face.

"Are you okay?" I asked.

"I want you to promise me something, Stuart," she sobbed, her face wrung with anguish. "I want you to promise you'll stay home tonight. Okay?"

"Maryse there's too much at stake."

"No. It's all a terrible joke." She lowered her head, overcome with emotion. "Please, stay home. I promise you, you won't lose your job. I promise, by tomorrow everything will be fine. But you must stay home, tonight." Then her eyes rose up to mine. "Promise me, Stuart?"

From the look on her face, Maryse was in torment. "Who were you talking to?"

She wavered. "It was—my husband. That's why I know he did not call René." Maryse returned her cell-phone to her purse and the tears began streaming, again. "I'm sorry about this, Stuart. I truly am."

I wanted to accept her words as gospel. But if her husband had not telephoned René, it made no difference to my situation. It was René who expected me to meet with Baudouin Rousseau. It was René who would fire me if I did not do so.

"You said your husband would not have ordered me to meet him tonight," I said. "Why not tonight?"

Slowly and hesitatingly, she said, "That is...not important."

"It is to me."

Maryse let go a long sigh. "Stuart… Look, he's having a meeting with François Chiappe, tonight." She spoke quietly, with a curiously dry, controlled note in her voice. "Obviously, it is not something you could attend. See what I mean? You showing up at Baudouin's tonight would only make trouble for him, and you."

She made sense. But René's threat kept reverberating in my ears.

"Can I ask you a personal question, Maryse?"

"Of course," she sniffed. "If it's not too personal."

"Why are you divorcing your husband?"

She pulled a tissue from her purse and blew her nose. "I'm not. Baudouin is divorcing me."

For many seconds I was stunned mute. Her husband was divorcing her? Impossible! Look at her. Maryse was a living, breathing dream-woman for any heterosexual man with blood in his veins. In particular, one who was used to painting on villa patios and wearing red Speedo's.

"He's divorcing you?" I echoed, in disbelief.

She tilted close, her warmth and pressure giving my magic-nightstick a renewed appreciation for life. "I'll make this up to you, I promise."

"You don't owe me anything," I quickly returned.

She leaned her head on my shoulder saying, "Yes, I do."

"Why does your husband want a divorce?"

Maryse settled back in her seat, and let go a long sigh. "Baudouin found someone else."

Someone else? Who could be better than Maryse? Even with red eyes and a runny nose from crying, she was the most beautiful woman I had ever seen.

"He's got to be sick," I declared.

"He is, Stuart. My husband is very sick," she said swiftly. Then Maryse turned toward me and wrapped her arms around my left one again. "I want us to be great friends."

Friends? My heart sank. How many times had I heard that statement? A dozen, at least. Every woman I'd ever known had said that same thing. I never really considered the possibility of Maryse and I becoming anything but friends. However, hearing her say those words felt like a boulder had landed on my chest.

"Why did you ask me out?" I said. "I mean, there must be a hundred guys working at the Louvre who would trade their souls for a lunch-date with you. Why me?"

She tilted closer and kissed my cheek. "Because you make me feel like I am twelve again."

I blinked, completely confused. "Twelve? Is that good?"

"It is absolutely wonderful!"

I had no idea what she was talking about. But I smiled, just the same. "Well, I'm glad I'm good at something."

"You always have been."

"I have?"

She nodded. "Those two summers were the best of my life. You would paint. I would watch—and fantasize."

I gulped, "You mean you know I was me?"

"I wasn't certain until Cesar told me about your uncle." She touched the back of one hand to my beard and lightly dragged her fingers across it. "I have to go out for a little while tonight. Wait up for me?" she entreated. "When I get back, everything will have worked itself out."

Wait up for me? Was this a friend type wait-up? Or was she making a promise of passionate ecstasy? No. That would be too much to hope for. I would wait up. She would arrive, only to tell me how tired she was and that we would talk in the morning. Whereupon, she would got to her flat leaving me expectantly disappointed in mine. That was the way my romantic life had always been. Why should this be any different?

With great reluctance, I pointed to the electronic display above the exit-door. "The next stop is where I get off tonight. I need my ears raised and my chin tucked."

"You're talking in riddles, again," she sighed.

"Sorry. It's bad American humor about getting a haircut and a beard-trim. I'll see you later."

Maryse gave my lips a quick kiss. "Promise you'll wait up for me?" Her fingers trembled. She continued in a whisper, her eyes blurred by sudden tears, "I don't want to be alone, tonight. Promise me?"

"Sure. I'll wait up."

After bidding Maryse a good evening, I got off at the Métro station, and made my way up the steps to the sidewalk. Her kisses were nice. She not wanting to be alone and wanting me to wait up was even nicer. But why me? If she wanted company or passion or a combination of both, why ask me when Molyneux was available? And if her husband had not telephoned René, as Maryse claimed, why had she called her husband a bastard? And what did 'fall-guy' have to do with anything? Something was not right. Had she lied to me? Unfortunately, the only way I could determine the truth was to visit Baudouin Rousseau. Something I was not looking forward to doing, but something I could not avoid.

* * * *

Two hours later, I reached my flat, clipped and cropped, with a bundle of semi-new clothes, under one arm.

My stomach let go a loud rumble as I stripped off my jeans and shirt. Despite the uncertainty of my future, my second-favorite organ still maintained a strong physical desire for satisfaction. I had planned to skip the evening meal. There were rules about confronting danger. The most important one had to do with facing one's foes on an empty stomach. In that way, upchuck would not occur in the heat of battle—or in my case, on the Mafioso's shoes when he pulled out his gun.

I slipped on my newly acquired denim slacks and green sweater amidst a series of painful stomach-growls. I rubbed my middle and reconsidered supper. It was only fair to give it a little French cooking. After all, the poor complaining thing had been patiently awaiting this evening's feast. It cannot be easy digesting coffee and rolls meal after meal.

I checked my watch. It was nearly the appointed hour for Mme. Flaubert's nightly culinary offering. It was also the last chance I would have to change my mind, again. Should I join the others and glut myself on French delights? Then, retire to my flat and await the arrival of Maryse? Or should I head off to face the second most dangerous man in the Corsican Mafia? I wanted to do the former. But I could not avoid the latter. Not with René's threat hanging over my head like an axe. With stomach gurgling in anticipation, I left my flat and hurried down the hall.

The light was so dim when I walked into the communal dining room I bumped into several of my co-habitants before finding a vacant spot in which to stand. But after a few seconds of blinking, my eyes accustomed themselves to the low light and I glanced around. The room was long and narrow. The source of the light came from a small, brass chandelier containing only one working bulb. This was suspended over a maple dining table, near the midpoint of the latter's length. It was a very large table. In fact, it ran nearly the length of the room and spanned nearly the width.

I counted thirteen chairs encircling it. Six were along two sides of the table. The thirteenth chair was at the head. However, there were only twelve place-settings. One chair, on the far side and at the end, stood before an empty spot. Did someone die? Or were the rumors of my impending demise at the hands of Baudouin Rousseau preceding me?

I looked for Maryse. But she was apparently still doing whatever she had planned to do that required me to await her return. I wish I would've been able to understand more of what she had said to her husband. Why had Maryse become so upset during their discussion of the telephone message René had given me? Why did she refer to it as a bad joke?

A number of the other residents were already seated at the table. The rest were busily chatting back and forth across it. No one, it seemed, wanted to wander far from their assigned seat. I spotted a vacant chair in front of the last place-setting on my side of the table, and quickly settled into it. Despite my dread of what was to occur at 10 o'clock, I smiled with anticipation over the forthcoming meal. Dare I hope for *Boeuf Bourguignon*? Or *Coq au vin*? Even *Cassoulet* would not be a disappointment.

I sniffed the air, trying to detect the menu's offering. No urine, fortunately. But I did detect plenty of garlic. There was also a hint of vinegar along with another elusively murky odor. What was that? Roasted rabbit? It had been quite some time since I last enjoyed *Lapin a La Cocotte*. No, it could not be rabbit. There was far too much garlic being used. Chicken? I shall not turn my nose up at *Poulet Provencal*. No. Again it was the excessive garlic. Perhaps, the pending meal was guinea fowl? Dear God, please let it be *Roast Guinea Fowl Alsacian*?

Outside the boarding house, a passing truck backfired. This caused me to leave my meal-ponderings in favor of renewed suspicions about Maryse. Why had she spoken Corsican when she telephoned her husband? Surely Baudouin Rousseau understood French. Obviously, because she needed to cloak her words by talking in a language I would not likely understand. So what was said, other than name-calling and a remark about a 'fall-guy'? Plenty. Her words were nearly rampant as they crossed her lips. And whatever was replied from the other end had upset her tremendously.

What about her meeting with Molyneux at Le Fumoir? Had he followed us there? Based upon her reaction to his presence, she had not arranged for his arrival. And why had she purposely silenced Molyneux with a warning-sign that I understood French? She later claimed he was not her lover. But if that was true, why was it imperative his remarks were not understood by me? And if it was so important I remain in my flat, tonight, why had René specified a particular time for meeting Baudouin Rousseau? And what about René's insistence that I not be late?

A raucous laugh broke my concentration. I glanced around the room, again. Someone to my right was complaining about the rising cost of living. As expected, it became the general topic of discussion. Raise wages, someone across from me suggested. Cut production costs, another spouted. Lower taxes and shoot the Prime Minster, was a third approach. Not having ever met the Prime Minister of France I was unable to evaluate the economic improvement his abrupt passing might make. But, on the whole, I liked the idea of a dead politician.

Mme. Flaubert entered the dining room. She was clothed in formal evening attire including a blue velvet gown and sparkling diamonds draped around her goitrous neck. As one might expect, our landlady's arrival coincided with frantic chair-leg scraping, by those still unseated. This was followed by the usual concerto of flatware hitting fired-clay plates by all concerned.

After greeting us as a group, Mme. Flaubert requested I rise and introduce myself.

I did my best, drooling onto my shirt only twice.

When I sat down she made the same request of the others, for my benefit.

One by one each stood and offered a brief recitation about professional and personal pursuits, as well as the length of their residency at her boarding house.

Acelin Desmarais was first to tell the tale. He was short and plump, probably in his late fifties. He claimed to be a financial advisor. But from the shifty look in his eyes, I suspect his professional leanings were closer to that of bookmaker. He had been living at Mme. Flaubert's for two months.

Ciprien Leveque was next to speak. He was tall and gaunt with a hatchet face. He, too, had been living at Mme. Flaubert's for two months. He was a sixtyish sales clerk in a men's clothing store. At the close of his recital, Ciprien winked at me. I did not wink back.

Maurice Bouvier was a hulking, square-faced man. He looked to be about my age. He worked as an automobile mechanic. He also had been living at Mme. Flaubert's for two months. He reminded me of one of the men I saw speaking with René and Avoyelles, outside the restoration room. Bouvier? Somehow that name was oddly familiar.

Didier Arceneau was quite elderly. He had a short, spare figure, a keen, smooth-shaven, ascetic face, topped by a mop of snow-white hair. His dress was a bit unusual, albeit elegant. It consisted of a swallowtail tuxedo replete with gray spats protecting his patent leather shoes. He owned a winery in the province of Provence-Alpes-Côte d'Azur. He was staying at Mme. Flaubert's during his annual vacation in Paris.

Herve Gravois was about forty and stocky. He gave the impression of being an amiable fellow. But I suspect he was something quite different when renting cars to tourists. He had been residing at Mme. Flaubert's for several years.

Marcellus Laroche was youngish, somewhere past thirty. He was sullen in nature. This probably served him well as a truck driver. When prompted by Mme. Flaubert, he admitted to having lived there nearly a year.

Gillet Chevalier had a squat, heavy body. His head was topped by a shaggy mane of dark hair. A thickly curled van dyke decorated what looked to be a receding chin. One of his front teeth was capped in gold. He claimed to be a barker at *Le Bal du Moulin Rouge*. He had lived at Mme. Flaubert's for only two months. He, too, looked like one of the men I saw speaking with René and Avoyelles.

Mme. Cossette Fortescue was a tall, thin, hard-eyed widow of middle years. She was blessed with a sour face and an equally sour voice. She wore glasses with lenses that looked like the bottoms of ashtrays. She began her recitation by stating, with admiration, that she had a stepbrother who was a physician. As she spoke, Mme. Cossette Fortescue expressed herself in affected sentences in which her lips formed the syllables with extreme care, one by one. It was as if she wanted what she said to be considered words of great price; words that must be lifted to the highest level of verbalized perfection. She closed her story by saying her husband had died on their honeymoon. I could not help but toy with the idea that her spouse's demise had actually been a suicide, and she was too embarrassed to admit it. Her facial expressions indicated that Mme. Cossette Fortescue found me as revolting as I found her.

Mademoiselle Fabienne Prideux was tall, red-haired, strikingly attractive and about twenty years of age. Although her figure was not svelte, she looked extremely fit. From any angle, one could not help but notice her provocative hips and more than ample bosom. She worked as a clerk in a law office. As Fabienne spoke, I noticed Didier Arceneau's eyes watching her lustily; not that I blamed him. Although Fabienne was not an uncommon name I had to wonder if she was the Fabienne with whom René was involved?

Mme. Jenay Simon was petite and elderly. She had bluish hair and an oval face, of delicate construction. Her lips where thin and she smiled easily. Her long fingernails were lacquered ruby red. She had recently sold her dress shop, and was looking forward to retirement. She, too, was offering an admiring gaze—but hers was upon Didier Arceneau.

Mademoiselle Madeleine Moreau was tall and lean. She was a waitress at the café below my flat. When she spoke, she opened her mouth so wide I thought it might be possible to dive down her throat. Tipping, she insisted in closing, was expected regardless of income. Instinctively, my hands went to my pockets in order to protect what little remained of mine.

Maryse Rousseau had not arrived by the time the others finished their tales. Mme. Flaubert seemed concerned by this and asked if anyone had seen her. I reported that Maryse had mentioned running an errand. My words seemed to reassure my landlady.

Mme. Flaubert picked up the small silver bell resting next to her plate and gave it a ring. Immediately, two young men in tight-fitting jeans and t-shirts appeared. Each carried a large kettle containing the garlic-ladened delight intended for our plates.

The distribution of food was a clumsy effort. But one probably used since Mme. Flaubert first offered rooms to let. A ladled portion was placed on the plate in front of the server. Then that plate was passed down the table to the last person not yet served. This, in turn, signaled that individual to hand his or her plate to the next person up the line until the server was handed another empty plate. This would be filled and the process repeated.

I was seated at the far end of one side of the table. So my portion of the feast reached me, before the others. I was stunned by the sight of it. Not only was my plate filled with gray muck, but it contained chunks of what looked like pink cable. I jabbed one of these objects with my fork. The tines entered after some insistence. Then I raised the morsel up to eye-level in order to examine it. It had rubber-like interior and its exterior had a curious pattern: like a collection of narrow rings joined together. Upon further consideration, I came to the conclusion that the morsel was like a segment of rat's tail. I could not imagine it.

Tonight's meal was not *Roast Guinea Fowl Alsacian*.

I set the morsel and the others like it aside. Then, I began to eat the remaining meat and vegetables.

I was so hungry, I gulped my food. However as the contents of my plate were reduced to only the cable-like pieces, I realized the mistake of being impetuous. In a wild bout of fancy, my imagination conjured up the image of the tenant, represented by the missing place-setting, having been butchered in Mme. Flaubert's kitchen for this feast. The cable-like pieces were nothing less than the overcooked pieces of his private parts. My stomach started rolling. My throat began calling the gag reaction. My tongue tried to tie itself into a bow.

I set down my fork, and softly prayed that what was in my stomach would remain there. When that failed to lull my surging innards, I quickly rose and excused myself.

Outside, with one hand gripping my gurgling belly, I hobbled toward the subway station. Never in my life had I experienced such a disgusting culinary composition. It had been so vile, the thought of death at the hands of M. Rousseau dangled before me like dessert. How in hell was I going to survive on the pittance paid me when I could not consume the evening meal supplied by my landlady?

"Monsieur, I beg of you!" a wheezing voice called to my back.

I stopped and turned to see Didier Arceneau struggling along the sidewalk, trying to catch up with me.

"I must discuss a matter of the utmost delicacy," he coughed.

"M. Arceneau," I returned, pointing toward the Métro station. "I am sorry. But I have an appointment that cannot be delayed."

"Tomorrow, then," he declared, halting his approach, one hand clutching at his chest. "At your flat."

I nodded. "Assuming we are both still alive." Then, I turned and hurried on my way.

* * * *

The ride to the rue de l'Ancienne-Comédie station was long and tiring. Shortly before ten o'clock, I got off the Métro merely a block from the address provided by René. I was surprised at what I saw. M. Rousseau's home was actually a ten-story apartment building. In spite of my stomach's ongoing complaints, I headed toward it.

I felt I had to be prepared for two reactions from M. Rousseau. One of him expecting my presence and the other of him being completely confused by it. If he had telephoned René, I would deny any romantic intentions toward Maryse in my best lisp and most effeminate hand-waving. If he had not left the message for me, then I would apologize for intruding upon his evening and depart. Either way, a man in his position would hardly want to draw any type of notoriety toward himself by exhibiting physical violence. That sounded convincing in a morbid, off-key sort of way.

41

By the time I was in the apartment building's elevator and on my way up to the tenth floor, I was nearly convinced there was nothing to worry about. Unfortunately, when the lift-doors opened and I saw the long hallway, I lost my courage—as well as the contents of my stomach.

For several minutes I vomited and vowed that a retreat would be in the best interests of all concerned. Then, as my stomach stabilized, I found spine enough to regaining my courage and I stumbled down the hall in search of apartment 1011.

Upon hearing my knock on that door a man, speaking in English, told me to enter.

I turned the knob, pushed open the door and stepped inside. The room was completely dark. A split second later, I heard a woman scream. I opened my mouth to speak. But before I could say a word, all sensibility left me.

* * * *

I do not know how long I was unconscious. I opened my eyes to the same dark room, sat up on the carpet and touched the sore lump at the back of my head. Although my hand did not come away with blood, someone had given my skull a determined blow.

I get to my feet and looked around, my head spinning. Although the lights in the apartment were off, I could still see my surroundings, because of the moonlight shining in through the windows. The living room looked like it had been searched. Furniture was toppled. Wall hangings were on the floor. Everywhere, there seemed to be the scent of something tart—lemony. Had I busted in on a robbery?

From the balcony, I heard voices. I turned in that direction and cocked an ear. The talk seemed to be coming from beyond the curtains, floating back and forth in front of the doorway.

I staggered toward the noise, pushing the curtains aside. But I found no one on the balcony. Then I heard the voices once more. They were louder now and quite frantic and insistent, coming from somewhere below. I went over to the balcony railing and looked down. Ten floors below, I could just make out a group of people huddled together in the darkened parking lot. Arms were waving. Fingers were pointing, upward. It was as if they were accusing me of something.

I stumbled back, intending to leave. But when I returned to the living room, the lights were on. Two men in suits were standing in front of the door with guns in their hands. One was tall, dark and of middle age with a strong and muscular build. His face was smooth with a broad nose and a firm-set jaw. The other was young, short, plump and had shifty eyes. From the grim looks upon their faces, neither was a jokester. So I took their implied threat seriously.

"All I did was have lunch with his wife," I explained.

"I congratulate you, Monsieur," said the older man, offering me a slight bow.

The other fellow was more formal in addressing me. "Police," he declared. "You are under arrest, Monsieur."

"For the Degas'?" I gaped. "I swear on all that's holy, I never knew my uncle was going to sell them."

"The charge is murder," returned the first man, looking at me askance as if his explanation should be extraneous.

I blinked, hoping this was another bad dream or some weird hallucination, a result of my head-injury. "Who in hell did I kill?"

"Baudouin Rousseau, Monsieur," returned the second, with a roll of his eyes. "As if you did not know."

I was struck dumb.

The first man said, dreamily, "A woman such as Mme. Rousseau is worth killing for, *N'est-ce pas?*"

I could have wept. "I don't suppose you'd believe me if I told you I was gay?"

"No," said the first man, who then winked. "But I am willing to let you convince me."

I shook my head. "I'd rather face the murder-charge."

Chapter 4
A Hole Deeply Dug for Dying

There are 18 million crimes reported in France, each year. Of those, less than 2% are prosecuted. Considering the population of France is less than 62 million, the probability of a tourist sharing space with a criminal is very likely. As such, being a person of interest in a crime is the norm for Parisians. But if one is an American in France, being a person of interest is the same as being guilty.

Immediately after my arrest I was taken to *Police Nationale* headquarters at 11 rue des Saussaies. Six hours later, I was still there shackled hand and foot, sitting in a chair in front of a desk occupied by a plump, sixtyish man with fish eyes. He had identified himself as Chief Inspector Claude Monet. His ideas concerning human rights, however, did not coincide with mine. Frankly, his ideas on the subject were more or less out of the stone-age. In his favor, however, the Chief Inspector did pride himself on being related to the famous painter. Yes, I did ask.

"For the hundredth time," I pleaded, "I did not kill M. Baudouin Rousseau."

"You lie!" he shouted back.

Chief Inspector Monet was not what I would call a spiffy dresser. He wore a black suit and a white shirt buttoned to the collar. His tattered necktie was also black. It lay coiled upon the desktop like a discarded rag. His scuffed shoes creaked when he walked. He was also not impressive in stature. He was slightly over five feet in height and nearly as wide as he was tall.

"Why would I kill M. Rousseau?" I returned, wearily. "What motive would I have?"

One of Monet's dark eyebrows arched slightly. "His money of course."

"What money?"

"The money his wife will inherit."

"That's ridiculous! Anything she inherits is hers. What good will it do me?"

"You intend to marry Mme. Rousseau, of course."

"Get it through your thick skull, Monet! I did not kill Baudouin Rousseau!"

"You were arrested in Baudouin Rousseau's apartment immediately after his death." He thrust a sausage-like finger at me. "Do you deny you this?"

I shrugged. "Obviously, I was arrested there or I would not be here listening to your stupid suppositions. But, it couldn't have been immediately after Rousseau died. Someone must've reported finding his body. How long did it take your bumbling men to get to his apartment from whatever bar they were carousing in?"

He glared at me, his bulging brown eyes unblinking. "Do not attempt to twist the circumstances, Monsieur."

"I'm not twisting anything. I'm trying to straighten your thinking. For hours now, I have been telling you I had an appointment with Baudouin Rousseau. I went there at the appointed time. I did not kill him."

"You expect me to believe that pitiful story about a phone message from M. Rousseau requesting your presence?" he scoffed.

"It is the truth. I told you before, I am begging you now. Ask my boss at the Louvre about it. Ask René. I'm sure he'll confirm everything I've said."

Monet made a dismissive gesture. "I did speak with René D'aubigne." He paused to rub his stubbly chin with the palm of one hairy hand. "In fact, it was just before you were returned to my office from your cell, this last time. M. D'aubigne flatly denies there was a message. Further, he denies having ordered you to meet Baudouin Rousseau."

"That lying bastard! No wonder he took the note back. What in hell does René have against me?"

"Probably, the knowledge that you are a habitual liar."

"All right. Forget René. Forget the note. Forget my explanation of events. Consider only the lump on the back of my head. It is the size of Godzilla's right testicle. Obviously, somebody hit me. Equally obvious, I was knocked unconscious. Even more obvious, that lump is why I was at the apartment when your men arrived and arrested me."

Monet smiled like a shark eying its prey, all teeth and eyeballs. "Do you take me for a fool, Monsieur? You did that injury to yourself when you realized you were trapped in the apartment with no way to escape."

"Don't be ridiculous! If I wanted to kill somebody, would I do it in France? And if I did come to France to kill somebody, would I kill a member of the Corsican Mafia? And if I did…"

He raised a hand to silence my protestations. Then in slow, deliberate words Monet said, "You are forgetting that I know about your romantic relationship with Mme. Rousseau."

"Again, I tell you... Maryse and I barely know each other."

Monet tilted across the desk sneering, "Now who is being ridiculous? You and she ate lunch at Le Fumoir café." Again the sausage-finger waggled at me. "Do you deny this?"

My shoulders sagged in defeat. "You got me on that one, Chief Inspector. We went Dutch treat at her invitation. But it could hardly be construed as a romantic rendezvous. I insisted she leave the tip."

"Hah! The romance came later, as we both know. When the two of you had a tryst in the Louvre's parking lot." The Chief Inspector darted a quick glance at his watch. "Deny that, if you can."

"Where could we have a tryst in a parking lot? Neither of us owns a car!"

His eyebrows shot up like a basalt version of the 'Golden Arches.' "I have a witness who swears you and Mme. Rousseau were on the asphalt between two parked cars humping away like there was no tomorrow."

"That is a lie! What do you take me for? Some sex-crazed lunatic who grabs a woman and tosses her down on the tarmac for a nooner in front of the entire world?"

"I must admit your lack of French breeding makes that event highly improbable," admitted Monet, not unkindly. "But the witness is adamant."

"What witness? Who would know us? If all you have is a lousy description..."

He cut me off with, "I have more than that, Monsieur. I have a sworn statement from Mme. Cossette Fortescue as to what she saw in the parking lot. She named both of you." He drew from his pocket a blackened, odoriferous pipe before saying, "Do you deny knowing Mme. Cossette Fortescue?"

"I knew that woman hated me. I could tell it in her voice. But to lie like that... What in hell did I ever do to her? How is it you have a statement from her?"

"She telephoned me shortly after your arrest. She felt it was her civic duty to report the event."

"Did it not strike you as odd that she knew about my arrest? Isn't it far more likely that she is trying to frame me?"

The detective blew out a weary breath, as he patted his pockets looking for his tobacco pouch. "Why not confess to Rousseau's murder, Monsieur?" persisted Monet, doggedly. "You are caught. You have no defense. *Finis.*"

"I am not saying another word until I speak with someone at the American embassy," I grumbled.

"Then you will have a very long, silent wait. Because no one is going to tell them you are here." Not finding the pouch, he stuffed the pipe between his teeth and noisily sucked upon its stem.

"I have a right to a telephone call!" I shouted.

His head wagged, as he returned the pipe to his suit. "This is not the United States, Monsieur. In France, you have only such rights as I grant."

Chief Inspector Monet fished the evening paper from the trash can next to his desk, and leisurely began turning the pages. Although he feigned an attitude of apparent idleness, every time I made the slightest movement his glance darted in my direction, causing a slight frown.

"Look at me," I blurted, when my frustrations with him peaked. "Do I look stupid enough to kill a member of the Corsican Mafia?"

"Frankly, yes." Monet dropped the newspaper into the trash and tilted back in his chair, his eyes suspicious slits. "Mme. Rousseau helped you do it, didn't she? It was all her idea, wasn't it? Tell me everything, and I will see what can be done to reduce your sentence."

"Of course she did not help me kill her husband."

His eyes shot open in surprise. "You admit you did it by yourself?"

"No! What I mean is, she was not even with me."

"So you agreed to meet her afterward, yes?" He half-rose to his feet, grinning at me. "You wanted her. You knew the divorce agreement would get her nothing. So you killed her husband in order for her to inherit his entire estate."

"Inherit what? Baudouin Rousseau was a gangster, not a financier!"

"A very wealthy gangster with numerous real estate holdings – including the apartment building in which you murdered him."

"Think about it, Chief Inspector… If I am a murderer, why would I hang around after killing Rousseau? Nobody is that stupid."

"Stupid or otherwise, you did. It is an undeniable fact. Otherwise you would not have been arrested." With a self-satisfied snort, he slumped back into his chair, plopped his big feet on the desktop and began humming. "The game is over, Monsieur."

You are probably wondering why I had not demanded an attorney to represent me. I had. And I did it when I first arrived at Monet's office. But all I got in return for my request was several hours being ignored in a holding cell, between venomous bouts of interrogation.

The Chief Inspector frowned angrily. Then his hands went to his face and he dragged his palms across it. Afterward, for many seconds, he stared down at his big belly, as if expecting it to explode.

"Who else is vying for Mme. Rousseau's favors?" he asked, in due course.

"How would I know?"

"You must've seen her with other men." He leaned on arm on the desk, tilting toward me. "How many men did she verbally parade before you, shaming you, taunting you? How many times did she do this before you finally agreed to kill M. Rousseau?"

"All right. Look at me. Take a damn good look at me! Do I look strong enough to push an armed gangster over the railing of his tenth floor apartment? I can barely haul my own ass off the pot!"

He rose up slapping his hands together. "Check one off for the brain dead American! It would, indeed, take more than you to have manhandled Baudouin Rousseau to his death."

I gaped for a moment, completely confused by his response. "Is that good or bad, from my prospective?"

"It merely means you had help, Monsieur."

"That has got to be the stupidest deduction ever made in the history of crime detection! Who in their right mind would help me kill a Corsican Mafioso? Would you? Do you know anyone who might? I sure as hell don't!"

"Your evasiveness tells me you know who her other lovers are," he smirked. Monet settled back into his chair, watching me with a disconcerting look of inquiring interest. "What was the arrangement? You would share her as well as her inheritance with them, once her husband was dead? Do not be ashamed to tell me all the hideously perverted details."

I was about to call him the dimmest bulb on the Christmas tree, among other things, when I remembered Dr. Molyneux. "Actually, there is another man."

He tilted toward me shouting, "You confess that he helped you kill M. Rousseau?"

"Of course not! I mean there is a man who I think is in love with Maryse. She denied it. But from the way she looked at him and he looked at her, I think she was lying."

He sank back into his chair. "Just one man? We are discussing a woman about to be divorced. A passionate young woman blistering with the fire of lust in her loins!"

"I don't know anything about her blistered loins. But a guy who probably does is Dr. Michele Molyneux. During the week he lives at Mme. Flaubert's. Not only did I see Molyneux holding Maryse's hands, but he kissed her cheek. Maybe it was him and Maryse your witness saw on the asphalt between the cars? That miserable old crone is blind as a bat."

Monet snickered. "I knew it was just a matter of time before I broke down your defenses. And I will do the same to M. Molyneux. In the end, he will testify against you for killing M. Rousseau and you will testify against him. Then, both of you shall testify against Mme. Rousseau. In the end I will have all of you."

"Why do you keep ignoring the fact that someone knocked me unconscious? How can I kill someone if I am unconscious?"

He rolled his eyes mockingly. "You, yourself, insisted a doctor examine your injury. A doctor did. And the doctor agreed with me that you could have caused that injury to yourself. End of story."

"But I didn't cause it!"

"I have heard that sob-story until I am sick to death of it," he returned, batting the air with both hands. "Admit it. Mme. Rousseau entrapped you with her charms. Using her own keys she let you into the apartment. Then the two of you…"

"Her keys? Why on earth would we risk being seen together on the Métro going to her husband's apartment if we were planning to kill him? I told you. I arrived alone. Ask anyone who was in that same Métro-car I sat in. They will tell you that Maryse was not with me."

"She drove in her own car, of course."

"Maryse does not know how to drive. Why would she have a car?"

"Of course she knows how to drive," he snorted. "Mme. Rousseau possesses a valid driving license and owns a new gray Peugeot. She garages it only a few blocks away from Mme. Flaubert's."

Again, I was struck dumb. Was Monet lying to shake my faith in Maryse? Or had she lied to me about something as innocuous as knowing how to drive?

"Listen to me?" I pleaded. "At least hear me out, please?"

His shoulders heaved with disinterest.

"I can recall knocking on Rousseau's apartment door," I explained. "I remember somebody telling me to come in. I opened the door. The next thing I remember is getting up off the carpet shortly before your men arrived. I'm trying to remember the in-between's but so far no luck."

"Don't lie to me!" His brow furrowed like a freshly plowed field and he turned toward me swiftly, his face suffused with sudden interest. "You must've felt the blow that struck you down."

"I know it sounds crazy, but I don't even remember being hit. But I must have been. I got the lump. Only I didn't feel it happen."

He stood up his lips pursed in thought. Then he began to pace beside the desk. With each step mumblings crept from between his moving lips, as if he were rehearsing a speech. I watched, and waited.

Eventually, Monet stopped and stared at me, his eyebrows knotted. "Was Mme. Rousseau aware you were going to visit her husband?"

"No. Yes. You see she told me not to go? But I did, anyway."

He blinked in confusion. "Told you not to go? Why?"

"Something about her husband having a meeting with François Chiappe."

"Did she tell you what the meeting was about?"

I wagged my head. "I told her what René had told me. That's when Maryse became upset and told me to stay home."

"Became upset?" Monet repeated, sharply. "Why?"

"I don't know. But she telephoned her husband. They talked at length. During which, she became even more upset. She said to forget about what René had threatened. She said that she would take care of it. She told me to stay in my flat."

He spread his arms beseechingly. "If that is the case why in hell did you go?"

"I had to know the truth!"

"What truth? Truth is not a consideration when evaluating your immeasurable stupidity."

"I thought Maryse might have lied. I thought Rene and Cesar Avoyelles might be in league with her against me. Only her husband could tell me the truth. I had to know!"

"Are you paranoid? Do you see people plotting against you all the time?"

"Of course I'm paranoid! I'm under arrest for a murder I did not commit!"

He tilted his head back and groaned at the ceiling. "The only truth is what I say it is." Then his chin dipped and he was glaring at me, again. "If you and Mme. Rousseau are just friends—as you claim. Why in hell would you care whether she lied, or not?"

I started to blurt what I had overheard concerning the murder plot, but I caught myself. Admitting that conversation, at this juncture, would only make matters worse. Not only had I not reported a murder plot. But any claim I might make concerning it would be construed a lie to protect the others involved in Rousseau's murder.

"I don't care about her," I returned. "All right, I do care."

Monet grinned. "So you finally admit you are in love with Mme. Rousseau, eh?"

"I admit—I guess I like her. Is that a crime?"

"Only if you killed her husband, in order to prove it." He returned to his chair and sat down. "Why would René D'aubigne insist you meet with M. Rousseau?"

"I assumed he was afraid that if I did not, M. Rousseau might send men to the Louvre – after me."

"M. D'aubigne thought that if such an event occurred, it could result in his own injury or perhaps death?"

"Possibly. I didn't ask him."

One of the inspector's dirty fingernails tapped the desktop. "If this alleged note exists, where is it?"

"René took it back and put it in his pocket."

"Why?"

"Why what?"

His arms flailed the air. "Why in hell did he take the note from you?"

"I don't know. I guess I'll ask him. I'll also ask why in hell he lied to you."

"Do not plan on that being anytime soon, Monsieur." He scratched his groin, and then added in a lower tone, the words coming swiftly. "Here is my difficulty. If I am to believe your story, then I must assume René D'aubigne is involved in M. Rousseau's murder. There is no other explanation for his lies. But what motive would he have? Did he do business with M. Rousseau? Does he, too, want to possess Mme. Rousseau? What? You, on the other hand, have a great deal of motive. Not only that, but you were arrested at the crime-scene."

"I know it must look bad, but I would never hurt anyone."

"Did M. D'aubigne have business dealings with M. Rousseau? Was M. D'aubigne preoccupied with Mme. Rousseau?"

"I don't know about business dealings. But I know René isn't interested in Maryse. René is having an affair with someone named Fabienne."

Monet jumped to his feet shouting, "Fabienne Prideux?"

I shrugged. "I've only overheard him talking to her on the phone. Do you know Fabienne Prideux?"

"It is I who will ask the questions!" he roared, settling back into his chair. Then he fell silent. After a few seconds the Chief Inspector said "Well, if he is having an affair with a young woman, obviously his finances are strained. That could tempt him into illegal activities. Who better than M. Rousseau to contact, under such circumstances?" He fumbled with his lower lip, drifting back into thought. At length he asked, "Did M. D'aubigne ever discuss M. Rousseau with you?"

"Only concerning the note."

"In so doing, did you get the impression he knew M. Rousseau personally?"

"Not as such. But he knew a great deal about Rousseau."

"Either he is lying or you are," sighed Monet. "You do see there can be no other explanation? But if he lied, why? Obviously, because he was involved in M. Rousseau's murder. But to what end? In your own words, he has no interest in Mme. Rousseau and is not doing business with M. Rousseau, therefore he has no motive. You, on the other hand, do."

I dropped my chin to my chest groaning, "I swear I am not lying."

Again he fell silent, thinking. After a minute or so he said, "Does D'aubigne talk to anyone else? What I mean is, persons who are not affiliated with the Louvre? Business associates, for example?"

"René and Cesar Avoyelles are well acquainted," I replied, raising my eyes back to his.

Monet gave a noncommittal nod. "Anyone else?"

I started to shake my head when I recalled the two men René and Avoyelles had met with, outside the restoration room. "I saw two other men. I think they were Bouvier and Chevalier—two tenants at Mme. Flaubert's. I saw them talking with René and Avoyelles."

He swung toward me like a gate on greased hinges in a high wind. "Those two thugs?"

"I might be mistaken. I really didn't get a good look at either of man during that conversation."

His fist hit the desk with a bang! "Now you have said something worthwhile!"

"I don't understand."

"Of course *you* don't. You are an idiot." He thumped his chest. "The important thing is for *me* to understand – and I think I do." He waggled a finger overhead. "It is starting to fall into place."

"Is that a plus or minus, from my view?"

"Did Mme. Rousseau at any time discuss her financial situation with you?" he asked, ignoring my question.

"No."

"She must have! You are her lover! You would've asked. She would've said."

"I am not her lover! She helped me get a flat at Mme. Flaubert's. Before that and after, we may have chit-chatted at work a few times. And, I admit, on the Métro she did push her boob against my arm when I asked about her pending divorce. Whereupon, Maryse told me her husband was divorcing her because he'd found someone else. And then she kissed me and told me to wait up for her because she did not want to be alone. But beyond that…"

"And you believed her about the divorce?" he interposed.

"I had no reason not to."

"I know for a fact Baudouin Rousseau filed for divorce claiming infidelity on his wife's part." Monet shook his head to emphasize his refute of Maryse's words. "It is in the court records. It cannot be disputed."

I can hear you snorting with amusement. Yes. Maryse lied to me when she claimed to have been faithful to her husband. She also lied when she told me her husband was divorcing her because he had found someone else. Well, I admit it. I was a sucker to fall for her lines. You are probably going to suggest that she lied about other things. I also agree with that. But you must admit, it is very hard to call someone so nicely packaged, a liar.

"When did Bouvier and Chevalier meet with M. D'aubigne?" Monet asked.

"Yesterday morning."

"Did you hear what was said?"

I wagged my head. "They were out in the hallway."

"Did this discussion appear to be friendly?"

"I didn't see any smiles. M. Cesar Avoyelles was involved in it. He should be able to tell you what was talked about."

The Chief Inspector made an impatient movement with one hand. "Let us assume—for argument's sake—you are telling the truth." He thrust a finger toward the ceiling for emphasis. "I say, assume! Then what first appeared to be a simple homicide for gain becomes a much more complex affair."

I had no idea what he was talking about. I knew from the overheard conversation there had been a diamond theft and that Rousseau was supposed to dispose of the loot. I also knew from that same conversation that Baudouin had been delaying the payout and at least two players were upset—wait! Bouvier! Buji had called the other man, Bouvier!

"I think you're right about Chevalier and Bouvier, Chief Inspector."

He snorted. "Of course I am right. I am never wrong."

"What I mean is, I think they were involved with M. Rousseau and they might be the ones who killed him."

His nose twitched. "Why?"

I did not dare tell him about the overheard conversation. But at the same time, I had to come up with a rational explanation as to why I thought those two and killed M. Rousseau.

"I—I overheard Bouvier talking with someone, a day or two ago," I lied. "At the time I didn't think it was important. But now I believe he and that other man were planning to kill M. Rousseau."

"What man?"

"Chevalier, I think."

"Where was this conversation?"

"I—I—Outside Mme. Flaubert's. They were talking as I went past."

He frowned. "And from two seconds of overheard conversation you came to the conclusion that they killed M. Rousseau?"

"We—I—I'm—I've got very good hearing," I returned.

"Are you absolutely positive the other man was Chevalier?"

I shook my head. "Sorry."

"Ears like a bat but eyes like a mole." Monet scratched his chin, thinking. "Did you have a key to M. Rousseau's apartment?"

"Of course not."

His feet hit the floor and the fat finger of accusation pierced the air between us. "Then how did you get in?"

"The door was unlocked."

"I suppose it opened like magic?" Monet said, making a mocking face.

"I told you, I knocked. Then I was instructed to enter."

"Instructed, how? In French? In English? In Corsican? How?"

I hesitated for many seconds thinking back. "In English."

"English? You are certain?"

"Frankly, no. But to the best of my recollection the words were spoken in English."

"Was it a man's voice or a woman's?"

"A man."

He slapped the desktop with the palm of one hand. "I know all about Baudouin Rousseau, Monsieur. He did not speak English! He spoke only French."

"But if he's Corsican…"

"Seventy percent of all Corsican's speak only French."

Obviously, Maryse lied again. If her husband had been on the other end of the connection, why was she speaking to him in a language he would not understand? Evidently he was not the recipient of her call. He was also not the one she had called a bastard. But if not he, who was speaking to her?

"All right, damn it!" I shouted. "It must have been in French. What difference does it make?" I leaned forward adding, "I'm certain Bouvier intended to kill Rousseau."

"I want you to think back carefully," he said, shifting in his chair to get comfortable. "I want you to put yourself outside M. Rousseau's apartment door." Monet steadied his voice. "Then I want you to tell me all you heard and saw and smelled—no matter how insignificant. Understand?"

I nodded. "I arrived a minute or two before ten o'clock. I knocked. A man told me to come in. I opened the door…"

"Stop! You have the door open. What do you see?"

"Nothing. The apartment is dark because all the lights are off."

"Of course you can see! The light from the hallway is shining into the apartment, over your shoulders. Concentrate. Think back. What is before your eyes?"

I shut my eyes and replayed those memories. "I see furniture."

"Good! Is it situated correctly or toppled?"

"It's like it should be."

"What else?"

"I see shadows around a table."

"People?"

"Yes."

"Excellent! How many?"

"One is sitting in a chair. Another is standing right next to the first. Then there is one other—much smaller."

"Male or female?"

I concentrated harder trying to ascertain gender from a blur of memory. "The one sitting and the one next are both men—I think. They look formidable. The other is slightly built, a woman—I think."

"Can you see any of their faces?"

I opened my eyes and wagged my head.

He smiled, almost giggling. "Then what?"

"I stepped inside the apartment, and..."

"Stop! You are in there. What do you see?"

I clenched my eyes and strained with concentration. "A curtain is moving to my left—the one in front of the balcony doors. They are all staring at me."

"The three you described? Can you now see their faces? Your eyes have adjusted to the darkness, you must see their faces!"

I shook my head. "No. But I see two sets of eyes—shining."

"And?"

"And I smell something. Cologne. Citrusy."

"And?"

"The women shouts at me."

"What did she say?"

"Nothing. It was more a cry of warning."

"And then?"

I opened my eyes and shrugged. "Nothing. It all goes black."

He leaned back in his chair rubbing his hands. "I've got it. Not all of it. But enough to make a surmisal. You saw two sets of eyes and yet you saw three people. Therefore the man sitting had his eyes closed. Why?"

"I don't know."

"Because he was dead or unconscious. Therefore we can assume the seated man was M. Baudouin Rousseau!" Monet thrust a finger toward the ceiling. "Finally you have helped!" Then he held up one hand to tic off its fingers with the other. "From this we know that at least three people were involved in Baudouin Rousseau's murder. The woman, the man standing next to the seated figure, and the one who struck you. All the furniture is placed properly. So what does that tell you?"

"France is underrated as a holiday destination?"

"It tells us M. Rousseau's apartment had not yet been searched," Monet declared. "And yet we know it *was* searched. So what had they been after?"

His pompousness was so great I could not help but bait him with something from the overheard conversation that would capture his imagination. "Diamonds?"

His eyes narrowed upon me, suspiciously. "Why would you say that?"

"Like I told you, there was that conversation I overheard on the sidewalk in front of Mme. Flaubert's."

"You got a lot of information in the two seconds it took you to walk past Bouvier and Chevalier, didn't you?" He settled back in his chair, stewing in silence. At length he said, "Now, that you are at M. Rousseau's we must ask ourselves why?"

"I told you…"

"I do not mean the reason you were given to go there! Why was it necessary for you to be there? Why would a group of people gathered in a man's home have wanted a stranger present? Why? Because you were to be what you American's call, the fall-guy; that is why." He thumped his chest. "Now do you see why I, Claude Monet, received promotion to Chief Inspector before I was thirty years of age?"

Fall-guy! Maryse had said it during her phone conversation on the Metro!

"Now," continued Monet, "what does that tell us? Answer, those gathered at M. Rousseau's apartment went there with the intention of killing him. Otherwise, why plan for someone else to take the blame? But what motive would a group of people have for murder?"

A female, uniformed officer came in carrying a piece of paper. "The initial autopsy report on Baudouin Rousseau, Buji."

Buji? The name snapped me out of my depression like a needle entering my backside, at the speed of light. Buji was the name mentioned in the conversation. What had Monet said earlier? A man having an affair with a young woman is going to be strapped for cash? That same man, therefore, would be enticed to partner with the likes of Baudouin Rousseau? Had this been the case? Was I actually talking to the man responsible for murdering Baudouin Rousseau? Suddenly I felt like the fly in the spider's parlor.

Monet took the paper and read it. Then he let go a series of curses ending with, "There is no chance of a mistake?"

She shook her head. "Both sodium amytal and thiopental sodium were found in Baudouin Rousseau's blood. These were administered in two massive doses, based upon the syringe injection marks. Someone with medical knowledge was involved, or so the toxicologist claims. He also claims the use of those drugs indicates a need to induce M. Rousseau to talk about something the dead man did not want to discuss."

"You mean, like Scopolamine?" Monet scoffed.

"There's no way to prove it either way," she replied, with a shrug. "The coroner said that sodium amytal and thiopental sodium work as effectively as Scopolamine. He also said there is no other reason those drugs would be paired as a treatment vehicle."

"As a *legitimate* treatment vehicle," corrected Monet. Then the Chief Inspector made a repugnant face, tilting his head toward me. "Release that idiot."

She strode over and quickly unlocked my handcuffs and shackles. Then the female officer left the room.

"I'm free to go?" I got to my feet.

"For the time being," returned Monet. "But do not attempt to leave Paris. Until my investigation into this matter is complete, you will remain here." He suddenly paused, thinking. "Mme. Rousseau was the woman in Baudouin Rousseau's apartment, of course. The man sitting is, obviously, her husband. That can only mean the other man was…"

"Was who?"

He glared at me shouting, "None of your damn business!"

"A doctor? The drugs mean a doctor, right? Molyneux, maybe?"

"Get out!" he shouted, pointing at the office door.

Typical French ingrate.

* * * *

I caught the Métro and arrived at the Louvre just a few minutes late for work. But no sooner had I reached my stool when René told me I was fired.

"What have I done, René?" I pleaded.

"Your behavior is unconscionable, M. Stuart," René D'aubigne curtly replied.

"My behavior? What about your lying to Chief Inspector Monet about that damned note? What about you telling Monet you hadn't ordered me to go to Baudouin Rousseau's flat?"

"Stop trying to confuse the issue. You murdered M. Baudouin Rousseau! Maryse told me all about it. How could you do such a thing? That poor child is so distraught she could not come to work today."

I made a pleading gesture. "René, I've killed no one. I was arrested at M. Rousseau's apartment, yes. But I am not his murderer. If you had only told Monet about the note…"

"Like I should believe your words?" he demanded, coolly.

"Why should you believe Maryse? She was there, too. If anyone is guilty of killing her husband, it's Maryse! I was just the fall-guy."

A look almost of sudden apprehension crossed his chubby face, and was gone. "Get out! Get your things and get out!"

In France, a worker can be fired without cause. No reason need be given for the termination. This, of course, is what keeps nepotism alive and flourishing among Parisian civil servants. It is also why arguing further with René would be a waste of time.

I grabbed up the few personal items I had there, and then caught the Métro to Mme. Flaubert's Boarding House.

Chapter 5
Sixty Million in Diamonds

The French love cheese more than any other food. In fact there are approximately five hundred different cheeses produced in France. These aromatic delicacies are created in either raw, pasteurized or *petit-lait* (whey) forms. Any country that can create so many cheeses must also be major player in the production of wine. In fact France is the world largest producer. Nearly six million tons of fermented grapes are bottled annually. Per capita, the French consume nearly 60 liters of wine each year. You might be thinking, if so much of a good thing is being produced why doesn't more of it reach the United States? The reason is political. Both wine and cheese are protected by the *appellation d'origine controlee*. In American terms, this means only limited quantities of a particular cheese or wine can legally be produced. The intention of the law is to stop mass production which, when running amuck, could ruin the subtle variations of the products between the various regions. But it also ensures that most of what is created in France remains there. For me, a nibble of Époisses de Bourgogne, a sip of Burgundy and life, other than mine, becomes beautiful.

When I arrived at Mme. Flaubert's I stopped at Maryse's flat and rapped on her door. I was feeling both anger and pity. I was angry because she had lied to me. I felt pity for her because she would live with the horror of being present when her husband was murdered, for the rest of her life. Disappointed when Maryse did not respond, I went to my flat and unlocked the door.

But no sooner had I stepped inside when two masked men grabbed me and shoved me across the room. Both were dressed in black clothing. The masks they wore were ski-types that allowed only the lips and eyes to show. One man held a silencer-affixed pistol. The other brandished a long-bladed knife.

"I've got no money," I told them, fanning my hands protectively. "In fact, I just got fired."

"What did you do with the damn diamonds!" the one with the gun demanded. He was thick-bodied with dirty running shoes on his feet.

"Diamonds?" I gaped, looking from one to the other. "I don't have any diamonds."

"We know you got 'em," growled the one with the knife. He was a giant of a man. On his feet were black, work boots with steel-tipped soles.

"I have no idea what you are talking about," I returned, as politely as I knew how.

The one holding the gun lunged forward and clubbed me on the jaw with the weapon's butt. The blow sent me spinning against the davenport.

"You were there when Rousseau bought it!" he shouted. "You searched the apartment afterward. We know you found the diamonds."

You are probably asking yourself, why doesn't the idiot—as Monet described me—leap out of the window to safety? The answer is an implacable one. My body is frozen with fear. Well, most of my body. One or two involuntary reactions to my terrifying circumstances are straining to make indelible remembrances upon my whiter-than-whites.

"I was arrested at Rousseau's apartment; yes," I told them, rubbing my swollen chin. "But I didn't search the apartment. It had already been searched when I came to."

"You lying bastard!" shouted the one with the knife. "I'm not about to let you walk off with our sixty-mill!"

He rushed forward and caught my right eye with a left hook. I hit the floor like a beer keg tumbling from a delivery truck. Then he squatted down, touched the tip of the knife blade to my left cheek. A flick of his wrist later and I recoiled; my left hand going to my face to cover a badly bleeding wound.

"Please believe me. I don't have your diamonds," I begged.

"Shoot the bastard," he growled to his partner, standing upright.

"If I had diamonds would I be living here?" I gurgled, in protest. "Look at this stinking dump! Would you live here with sixty million stashed somewhere?"

He kicked me in the ribs, causing me to curl up into fetal fashion.

"I swear I don't have your diamonds." I whimpered.

The one with the gun jumped forward and tried to kick me in the groin. He missed his mark and caught my right thigh, instead. With another whimper, I twisted away, clawing at the injured limb in agony.

"We're out sixty million!" shouted the one with the knife. "That means somebody's goin' down!"

I struggled to me feet and turned to face them. "Killing me won't get you anything," I choked. "Neither will beating me. I don't have your diamonds. I don't know where they are. If I did, I'd give them to you."

The one with the pistol cocked it and took aim at my head. I closed the one eye that was not swollen shut and prayed, expecting to die.

"Wait," said the one with the knife. "Maybe we've been taken for a ride. Where'd she get the idea this joker had the diamonds? He was out cold, when we left; remember? We saw the cops rolling in as we drove out. He wouldn't have had time to do a search."

"Who else could have 'em?"

"Only you and me searched the joint—as far as we know. But what if somebody came back after – I mean after the cops left? Or got there ahead of us? What if they already knew where the diamonds were and held out on the rest of us? Get what I mean?"

I opened my good eye to study the pair.

"Her?"

"Maybe. Or Buji. But she had to know, didn't she? He'd have told her, wouldn't he?"

"Why? Baudouin dumped her for that other bitch, remember?" said the one with the gun. "For my money, that one's the one who'd know. You can't make me believe she'd sit tight and wait for him to come around with the news. She'd have ragged his ass until he talked."

"Maybe. Or maybe it was the quack? Think about that. Who told us them drugs was the only way to get Baudouin to talk? Who pumped the juice into him? We all knew Baudouin was ready to kick it. What if it was all a setup? Baudouin gets put out of his misery, and the doc walks off with the stones."

"That's right. He'd have known the risks. He'd never have pumped his pal full of juice without first finding out where the stash was."

"I say we meet with the others. One of 'em has the diamonds. That, I'm sure of. So one of 'em comes across or we knock 'em all off." Then he pointed at me. "What about him?"

"What about him?" The one with the gun grinned at me. "You'll be a good little boy and keep yer mouth shut, won't ya?"

"If you go to the cops," chimed his partner, "we'll spend a week killin' you."

"I won't say anything to anybody," I quickly returned.

After they stormed out of my flat, it took me many seconds to hobble the short distance over to the open door. My ribs and leg ached. My face was bleeding, and throbbing. I felt like I was on my way to hell climbing aboard the express down-elevator. What worried me most was the amount of blood running out of the knife wound.

There was no point in trying to get an ambulance to my flat. My French was fluent. But I still had an American accent. That would mean I would wait for help until I bled to death. I staggered out into the hall intending to go outside and flag down a taxi. Assuming the driver did not mind a little leakage from his passenger, I might be able to pay him passage to a hospital.

Fortunately, my luck took a change for the better, then. Sort of. Dr. Michele Molyneux was coming down the steps carrying his Gladstone bag. If the comments those goons had made about a quack were accurate, I might be looking at Baudouin Rousseau's killer. As far as I knew, he was the only physician being friendly with Maryse Rousseau. The question in my mind was, would he also kill me if I asked for help?

"What happened, Stuart?" he gasped, rushing over.

I started to tell him I would catch a taxi, rather than delay his departure. But Molyneux slung my arm over his shoulder and half-carried me back into my flat.

"Did you fall?" he asked, settling me on the davenport.

"I was attacked. Two men. They thought I had diamonds."

He gave me as surprised look. "Diamonds?" Then Molyneux opened his medical bag and took out gauze, a bottle of something pink, a suturing needle, a small clamp and a packet of sutures. "Where would you get diamonds?"

"That's what I tried to point out to the pair who worked me over. They had the idea those diamonds should've been at Baudouin Rousseau's apartment. You're a friend of Rousseau's, aren't you?"

"I was a very good friend. I was stunned when I heard about his murder this morning." Then in one stride he was leaning over me. "This is going to hurt," he warned, as he daubed the pink antibiotic onto the wound.

He was not exaggerating. It felt like flames were enveloping my cheek. But I managed to sit still.

Then he opened the clamp and positioned it, closing the wound. "You're lucky you did not lose that eye."

Remembering the toxicology report on Baudouin Rousseau, I said, "I hope my luck is still holding."

"You'll have to sit very still. It will take four sutures to close this. The wound is cut to the bone. I'll be as quick as I can. The clamp is temporary. It will stop the bleeding, until I finish suturing. I don't have any painkiller. Can you stand a lot of pain?"

"I have so far."

He grabbed up the needle and affixed the thread-like suture. Then he leaned over me and made the first puncture. Tears flooded my eyes. It was not just from the pain. I wanted to cry like a baby from all I had endured over the last twenty-four hours.

"According to Chief Inspector Monet, Baudouin Rousseau was hopped up on drugs when he died," I winced.

"Nonsense."

"Not fun drugs. Truth-serum type drugs."

"More likely pain-killers," Molyneux countered, tying off the suture. "Truth serums are strictly movie stuff."

"Why pain killers?"

"Baudouin was dying of cancer. He was in a great deal of pain. He could no longer sleep, because of the agony. At best he would doze in a chair after being injected with painkillers."

His response surprised me. Maryse had made no mention of her husband's illness. She had agreed with me when I suggested Baudouin was sick. But I had meant that as a dig against his decision to divorce her.

"Does Maryse know?" I asked.

He quickly moved onto the next suture. "Of course."

Maybe Monet had it wrong, at least in terms of motive. Had Maryse and the others been there to help Baudouin Rousseau kill himself? Assisted Suicide? But if that was the case, why would they need a fall-guy? And why were they all there? Would it not be more likely that a mercy killing would be done with as few people around, as possible?

"What about his mistress?" I asked. "Did she know about his cancer?"

Molyneux eased up, straightening his back. "There was no mistress, M. Stuart."

"But they were divorcing—Maryse and her husband."

"In Baudouin's physical condition, a woman was the last thing he would've desired."

Who was lying? Maryse had told me her husband divorced her after finding someone else. Monet had claimed Baudouin had divorced Maryse because she was unfaithful. Now, Molyneux claimed Baudouin would have had no interest in a mistress. Molyneux's contention indirectly supported Monet's claim. This left Maryse as the liar. But what if they all were lying?

"I was at Baudouin Rousseau's apartment, last night," I remarked. "I went there to have a meeting with him. Somebody knocked me out, as I went in. When I came to, I was arrested by the police. In between, Baudouin Rousseau was murdered. Were you with him last night?"

He picked up the second suture and threaded it into the needle. "What makes you think that?"

"It wasn't an accusation. I just remember seeing three people—two men and a woman."

He swallowed thickly. "You can identify them?"

"I couldn't see their faces. Just shadows, more or less."

"Well, I assure you I was not one of those shadows. I wish I had been there. I might've been able to help Baudouin. In fact, I was with Maryse. She was very upset about certain things and wanted to talk."

"What things?"

"I'm afraid, as her physician, I cannot divulge that."

Her physician? She had told me he was just a friend. So why would she lie? If not her, why would he? If he did not want to discuss it because she had asked him to keep her remarks between them, then why not tell me it was none of my business?

Molyneux pushed the needle through my skin. "Did you search Baudouin's apartment?"

"Everybody seems to think I searched his apartment," I winced. "But it wasn't me. The fact is, it was the two who banged me around."

He tied off the thread, scowling. "How could you know that if you were unconscious?"

"They talked about it in front of me, after giving me what you're patching."

"Did you recognize these men?"

"No. They wore ski-masks."

"Balaclavas?"

"I guess that's what they're called. But if those guys were there, I know they weren't either of the two male shadows. One of them was too tall. The other was too wide. So that means, there were at least five people watching Baudouin Rousseau die. Why?" I paused, waiting for him to comment.

When Molyneux made no remark I continued with, "I take it you prescribed the pain-killers Baudouin was taking?"

The third suture was made and tied off. "No," returned Molyneux. "I was not his physician. I was merely his friend."

"According to the toxicology report on your friend, he'd been injected with sodium amytal and thiopental sodium; more than once."

"Sodium amytal is used to treat insomnia. Thiopental sodium is an anesthetic." He let go a long sigh. "As I surmised, the intention was not to induce talk but to ease Baudouin's discomfort."

"That being the case, it must've been an accidental death," I concluded. "You know. Rousseau injected himself with a bit too much and his heart gave out."

Molyneux laughed, dryly, picking up the last suture. "A physician's nightmare, I can tell you. The drug companies provide guidelines for their products. But those are not foolproof. An allergic reaction or an inter-drug reaction can be deadly."

I decided to bait him with, "Sixty million was the number."

"Number?" Molyneux echoed as he threaded the suture into the needle.

"The value of the diamonds Baudouin was supposed to have. Where would anyone get that much in diamonds?"

"When we finish," he said, "I'll telephone the police."

"It won't do any good. Not for me. Not for any American. You know that. They'll come because you called. But the report will be dusted as soon as they get outside."

Molyneux tied off the last suture and then removed the clamp. Afterward, he backed up to assess his tailoring. "Don't wash anywhere near the wound until tomorrow. I'll give you something for the pain so you can sleep."

"I won't need it."

He offered a crooked smile. "I get the feeling you don't trust me, Stuart."

"It's not that," I lied. "I'm tougher than I look."

"Right now the nerves in the area of the wound are stunned from the injury. Once they begin to seal back together, you'll be in absolute agony. I give you my word I am not going to poison you."

I did not know whether to believe him, or not. I had no proof he was a party to what happened at Baudouin Rousseau's apartment. The autopsy suggested a doctor. The goons who cut me referred to a 'quack' having injected Baudouin. That probably meant a physician but it could also mean someone who was not a physician but acted like one. The only thing indicating Molyneux was actually involved related to his friendship with Baudouin and Maryse Rousseau. But why would any physician have taken part in a diamond robbery? Obviously, all who were there had been involved in the robbery otherwise there would be no reason for the search. In any event, the odds were very much against Molyneux deliberately doing me harm. Had he wanted me dead he could just as easily claimed he had some painkiller and injected me with something lethal.

"I could use a nap after what I've been through," I admitted.

He went back to his bag and dug around for a few minutes. Then he returned with a packet of two pills. "Take one and lie down. It will make you sleep for probably twelve hours or more. Take the second one only if needed. The bleeding has stopped. I'm not anticipating any infection. But if you see a puss-like fluid oozing from the wound, get to a doctor right away. An infection that close to an eye must be considered very serious."

As he put away his needle and other materials, I tore open the packet of pills and took out one of the tablets. Then I plopped it into my mouth and swallowed.

"How much do I owe you?" I asked him.

Molyneux picked up his bag and came over to me. He gently patted my shoulder. "Don't worry about that, Stuart." Then he started away and stopped, turning to face me. "I am sorry about this."

"It wasn't your fault."

As he left my flat, Didier Arceneau rushed up to him. "Thank you for the prescription, Buji. It is like I am sixteen, again—at least in one area."

Buji? Had I heard the elderly man correctly?

The doctor smiled. "I still think you are taking a foolish risk, M. Arceneau. At your age a young woman is a very dangerous hobby."

"But one worth the trouble," the old man returned, patting the doctor on the arm.

As Molyneux moved off Arceneau strode into my apartment, and shut the door.

"You called him 'Buji'," I remarked.

The elderly man shrugged. "Of course. We are old friends. Among intimates it is not unusual to use terms of endearment."

Was every man in Paris nicknamed Buji?

With a groan I stood up and pointed at the door. "I'm sorry, M. Arceneau, but whatever it is I cannot help. I think I'll be dying in a few minutes."

"But I've been trying to reach you all morning, Monsieur," he pleaded. "Surely you can give me five minutes?"

"Look at me. Two killers pounded my face to oblivion before giving me a knife-point tattoo. I may have just taken poison. And if I hadn't been a quick leg-jerker, my balls would be somewhere up near my ears."

He grimaced as his eyes scanned my face. "I noticed you were injured, of course. But I thought, perhaps, you had attempted suicide." He frowned. "Is the poison you took always fatal?"

"Uh, no."

"Then it is a very poor choice for suicide."

"I am not trying to kill myself. I was making a bad joke."

"It would not surprise me if you had attempted suicide. It is a practice in this flat. I think you are the third to make the attempt. Your immediate predecessor, succeeded." Arceneau pointed up at the hole in the ceiling. "He screwed a huge hook into a joist and tied a rope around it. Then he hanged himself." The elderly man pointed down at the circular bare spot on the floor, beneath the hole. "He dangled there for over a week, his body twisting and turning in the breeze through the open window. That spot is where his hobnail boots scraped round and round. We all thought he was just dancing—until the smell."

"Wonderful," I groaned. "I'm looking forward to that embellishment of tonight's dreams. Did he leave a note?"

M. Arceneau nodded. "Something about rats, I think. But after last night's culinary debacle cutting one's throat might not be a bad idea." One hand went to his belly and he belched, loudly. "Her cooking has declined to the point where I may have to forgo my vacation next year."

"I'm relieved to hear our gracious landlady held sway in a kitchen, at one time."

The old man made a bleak move with one hand. "Only just—and quite tenuously. But she is very reasonably priced."

"You mean rooms, I take it?"

He winked. "Any way you would like to interpret it, or so I am told."

I slumped back down on the davenport, not having the energy to argue. Despite his advanced years, I lacked the strength to force him out of my flat. Between the exhaustion from my injuries and the medication slowly spreading through my system, I could barely move.

"I thought we were eating rats," I told him. "I had a plate full of what looked like tails."

"That would not surprise me," he returned thoughtfully.

I gave a feeble shrug. "I'll give you five minutes. Then I intend to die whether you're finished, or not."

He belched, again. "I was—thinking of you and I—sharing a very special experience."

I blinked my good eye, completely astounded by the implication of his words. Was I actually being propositioned by a geezer in a two hundred year old tuxedo?

"M. Arceneau…" I began. "As flattering as it sounds…"

"I offer my money for what you do best, Monsieur," he interjected. "Paint."

Paint? I was not sure whether to be disappointed by the clarification, or relieved. I got to my feet not believing what I had heard. "You're offering me a commission?"

He tiptoed closer, glancing about as if afraid his next words might be overheard by invisible listeners. "You have, perhaps, noticed Mademoiselle Fabienne Prideux?"

I nodded. "She is the type of woman a man would have trouble not noticing—from any angle."

He grimaced in pain as one of his hands clenched at his shirt. "She is perfection," he whimpered. "So firm, so round, so fully-packed!" His mouth quivered and his knees began to shake. "The mere thought of her causes me to… to…"

"You want a painting of yourself to give to her?" I interrupted.

"Excuse me," Arceneau groaned. He took a tiny, brown bottle from his vest. From within he withdrew a petite white pill. "Nitro-glycerin. I, uh, sometimes get a little overstressed when I think about her." He placed the tablet beneath his tongue and closed his eyes. "Unfortunately, right now I am in short supply on the big-bang front."

"Do you want me to get you a doctor?"

He opened his eyes and made a despairing gesture. "There is nothing he could do. And there is nothing I can do. She possesses my soul because I lust for her body. Each night after saying prayers, I lay in my bed thinking about her. Sometimes all night, I think of her—every inch of her —every curve of her—every hill and valley, nook and cranny of her." He paused, nearly breathless, his entire body quivering. "Sometimes I don't sleep for days!"

I grabbed him by the shoulders, fearing he would fall over. "You'd better sit down."

"It is not necessary, Monsieur," he returned, backing out of my grasp. "But I had better get to the point of my visit before I need another Nitro. I want you to paint Fabienne's portrait, twice over: a big one and a small one."

"Of course I will do this, M. Arceneau. But are you certain you want to hire me? There are many other artists in Paris who are far more experienced at portraiture."

He pointed to the five canvases I had hung on the walls. "Mme. Flaubert was kind enough to let me see your creations after you settled in. I was very impressed. You are a true talent."

I was slightly irritated. How dare Mme. Flaubert open my flat to the scrutiny of the other residents? On the other hand, she did own the place and had she not shown my paintings to M. Arceneau, he and I would not be discussing a commissioned work.

"Naturally," he continued, "I will advance whatever funds are needed."

"That would be a blessing," I told him, in genuine appreciation.

He dug out a fat wallet and withdrew three hundred Euros. "Will that be enough to get you started?"

I took the money nodding, and grinning, the pill making me feel drunk and giddy.

Then the elderly man made a crooked face as if thinking about something unpleasant. "There is one complication." He glanced around, again. Satisfied no one else was in earshot he whispered, "I would like the big one to be of her *dans le nu.*"

I giggled drunkenly. "Naked?"

He nodded. "The other, I want of her in a nightgown—something very tasteful." He cleared his throat, nervously. "It is for her, the little one. The big one, of course, is for me." Then he began trembling and grabbed my arm. "Monsieur, in that big one I want all the goodies. Price is no object. Hit me with everything she's got, straight on; life size, full-color, 3-D!"

"The big kahuna for you and the little kahuna for her," I slurred, feeling sleepily intoxicated. "No problem-o. When can the beauteous Fabienne strip off for the initial sketches of her goodies?"

He blinked in confusion. "Kahuna? But I wanted portraits."

"Sorry," I giggled. "Bad American slang. Big painting and little painting. Big one, all the goodies. Little one, a light brush-over on the goodie-front. Gotcha'!"

"Ah, yes. I shall remember kahuna." He turned partially away, one hand waggling in the air. "Unfortunately, there is a slight snag."

"Not from the pill I took. That puppy is pure pleasure. Whew! I am flying high, today!"

He twisted back and offered a sheepish grin. "I have not yet told Fabienne about the portraits."

"Ah, I see. Well, tell her I'm a poofter and I'm sure she won't mind letting the bare leg waggle."

He backed away suddenly ill at east. "I did not realize you were one of those."

I fanned the air with both hands attempting to reassure him. "No. I'm not. But that usually works to get a shy female model naked. I can't tell you how many times I pulled that in school. I never got anything other than visual experiences. But what trips those babies were!"

His face suddenly went glum. "I tried taking Fabienne on a trip, once. No luck. She insisted upon separate rooms. Nevertheless, I am now confident in my quest. With you and I in agreement, I shall get everything I'm after." He winked and tapped the side of his nose. "Tomorrow night I will make the proposition." He glanced around again. "Mademoiselle Fabienne will be visiting my flat. I will, of course, be serving Champagne and caviar. In the course of the evening, I will broach the subject—as you suggested." Again, his body started trembling. "And then I shall attempt to broach her!"

"Only on a safe-sex level, I hope."

He backed away, batting at my concerns with one hand. "At my age, sex is never safe at any level. Especially with a young woman who has the biggest set of…"

"With respect, M. Arceneau," I interjected, drunkenly. "Considering all the circumstances, I would not get your hopes up."

"Getting it up is no problem," he wheezed. "The difficulty is getting it in over her objections!"

"Ah, I see. She is the fickle type."

He nodded, still wheezing with excitement. "But once Mademoiselle Prideux hears about the portraits she will realize my intentions are not frivolous."

"Ah, so you plan to marry her?" I slurred. "You've got guts, I'll say that for you."

The old man seemed to vibrate as he grabbed onto my arms to steady himself. "Marriage, hell! I intend to bonk her or die trying!"

I reached out and nudged him toward the door. "Now, I think we'd better part ways. I'm starting to see three of you and those spats are a real turn-on."

"Thank you, Monsieur," he returned, backing away. Then the elderly man put more passion into his tone. "I think tomorrow night will be one of those nights." With that, he turned and left, closing the door on his exit.

I staggered over to the door and set the lock. I was looking forward to twelve hours of uninterrupted, drugged sleep. But upon awakening, I intended to telephone my uncle. Since he was profiting from the forgeries I had innocently painted, why shouldn't I enjoy the fruits of my youthful labors? Considering the 'Degas' and their implications, I felt sure he would cough up enough Euros to tide me over until I returned home, to avoid my letting Cesar Avoyelles in on my uncles not so little secret. The money, of course, being a secret not shared with my mother.

Suddenly, wooziness settled upon me. I hurried back to the davenport and pulled it open. Seconds later I was lying upon the mattress, drifting off into sleep. But no sooner did my dreams begin when I was awakened by angry voices.

"What are you playing at, Buji?" demanded a woman. Her voice was bitterly accusatory.

"Calm down, you frigid bitch!" was the man's impatient reply.

"Don't call me that!"

"All right—Maryse, my love."

Maryse? Did I hear, Maryse? I half sat up trying to focus upon the sound of each voice, hoping to link the woman's to Maryse Rousseau's. But the painkiller was in high gear and I could barely force myself to remain awake.

"François Chiappe is asking questions," the woman hissed.

"If nobody talks he won't find out anything."

"I'm not willing to bet my life on that. I want my cut of the sixty million and I want it now."

"You'll have to wait like the rest of us, you frigid cow. Until we can locate the stones!"

"I didn't risk my neck stealing those diamonds to be pushed aside. You know where the diamonds are! You must know!"

"I don't know any more than you or the others."

Dear God! How terrible. Not only had Maryse Rousseau's husband been murdered; not only had she been involved in the diamond heist; but, Maryse is frigid!

"Didn't that damn quack find out where the diamonds were before killing him?" she snapped.

"It was an accident. We…"

Her voice cut in, seething. "Accident, hell! The newspapers said Baudouin had been tossed off the balcony."

He growled, "That must have been Molyneux's doing, after we all left!"

"You were still there when I went."

"I didn't help!"

Dr. Michele Molyneux? So he had been there, after all! Which begged the question, who had not lied to me, or about me, or because of me?

Her voice rose shrilly. "Three months of waiting for nothing!"

He paused for many seconds. "There were six of us in that apartment. You, Molyneux and I were in the front room with Rousseau. Those so-called experts you brought in to help us pull the robbery were searching Baudouin's apartment. That damn Stuart was out, on the floor."

"So what?"

"Think about it. If the diamonds are not in Rousseau's apartment, and I don't have the diamonds, and you don't have the diamonds – then…"

"You think Bouvier and Chevalier found the diamonds and their threats are just an act?" she asked.

"They threatened you?" he gasped.

"I thought they were going to kill me. That's when I told them the American had the diamonds."

Thanks a lot, Maryse! Couldn't you have just said you didn't know where the diamonds were?

"I just had a thought. Maybe if we cut a deal with Chiappe?" Buji suggested. "That bastard gets the heavy end in exchange for recovering the stones. What do you think?"

"If we get him involved he'll want to know who was there when Baudouin died."

"So we tell him—leaving ourselves out."

"That would mean a bigger cut. But what if Molyneux or those other two talk about us being there, when Chiappe is questioning them about the diamonds?"

"We'll forewarn Chiappe to expect the three of them to try and implicate us."

She muttered, "If Bouvier or Chevalier or Molyneux have the diamonds, why would they hang around?"

"They'd have to. Otherwise the finger of guilt would point at them. Don't worry. Chiappe will know how to handle them."

Silence fell between the pair for nearly a minute. Then she sighed heavily. "I'm still not convinced Baudouin didn't sell the diamonds."

"Why would he lie to us? Bouvier and Chevalier wanted to kill him."

"He was in so much pain he did not care. But I've been thinking… The past few weeks when I was with him, he was doped to the heavens. Nothing he said made much sense." She hesitated a moment before adding, "But one night he started giggling about having a Van Gogh."

"What Van Gogh?"

"I don't know. But considering what they go for, I got to thinking that maybe he swapped the diamonds for it."

"He wouldn't get a Van Gogh for a mere sixty million."

"He might if the seller was pressed."

"But there's no Van Gogh in his flat," Buji returned.

"Maybe somebody else is holding it?"

"Her?"

"More likely him."

"Him, who?"

"Before he got sick, Baudouin intended to take control of the Corsican mob. What better way to ensure his succession than by handing that painting to his boss?"

Buji's voice went mournful. "Mme. Chiappe is an art collector, isn't she?"

"See what I mean? Getting Chiappe involved might backfire."

More silence.

She taunted with, "I suppose you could ask your rich pal to step in. He might have the connections to find out if Chiappe has the Van Gogh."

"There are too many involved already!"

Then she laughed caustically amidst the scraping sound of chair legs moving across a floor. "One more or less makes no difference, as far as I'm concerned. Not when were about to split a pile of nothing."

I closed my eyes, and let sleep overwhelm me. Or had I already fallen asleep and what I assumed were voices had merely been a dream? And what about Maryse Rousseau? Liar or not, my nightstick was hanging his head because of her being frigid.

Chapter 6
Another Murder

There is an old French adage that says, *Amour de garse, & faut de chien ne dure si l'on ne dit, tien.* Roughly translated it means, 'Whores and dogs adore a man only when he feeds them.' As far as I was concerned, Maryse Rousseau fell into that category—at least in a frigid sort of non-canine way. I had fed her with my stupidity, and in return she had fawned upon my gullibility with her lies. In the end, as the proverb suggests, I was the one who was betrayed.

My drugged sleep lasted a mere nine hours. I got out of bed stiff and sore like an old man, a few hours after sunrise. The overheard conversation, from the night before, was hazy in my mind. But I clearly remembered the reference to Molyneux, the Van Gogh and Maryse's sexual dysfunction. How could a woman with so much be interested in using it so little?

You're probably thinking I should inform Monet about the latest overheard conversation. Unfortunately, that would require me to admit there was a previous conversation which in turn would lead to yet another round of interrogations. As enjoyable as that might sound to you, I am not up to it. Besides, why should I help him? I'm the idiot American, remember?

I pulled on my robe, grabbed clean clothing and my towel. Then I hobbled up to the third floor to attend my morning ablutions.

Thirty minutes later I was back in my flat, dressed in very worn but clean denims, a slightly stained sweatshirt, clean underwear and white socks; the cleanest of which had only one hole.

Despite my physical misery, I was somewhat optimistic about the day's events. First I would telephone Uncle Stuart and ask him to wire money. Should he be hesitant, I would remind him of the profits he earned when he sold the 'Degas' to Cesar Avoyelles. Then, after collecting those much-needed funds from Western Union, I would open a bank account. After that, I would treat myself to a well-deserved breakfast. Perhaps, *Café au lait*, a glass of orange juice, *tartines*, and *fromage blanc?*

The breaking sun shining in through the window beckoned me over. I made the short, limping trek and stared out at silver drops of dew glistening upon the gray weeds growing between the chinks in the alley's black pavement.

What a day! Not a cloud in the sky.

As my eyes drifted, I noticed the gathering of birds on the window ledges of the old warehouse. Their numbers had become substantially smaller since the day I moved in. This morning there were only three of the black-feathered creatures. The reduction in their numbers could be chalked up to the rising cost of food in Paris. Anything that walked, crawled or slithered was going into the family pots, these days. God help any parakeet who slips its cage or the pup that breaks its leash.

The rats looked happy, as they rummaged among the garbage cans. I suppose I would be too if that was all I needed to earn my keep. But like the birds, their numbers had also decreased. On the day I moved into my flat, there had been over a dozen among the garbage cans. Now, there were only seven.

There could be many explanations for this diminishment of a very rugged species. Poisons. Traps. Or perhaps a large cat with a nasty attitude. However, the memory of Mme. Flaubert's culinary catastrophe suggested a more likely reason. Not that a rat would die from her cooking—unless, of course, it went into the pot.

My cheek still burned from the knife wound. I went over to the mirror and was appalled by what I saw. My chin was blue and swollen with a huge bruise. The stitches dangled like black worms trying to flee the red, swollen wound just beneath my eye. The other eye was blackened back to my ear and barely open. On the plus side, looking this bad might provide opportunities to earn a few Euros as a beggar. What was the name of that Sherlock Holmes story concerning a man who temporarily disfigured his face in order to gain the financial sympathy of passersby? Something about a twisted lip, I think.

As I left the window, I checked my watch. It was time for Uncle Stuart to be up, whether he wanted to be or not. He was probably lying in bed, sipping his morning cocoa and wondering how to spend his money. He had probably received a hundred thousand for each of the 'Degas', sold to Avoyelles. What he received for the Van Gogh's and other paintings I had created probably ran into millions. Therefore, a request for twenty thousand Euros would not be out of line. I left my flat and went in search of a public pay phone.

Coin operated phone booths are a thing of the past in Paris. The booths still exist. But the coin-insert slot is absent. To make a telephone call these days, assuming you are like me and do not own a cellular phone, you enter the *cabine téléphonique* and use what is called a *Télécartes*. These are prepaid cards embedded with a computer chip detailing the balance available for purchasing a call. Using the card causes the chip to be decremented by the price, not unlike the American gift cards sold by retailers.

You can purchase the *Télécartes* in various denominations. The usual source of supply is the nearest *Tabac* shop (Who knew patronizing a tobacco seller during your trip to France, would be necessary for a non-smoker?)

Acquiring the card is a minor inconvenience. There are *Tabac* shops on nearly every corner in Paris. Why not? Smoking tobacco in France is the second most popular national pastime.

I will let you think about what might be the number one pastime.

The cards do serve the telephone companies well. Not only are they non-refundable, but they have stopped the robbing of *cabine téléphoniques*. However you must be vigilant in guarding your *Télécartes*. If not, this digitized delight will disappear. Not for the reason you are assuming. Curiously, these little items have become collectables for the average Parisian. Consequently, should it be stolen, your well-spent purchase will likely resurface as a new display-item on the wall of some French flat you have never visited.

Several blocks away, I found the object of my search. I stepped inside, dialed my uncle's telephone number in Sao Paolo, Brazil and then rattled my Télécartes through the scanner. After what seemed like an eternity of ring tones, someone answered at the other end of the connection.

"I'd like to speak with Stuart S. Stuart, please?" I said, into the handset. "This is his nephew—Stuart S. Stuart—calling from Paris, France."

For the next two minutes I listened to a rapid mix of Spanish and Portuguese erupting from the screaming lungs of some woman who claimed to be my uncle's maid, menial and general bed-warmer. Bits and pieces of her frantic diatribe I recognized. But the bulk of what she ranted eluded me. According to my rough translation, my uncle was a low-life bastard who had ditched Sao Paoloean womanhood—presumably her—in favor of a Russian hottie with bleached hair and plastic boobs.

When the woman paused for breath, I asked where Uncle Stuart might be, if not in Brazil. That resulted in another multilingual tirade that meant - in the broadest sense— (I'll let you think about that one too) my uncle had flown to Siberia with the blonde bimbo.

As you can imagine, his absence was not good news. How could I possibly locate him in Siberia? That part of the world was almost completely lacking in telephone service, not to mention English speaking residents. And should I find him by some miracle, would Uncle Stuart have enough cash along to satisfy my needs? And if he did and agreed to wire it, would any of it actually reach France? Russians have a very strange view on exchange rates and percentage cuts for services rendered. A twenty thousand Euro request to my uncle would likely net me only two or three Euros by the time the Russians took their percentages.

I asked the maid when Uncle Stuart was expected back. Again the line throbbed with vehemence new and not so new, to my limited Portuguese vocabulary. She was certain my uncle would return. But the maid did not know when. Regardless, she had honed a large knife to a razor's edge and intended to use it upon his arrival. The next few words were difficult to understand. But she was either going to use the knife to slice up a gopher, or my uncle could expect to find gonads on the menu—his own. As I rang off, I crossed my legs in sympathy.

Where did that leave me? I had my pay for the week less expenditures, plus the three hundred Euros M. Arceneau had advanced, plus a few coins from the week-before's pay packet. Not much. But it would keep my head above water for another week, or so. Just barely.

I stepped back onto the sidewalk and considered what to do. Breakfast was definitely out. Probably lunch was well. Not to mention supper. Despite my complaining stomach, I was not yet desperate enough to face another meal from Mme. Flaubert's kitchen.

Then I remembered Cesar Avoyelles' interest in my paintings. Assuming Maryse had not lied when she claimed not to understand my references to the Degas and Avoyelles—a long-shot at best – there was a chance Cesar actually did not know he had been swindled. Following that line of reasoning—well, that desperate line of reasoning—Cesar Avoyelles might be willing to advance me funds against the sale of my artwork. Or he might tell me to get stuffed. I limped off in the direction of the Métro station. I was still optimistic. But not nearly as when I awoke.

* * * *

M. Avoyelles was surprised to see me when I entered his gallery two hours later. I could not blame him. Unless the mirror had lied, I was a frightening sight to behold.

"Dear God, what happened to you?" he greeted me, rushing over with arms outstretched in pity.

"I did a little dance number with a couple of guys who knew more steps than me," I returned. "M. Avoyelles, I was wondering…"

My nose suddenly detected the lemony scent of his cologne and I stopped short, not sure how to proceed. He was wearing the same scent I had noticed when I regained consciousness at M. Rousseau's apartment. Had Cesar Avoyelles been there?

Avoyelles bridged his lips with a raised forefinger to silence me. Then he took me by the arm and quickly escorted me to his office, at the rear of the gallery.

"I heard about your arrest," he confided, after shutting the door. "I must apologize for dragging you back here, so abruptly. But you look like death warmed-over."

"Now that you mention it, I feel that way."

He made a beseeching gesture. "That is not to say you are unwelcome. But my clientele never sees the gritty side of an artist's life." He made a disgusted face. "Frankly, one look at you might send them running." Then he winced, as his eyes rescanned my swollen face. "Stuart, are you sure you should you be out? Someone dying of fright at the sight of you in my galleria would not help business."

"I was not charged in M. Rousseau's murder, M. Avoyelles," I announced. "I was questioned. But, then I was released. I did not kill him. I swear…"

"Of course, you didn't kill him," he interposed, mildly. "I knew the police had made a mistake immediately." Avoyelles smiled apologetically. "Nevertheless, I could not convince René of your innocence. He is adamant in his refusal to reinstate you. I am sorry." One of his hands lazily drifted through the air. "You said two men beat you. Were they the police officers who interrogated you about Baudouin?"

"No. It was a pair of lunatics who were waiting for me in my flat. They thought I had sixty million in diamonds."

His eyes widened in surprise. "Diamonds, you say?"

There was a knock on the office door, and then it opened. A bottled blonde stuck her head in. "Mme. Chiappe is here, Buji."

I almost swallowed my tongue. Buji? First, Monet. Then Dr. Molyneux. Now Avoyelles! Considering the scent of his cologne, I felt I must now be face to face with the insufferable Buji from the overheard conversations.

"Give Mme. Chiappe some coffee and a sweet-roll," returned Avoyelles, casually. "I'll be with her in a few minutes."

After the blonde left, I made a retreating step. "Buji?"

He rolled his eyes. "A moniker of affection, I'm afraid. She, some-how, got the idea that I am interested in her. You know how it is. A young woman. A mature man. Several bottles of Champagne." He shrugged. "I'm afraid I was seduced."

"Meaning you did put up some resistance?"

He laughed. "None at all, actually."

"I guess I should've paid a call on you instead of Baudouin Rousseau."

Cesar gave a grim nod. "I wish you had, for both our sakes. Chief In-spector Claude Monet left here just before you arrived. From what he suggested, I damn well need an alibi for that night. I did point him to the young woman you saw. But he seemed unplaced by her words. Had you and I been together, there would be no worries for either of us."

"At least you had someone to offer words. Monet chewed on me for hours."

"I'm afraid Baudouin's murder has powerful political implications," he said, letting go a long sigh. "He was well known by the current Prime Minister and regarded, despite Baudouin's professional affiliations, as the P-M's personal advisor. There will be hell to pay if Baudouin's murder is not solved quickly."

"Are you telling me the Corsican Mafia is running France?"

He shrugged. "The failing economy has all but ruined me."

His story about Monet sounded believable. Perhaps I had jumped to a wrong conclusion based solely upon a common nickname.

"Did she say Mme. Chiappe?" I asked, tilting my head toward the door. "François Chiappe's wife?"

Avoyelles' brows suddenly twisted down. "You know François?"

I shook my head. "Just what I've read about him. Those articles did not make Chiappe out to be much of a humanitarian."

Cesar Avoyelles laughed, and retreated behind his desk. "Mme. Chi-appe has taken an interest in art, of late," he explained, and settled into a luxurious-looking, leather chair. "Price is no object, or so she claims. During the past few months, I have sold her a number of paintings." Then he pointed to one of the tulip-shaped chairs fronting his desk. "For God's sake, take a seat. You look like you're in agony."

I did as instructed, trying not to whimper as bruised flesh settled into preformed, red plastic. Then I let my eyes wander. The office walls were carefully decorated with French landscapes. The artists represented were

Pierre Patel, Gaspard Dughet, and Julien Dupre. There was one solitary Joan Miro abstract. The latter was titled, *The Village of Prades*. It hung on the wall directly behind Cesar's desk.

"These diamonds that were mentioned," he said, tugging at one ear. "Did those terrible men say where the diamonds had come from? Or, why they thought you might possess the stones?"

"No. But those goons were at Baudouin Rousseau's the night he died. The pair even discussed how they had searched his apartment for the diamonds."

"Indeed?" He fumbled with his lower lip, thinking. "Not to be offensive, but do you have the diamonds?"

"Of course not!" I returned, indignantly. "If I'd had the damn things would I look like this?"

"I did not mean you had stolen the diamonds from Baudouin. I just thought, perhaps, Maryse might've given them to you."

"Don't even mention her name. That woman pointed those goons to me claiming I had the diamonds! I'm lucky to be alive!"

"Maryse?" he scoffed. "Nonsense."

"All I did was share lunch with her—at her request. Since then my life has gone down the toilet. I'm out of a job. I can't leave Paris. I've had my brains kicked around for diamonds that probably no longer exist. Never again will I go anywhere near Maryse Rousseau."

He frowned with concern. "You said the diamonds might no longer exist. What did you mean?"

I had put my foot in my mouth, again! When would I learn to think through my words before speaking?

"Since getting my can kicked, I did some digging," I told him, purposely lying. "Rumor has it that Baudouin Rousseau traded the diamonds for a painting. A Van Gogh."

I watched the corners of his mouth curl up, slightly. "Indeed?"

"Sixty million buys an awful lot of art."

Then he smiled, "But not a typical Van Gogh." He snickered softly, tugging at his nose, as if he was now privy to where the diamonds might be found. "Even so, that is completely out of character for Baudouin."

"Why?"

Avoyelles formed the fingers of both hands into a teepee. "I'd known Baudouin since we were kids on Corsica. He would never trade a sure thing like diamonds for a painting whose value might or might not match the price he expensed. Particularly with so many forgeries being passed off as genuine, these days."

His mention of Corsica brought to mind Maryse's telephone conversation on the Métro, and Monet's claim that Baudouin Rousseau spoke only French. Had she called Avoyelles, instead of her husband? Unless Monet had his facts wrong or lied, Baudouin Rousseau did not speak Corsican. But as a child on Corsica, how could Baudouin not know that language?

"Do you speak Corsican?" I asked.

"Of course," he returned. "It was all we spoke as children. I had to learn French as an adult—not so easy."

"I assume Baudouin was in the same proverbial boat?"

He laughed. "Indeed."

So much for Monet's claims. Had he also lied about Maryse?

Cesar Avoyelles crossed his arms and made a confused face. "I wonder where those diamonds came from—originally?" Then his eyes widened and he jerked erect in his chair. "I have it! The Lucien Falize robbery, a few months ago. The men who attacked you must have been involved in it. But if that is true, then Baudouin was also involved. As far as I know, none of the thieves were ever identified!" Then he slumped back, once more looking confused. "What makes you think Maryse told them you had those diamonds? Are you saying she was also one of the thieves?"

"That's the way the facts stand."

"But that is so unlike her. Baudouin, I can see pulling that job. But Maryse? Never! Baudouin would not have allowed it, even if she had been willing—which she would not!"

"From what I've heard, she is not the gentlewoman she appears to be."

He gave a noncommittal nod. "I suppose anything is possible." Then he tilted across the desk, earnestly. "Do you think she has the diamonds? What is your opinion?"

"I would not be surprised."

He fell quite, again thinking. Eventually he said, "But you were there – alone, were you not? In Baudouin's flat? At least for a period of time."

"The truth is, I was knocked out when I arrived. I barely regained consciousness before the police showed up. Then I was arrested and dragged to the cells."

"But if you satisfied these terrible men that you did not have the stones, then they will go back to Maryse." He gave his head a worried shake. "I don't like that idea."

"I don't either," I returned. "But better her than me."

"I wish I knew who was involved in that robbery."

I decided to tempt fate and bait him. "They mentioned someone named Buji."

He leaned across the desk, gaping. "Buji?"

"That's the name of the ringleader, or so I gathered from what those goons said."

He laughed softly. "Ah, that explains why you went dead-white when you asked about my nickname. I thought you were going to faint."

"I nearly did."

"Well, whoever this Buji is, I assure you I am not he." Avoyelles hesitated a moment before adding, "Did they say anything that might identify Buji?"

I shrugged. "Not in front of me."

He tilted back in his chair clucking his tongue. "You notified the police, of course?"

"No. Frankly I'm not sure I can trust them."

Again, he leaned forward. "What do you mean?"

"While I was being interrogated by Chief Inspector Monet, one of his female police officers called him Buji. For all I know, he's the ringleader."

Cesar Avoyelles stood up, came around to the front of his desk and perched on one corner. "Stuart, you cannot possibly believe that Chief Inspector Monet would involve himself in anything illegal."

"I wouldn't trust him with my wallet even if I had it super-glued to his ass."

"I think your speculations concerning his ethics are much too broad. Buji is a very common nickname."

"What about Maryse, as names go?"

"Also quite common. In fact, I was married to a Maryse—the frigid bitch!"

I may not have gone white, but I certainly paled to gray at the sound of his ex-wife's description.

"Monet is an unpleasant sort," continued Avoyelles. "But he is honest."

"The man is a megalomaniac!"

Cesar Avoyelles waggled a scolding finger. "Be that as it may, I assure you, he is not the Buji discussed."

I was far from convinced, but I did not argue the point.

Cesar Avoyelles stood up, once again frowning. "If you get any ideas about those diamonds, I would appreciate hearing your thoughts."

"Right now, I've got other worries.

"What do you mean?"

"Rumor has it that François Chiappe is trying to find out who killed Baudouin. Is it a fair assumption that he's going to take revenge?"

"Absolutely."

"Then I won't make any long-term plans."

He laughed. "What do you mean?"

"Since I was the only one arrested, Chiappe cannot help but suspect me."

"Don't worry. François has people everywhere. He will have already heard about you being released."

"But will he believe I'm innocent?"

One hand tugged at Avoyelles' left ear as he fell back into thought. After a few seconds he said, "You did not actually speak to Baudouin that terrible night?"

"No," I replied. "I was out of the game before the play started."

He offered a pained expression in return for my words. "I am surprised, to some degree, that Baudouin got involved in that theft."

"I don't know what you mean."

"Baudouin was already terminally ill. Cancer. In terrible pain. So I am surprised he had an interest in the diamonds."

"That's what Dr. Molyneux mentioned. That he had cancer."

His brows arched in surprise. "Molyneux? When was this?"

"When he was sewing up the gash in my face, yesterday."

"Did you mention the diamonds to Michele?"

"I may have. I don't remember. I was in shock, at the time."

He hesitated as if trying to carefully form his next words. "Did Monet mention why he thought Baudouin had been murdered?"

"According to the toxicology report, Baudouin was drugged. Apparently the last injection was fatal. The coroner's theory is that the drugs were intended as a truth serum."

"Truth serum?" he scoffed.

"Monet did not believe it, either."

"Still, I find that very odd."

"Why?"

"I don't see Baudouin patiently watching someone give him an injection—unless it was something Baudouin wanted."

"Assisted suicide, you mean?"

He nodded.

"But if that's the case, why were all those people there?"

Avoyelles leaned over his desk, intently. "You saw them?"

"I saw only shadows—not faces. Two men – presumably one was M. Rousseau—and a woman. I didn't see the goons who pounded me. But they admitted they were there."

His mouth opened in surprise. "A woman? You are certain?"

I shrugged. "Maryse. I caught just a glimpse."

"But if you did not see her face…"

"Monet is convinced that woman was Maryse."

"Have you discussed this with her?" Avoyelles asked.

"No, and I don't intend to."

Avoyelles clucked his tongue. "Give her a chance to defend herself, Stuart." He shook a finger at me. "Remember, you were falsely accused."

"She lied to me. And that's not a falsehood."

"To what end?"

"For starters, Maryse said her husband had a mistress. But Dr. Molyneux said that wasn't the case."

He tilted back, thinking. "There were rumors of Baudouin having taken a lover after he and Maryse split up. For myself, I did not believe it. But, then, I did not believe Baudouin would divorce Maryse. He absolutely adored her."

"A man does not divorce a woman he adores."

Cesar Avoyelles considered my words and then shook his head. "One would think not. Unless…" Then he splayed his hands. "Well, why don't you tell me what brings you here?"

"I'm short on money."

He made a despairing movement with one hand. "I'm sure your uncle would gladly help."

I shifted in the chair, disappointed that he had not offered to assist. "I telephoned Uncle Stuart. But he's in Russia. Apparently, he's working on something blonde and not silicone-free. Which leaves me looking for help from you."

Cesar Avoyelles crossed his arms. "Of course I would like to help. But…"

My heart sank. "But you cannot?"

"If we could come to some sort of arrangement, yes. As I mentioned earlier, the economy has strained my finances to the breaking point."

"I guess that means you are no longer interested in my paintings?"

"Of course, I am. But right now I need a dramatic influx of cash."

I started to get up. "Well, thanks anyway."

"Don't leave, Stuart. I can still be of assistance. The question in my mind is how best to proceed?" He fell silent, studying me. Eventually he said, "I could advance you five thousand Euros."

I felt like I had died and gone to heaven! "M. Avoyelles, never in my wildest fantasies did I expect that much!"

"Then I would pay another five thousand more when you finish."

I blinked. "Finish? Finish what?"

"There, of course, will be a bonus depending upon the amount received from its sale. And there will be future opportunities for a great deal more money – hundreds of thousands per year, at least."

"Can we get back to the 'finish' part?"

Avoyelles' face became stern. "I am in need of a Matisse, Stuart. Mme. Chiappe is a great admirer of Matisse. And I do not want to disappoint her. Unfortunately, Matisse's works are so expensive. And they are very difficult to come by. You do see my predicament?"

My stomach dropped, hit my feet and then bounced out of sight. If I had been carrying a gun I would have shot myself. It was all clear, now. There had been no swindle regarding the Degas. Avoyelles and Uncle Stuart were in cahoots! My uncle supplied the paintings. Avoyelles sold them to unsuspecting collectors like Mme. Chiappe! Then the two of them split the proceeds.

"You want me to forge a Matisse so you can sell it to a Mafia Don's wife?" I choked.

He laughed. "Exactly."

I jumped to my feet in a panic. "I can't do that!"

"Why not? You painted a dozen or more forgeries for your uncle."

"Those were replicas. Pastiches. Pieces I did as part of my studies."

"And very good, they are. So good, even the experts cannot tell them from the real ones." He waggled a finger at me. "You have a rare gift, Stuart. Capitalize on it."

"I can't do anything illegal."

He splayed his hands. "Unfortunately, that is the only arrangement I am willing to make."

"But the money would be a loan. As soon as I get in touch with my uncle, I'd repay it."

"Stuart, I am overextended. I fight with the banks daily. If I don't come up with a substantial sum very soon I will lose everything."

"When you say substantial…"

"I need three million."

I fell silent, thinking. What if his financial desperation was at the heart of my troubles? What if he, with the assistance of Maryse and René, had orchestrated everything just to get me to this point—broke, desperate and here?

"For arguments sake," I said. "What happens when Mme. Chiappe realizes she's been cheated? It's not like she has to run to the police, for justice. Her husband is infamous for rendering his own brand of unpleasantness. I do not—I repeat—I do not want to go through what I did last night!"

He offered a reassuring smile. "There is nothing to worry about, Stuart."

"For you, maybe. But I'm the type who worries about little things—particularly when those little things are bullets in the guns of Mafiosos."

Avoyelles tented his fingers. "It won't come to that."

"How can you be sure?"

"Because I have already sold her several of your paintings."

One hand went to my stomach as a wave of fear driven nausea hit me like a pile-driver. "Are you insane?"

"She has had them examined—at my insistence. In each case, the experts reported back that she had purchased exactly what I had claimed the painting to be. Your Klimt, *Profile of a Girl*, is her favorite."

My uncle had me create three of those. At the time, of course, I just assumed he was intent upon me mastering Klimt's techniques. And, I guess he was.

"Wonderful," I said, dryly.

He struck his hands together and then splayed them palms up. "Unfortunately, the few hundred thousand I get from her, here and there, is barely enough to forestall my creditors. I need to sell something big. Once done, I will be free of them."

"Meaning the Matisse?"

His eyes fixed me like a butterfly pierced with a pin. "I have already quoted her three million for it. She said the money was not going to be an issue. All we have to do is deliver a painting."

I slumped back into the chair. "I guess I don't have much choice."

"We all have choices, Stuart. The trick is to make the right one at the right time—as you now are doing."

"Then you must've known the 'Degas' were not genuine?"

"Of course!" The gallery owner stood up, rubbing his palms together greedily. "Your uncle and I are partners. He provides the forgeries. I sell them."

"Poor René. He was convinced the Degas was genuine."

"Far better qualified experts on Degas than René were equally convinced." He beamed at me. "I sold two of your Miros just a few months ago; not to the same collector of course."

Hand Catching a Bird. I remembered that one, well, too. It was a favorite of my uncle's or so he said at the time. That was why he had me do two a day, for nearly a week.

"Should I assume one of those went to Mme. Chiappe?" I said.

His head wagged. "But I expect she is out there right now, convincing herself to buy it."

"Sounds like I've finally found my niche in the weird world of art."

The gallery owner winked. "You won't regret this, Stuart. I promise you."

I already did.

"The oils of today will be spotted by any half-bake Matisse expert," I warned. "My uncle created his own by grinding the pigments with oil and then adding thinner. I know the technique. And I can probably mix a palette that will pass. But one mistake will mean the game ends with you and me facing François Chiappe's gunmen."

"I know several discrete contacts with expertise in that area," returned Avoyelles, casually. "Leave it to me. I will have the tubes delivered to your flat in a few days."

"The canvas will be another issue. I understand the chemical aging process. But I've not actually done it."

"I have a canvas of the right age and size. It's been scraped down. But you know how to lay a new base in Matisse's style, I'm sure."

I shrugged, as if carrying a truck on my shoulders. Laying a base in Matisse's fashion was old business, to me. My uncle had been very particular about the way I prepared each canvas. I spent an entire month painting, scraping off paint, and relaying a new base in the styles of various masters. Little did I know…

"Then all that's left is to decide on the subject matter," I told him.

He shook a warning finger. "Don't get too creative. Keep it simple. I want something in line with what Matisse was creating at the turn of the twentieth century. I am not trying to break the bank with this one. I'm just trying to get myself clear."

"Something like Matisse's *Woman in a Hat*?"

He nodded. "But not a variation on that particular one. To get the money I need, something unique." Avoyelles put his hands akimbo at his hips, his face looking eager. "How long will it take?"

"Five to eight weeks," I told him. "Assuming I can rent a studio. My flat doesn't offer the necessary lighting. There is also a chance Mme. Flaubert will take the same attitude as René, and I'll be dumped out on the street. She is very fond of Maryse."

"I will speak to Mme. Flaubert about your flat," he returned. "There will be no repeat of René's foolish behavior. I hold the mortgage on her boarding house." Avoyelles opened his desk and took out a ring of keys. After selecting one, he tossed it to me. "I own a building with a studio on its top floor. It is at 23, rue de Lille. There is a cigar shop on the main floor. The manager uses the second floor for inventory storage. But access to the studio is through a blue door at street level that goes up steps leading directly to the third floor. There will be no issues over privacy."

I dropped the key into my pocket offering appreciation. "If you own so much property, why are you worried about the banks?"

"Everything is pledged as security for something else. When the economy was good, all I needed to do was continue buying. Financing was easy to obtain. Revenues from past investments covered the new ones. But when the economy tilted, the leaseholds on several of my larger investments went belly-up. That had a domino effect putting everything I have into jeopardy."

"Is anyone using the studio now?"

He shook his head. "It has not been used in over a year. It is not far from Mme. Flaubert's." His brows arched. "We are agreed on the price for the Matisse, I take it?"

"Yes. But could you have the paint delivered to the studio? I would prefer not to be seen carrying the tubes around."

"No problem."

He turned to the Joan Miro painting on the wall behind his desk. It was title, *Blue II*. Then he pulled the painting aside on a hinge to expose a wall-safe. After twirling the combination knob back and forth several times, he pulled open the steel door. From within he took out a bundle of cash, and turned to face me.

"The advance," he said, tossing the money. "But if you need more, let me know." He closed the safe. When he was facing me, again, Avoyelles said, "A few months from now, you will be rich enough to get a house of your own. A year from now, you will be spending a great deal of your time on the Riviera—at the best hotels with the most beautiful women."

I stood up feeling like the crook I was about to become. "I'll be in touch, M. Avoyelles."

He came around the desk and escorted me out of his office. "Don't look so glum, Stuart. I know exactly how you feel at this moment. But it will pass."

"The last day I worked at the Louvre, I noticed two men join in when you and René were speaking."

"Bouvier and Chevalier you mean?" he asked, candidly.

"They live at Mme. Flaubert's," I said, trying to be cagy. "I never realized they were art-lovers."

Avoyelles laughed. "Hardly that. They had business with René."

"What kind of business?"

He shrugged. "I have no idea. They told him everything was set and as I left, they followed. I'd never met that pair before. But I was very surprised René was doing business with them. I don't think those men are honest types."

Neither were we.

* * * *

I was nearly to the Métro station when I man's voice called my name. I turned to see Dr. Michele Molyneux hurrying along the sidewalk, toward me. He looked quite gray, as if terrified of something or someone. I hoped that his demeanor related to worry over my health, and not surprise that I was still alive.

"I stopped by your flat this morning, but you must have already gone," he declared. Then he tilted closer to get a better look at his stitchery. "No infection, that is good. But it will be sore for another two weeks. After a week, the sutures can come out. Again, I am very sorry about this."

"Who has the diamonds?" I asked.

He blinked in surprise. "I beg your pardon?"

"Does Maryse have the diamonds? I know you're involved."

91

"Stuart…" he began.

I cut him short with, "You were the one who doped-up Baudouin Rousseau. Don't deny it. It was you, Maryse, Buji and the two who busted my head at his place, that night."

"Stuart, if you value your life stay out of it. I give you my word, you will not be bothered again. But you must stay out of it."

A Maroon Citroën swerved from its path and jumped the curb. I jerked toward it. A moment later, Molyneux gave me a shove, sending me tumbling into an adjacent shop. When I got to my feet, Michele Molyneux lay on the sidewalk, his entire body quivering. The car had already sped away.

"Dear God," I said, hurrying over to him.

As I squatted down beside Molyneux, a crowd gathered. His eyes flickered open and he smiled at me.

"Who has the diamonds, Michele?" I whispered.

He blinked. Then, in a voice barely discernable, "She has them."

"She?"

His eyes shut, his breathing stopped and he went limp.

"Is he all right, Monsieur?" called the clerk from the store, as he came running over.

I stood up shaking my head. "I think he's dead."

"The driver deliberately tried to kill you and your friend!" the clerk went on. "I saw the whole thing."

I backed away from Molyneux's corpse, horrified.

"I'll call the police," he clerk said, and hurried off.

I pushed my way through the gathering crowd and crossed the street. I was not sure whether the driver of the Citroën intended me or Molyneux as his victim. But I assumed it had been Molyneux. Had the two who worked me over started making good on their threat to kill the others? Or was this the result of Buji's suggestion to get François Chiappe involved?

* * * *

It was almost another hour before I reached my flat. I went in, shut the door and set the lock. I wanted to seal out the entire world. I wanted to find a place to hide, a deep cave to crawl into. A pit where I could pull the rocks over me so I would never be found.

"She's going to be trouble."

It was Buji!

"Maryse is just talk."

It was Bouvier, again. The one from the first conversation.

"Talk didn't kill Molyneux," Buji returned.

"You can't think she did that?"

"I wouldn't put anything past that bitch!"

"I can see Maryse killing you, maybe. But not Molyneux."

"He killed Baudouin, didn't he? That cut us all out, didn't it? When we all got together last night it was clear that none of us had the diamonds. So, she probably thought there was nothing to lose."

"Or that Molyneux lied about not knowing where Baudouin hid the stones."

"It's too late if he did."

"She must have gone berserk. She was in love with Baudouin, remember."

"She was in love with me, once," muttered Buji, sadly.

"We have bigger things to worry about than your pitiful love-life. François Chiappe has his people digging, Buji. He'll kill us all, if he finds out what went down with Baudouin."

"Maybe he already has found out? Maybe it was his people who killed Molyneux?"

"Maryse told him?"

"The idea of involving Chiappe did come up in conversation with her," Buji returned. "You know how vindictive she is. With the diamonds being unrecoverable, what would she have to lose by pointing Chiappe at those who killed her precious Baudouin?"

I stood up and I ran out of my flat, down the hall to the stairs, and outside. Then I rounded the front and hurried into the café's entrance.

The place was crammed with people. Every booth and table was occupied. It took me a few seconds to acclimate myself as to the location of my room in relationship to where I was standing. There was the alley. There were the garbage cans just outside my window. That could only mean one of the tables across from those cans must be where the plotters were seated. But I saw only women in that area.

"It will be a twenty minute wait for a table, Monsieur."

I glanced over at the voice to see the maitre d' checking the register. "No, thank you. I was to meet some friends here. Unfortunately, I was detained. Did you see two men leave together, just moments ago?"

"I'm sorry, Monsieur. None of our guests have departed for at least ten minutes. Perhaps your friends have not yet arrived? I could arrange a place for you at the bar, while you wait."

I declined his offer and left the café, completely confused. The maitre d' had no reason to deceive me. Therefore, the voices must have come from somewhere other than in the café. That could only mean Mme. Flaubert's Boarding House. But where, within Mme. Flaubert's? And who was Buji among those in residence? I had met all the tenants before that unforgettable dinner. Bouvier must be one of the voices, assuming his name was not another common one. Maryse, of course. But which one of the tenants could be Buji?

From somewhere a saxophone played. The sound was mellow, almost depressing. A breeze gusted, carrying laughter and the scent of flowers. I looked around as if expecting to see someone or something that would link the voices I had heard at dinner to that of Buji's. But no other people were in sight. A trumpet joined the sax. It was muted, offering up a nasally blur of sound. Then a woman started singing.

"Buji must be someone living at Mme. Flaubert's," I told myself. "But that damn echo in the voices is going to make him hard to pin down."

A car horn blared. Startled, I jumped. Then I hurried back inside Mme. Flaubert's, and up to my flat. When I arrived, the voices had gone silent.

Chapter 7
Telling Tales

The Black Death arrived in Paris in 1348. It killed as many as 800 people a day. In 1466, 40,000 Parisians died of plague. In August of 1572, the St. Bartholomew's Day massacre occurred. This killed at least 10,000. Then Cholera epidemics struck Paris in both 1832 and 1849 claiming tens of thousands of lives. In the chaos caused by the fall of Napoleon III's government, 20,000 Parisians were butchered. Despite this, François Chiappe's resilient ancestors managed to survive.

That depressing thought nagged at me, during the following three days of preparing the studio. While I swept, dusted and then went in search of what I would need to make the place functional, I could not shake the feeling that François Chiappe's men were on their way to kill me. I had not been involved in Baudouin Rousseau's untimely demise. But would the Mafia Don believe me? If not, how could I possibly convince him?

The tubes of paint and the canvas promised by Cesar Avoyelles arrived. I examined each color carefully. All had been masterfully created. Now, all I had to do was create the Matisse. From a forger's prospective, I had a multitude of options. Because Henri Matisse, like most artists, went through a number of creative phases.

In his early works, Matisse experimented with Pointillism. This style of painting is created using small distinct dots of color. The resulting creation seems to emerge from disparate points. In about 1905 Matisse became involved in the Fauvism movement. These paintings were characterized by wild brush-work and discordant colors, while keeping subject matter extremely simple although slightly abstract. Matisse abandoned this for a brief dip into Orientalism. This style of art refers to the depiction of Eastern motifs. After the close of World War I, he took up what is referred to as the 'return to order.' This form rejected the extreme avant-garde of previous years, taking its inspiration from traditional art forms. Finally, nearing the end of his life, he created what are called cutouts. These were abstractions built of Gouache and paper to form a type of decoupage. Despite Avoyelles request that I do something similar to Matisse's efforts at the turn of the twentieth century, I wanted to offer something along the lines of his early works. Something I could take pride in, albeit silently.

After doing about a dozen or so sketches in his various styles, I finally settled upon a boating scene using the Pointillism technique. I intended to paint a young couple in a poling boat. The young man would be maneuvering the vessel along a river. The young woman would be lounging in the boat, her face toward him, dragging her hand through the water. Trees and brush would be the landscape on the far side of the river. The point of view for the painting would be on the water itself, near the boat.

I chose Pointillism because it was a less-used form of painting and so there would be fewer of Matisse's works to compare it against. Although Matisse was probably the best known for its use, others who experimented with this technique were Camille Pissarro, Gaetano Previati, Angelo Morbelli, Charles Angrand, Hippolyte Petitjean, and Henri-Edmond Cross. There were others, still. And their techniques were generally similar. All resulted in a grippingly unforgettable paintings. But Matisse's version of Pointillism is, to my eye, the most intriguing. That, for me, would be the personal challenge.

Although I was familiar with Pointillism, having spent many hours studying paintings done in this manner, I had never actually used the technique. I had suggested it to my uncle, during my mentoring period. But he felt it was far too time consuming to be a profitable approach to art. Also, this type of painting would offer unique challenges that, if failed at, would result in an artistic catastrophe. However, the allure of Pointillism was irresistible. If I could master it, my revival of that style might change what the critics thought of my own paintings.

On day five of my exile from Mme. Flaubert's, Cesar Avoyelles arrived at the studio with the second batch of paint-tubes. I could tell he was very excited about what he hoped the Matisse would be. And despite my continuing moral battle over forging the work of a great artist, I could not help but share his exhilaration.

"What have you come up with?" he asked breathlessly, handing me the box of paints. "I can stand the wait no longer. I must see what you're doing!"

I set the tubes on the worktable next to the easel and then uncovered the canvas I had been working on.

"Sweet Lord!" he cried, his eyes wide and bright. "This is perfection! Better than I could have hoped for!" Then his eyes came up to mine. "But are you certain it will fool an expert? Pointillism is extremely difficult."

"You know Matisse. You tell me."

He crept over to the canvas and studied what I had painted, inch by inch. After what seemed like a lifetime he stepped back, grabbed me and kissed both of my cheeks.

"You are a genius!"

"I'm a thief," I returned. "But I'm a thief who is about to set the art world on its ear. Somehow that makes what I'm doing feel right." Then I pointed at the canvas. "By the time I am finished, the value of that painting will be fifty times what you quoted Mme. Chiappe."

"Where are your sketches?"

I retrieved the pad from behind the easel and handed it to him. He quickly paged through it until he found the sketch of what was on the canvas. His voice was breathless as he uttered, "You are going to make both of us very rich, Stuart."

"We're a long way from that."

He began to pace like a kid waiting to go outside in order to show off his new bicycle, holding the sketchpad with one hand and wildly gesticulating with the other. "Do you know what the news services will say when I announce the discovery of a never-before seen Matisse Pointillism?" He was so excited his face had taken on the color of a pickled beet. "It will be like reporting the planet is going to explode! Once the press picks up on it, I will be inundated with offers." His arms rose and fell, the pages of the sketchbook flapping like paper wings. "Even if Mme. Chiappe has the money I would not dare attempt a private placement. My God, I would be crucified by the other potential buyers! We will have to offer it at auction."

"Is there some way we can have this secretly examined by a Matisse expert? I don't mean to have it certified. But for someone with the right background to take a hard, long look to make sure we don't end up in jail?"

He fanned the air, dismissing my concerns. "You concentrate on painting it. Leave its provenance and examination to me. I have a contact who will give it a discrete and very thorough scrutiny after you have finished. If there are flaws, he will spot them—and remain quiet. You will then correct those issues and he will reexamine it. The process will continue until the Matisse is perfect." Avoyelles stopped to look at me. "He is expensive. But if this turns out like I think it will, his fees will be insignificant!" Avoyelles' face became expectant, his body trembling with anticipation. "When? When will it be done? For God's sake, I won't get a wink of sleep until then!"

"Another six weeks, I think. Then a week to age the results. Then…"

"Six weeks?" he moaned. "How do you expect me to wait six weeks? I will go mad with anticipation!"

I made a defeated movement with both hands. "I cannot do it any quicker, Cesar. If that is too long, I will do something that should satisfy Mme. Chiappe. But even so, that still would take at least four weeks. For such a small delay, with such profit potential…"

He batted the air, to silence me. "I know, I know—it's just that I was not expecting something so wondrous! Take all the time you need. But keep me informed." Avoyelles drew in a deep breath and then exhaled noisily. His excitement was so great, his cheeks were coated with perspiration. "God, I will have to hire a media team to handle the exposition!" His arms suddenly flailed the air sending the sketchbook pages flapping again. "I'll have to purchase a new wardrobe! I can't let the public see me in these rags, announcing an art-world miracle! Wait! Maybe I should get a facelift? It would be healed in six weeks. And liposuction! Sweet mother of God! If we pull this off we'll live like kings!" He waggled the sketchpad in front of me. "Can I keep this?"

I nodded. "But I wouldn't get careless. Should that sketch be discovered everything will be lost."

He started to leave and then stopped. "Oh, Maryse has telephoned me at my office several times. She's concerned about you. She says you haven't been back to Mme. Flaubert's for nearly a week."

My heart skipped a beat at the news of her interest. However, I was resolved to have no more involvement with Maryse Rousseau.

"I have nothing to say to her," I told him.

"You might be treating her too harshly," he cautioned.

"How? She lied to me, again and again. Then… Cesar, the thought of her watching—if not actually participating—in her husband's death…" I made a despairing movement with one hand. "I cannot stomach it."

"Stuart, I cannot believe she was there. Not Maryse. I know you said you saw a woman. I know Monet is convinced of her presence, when Baudouin died. But neither of you know her as I do. I tell you, she would not have been there."

"I know for a fact she was there," I snapped, recalling Buji's listing of who was present that night.

He nodded pensively. "Just the same, you should give her a chance to explain."

"To what end?"

"Are you short of money?" he asked, after a moment of silence. "Do you need me to pay your rent?"

"No. I've already remitted that through the end of the month. But I'm staying here, for the time being, because I'm engrossed in this project. I cannot tear myself away from it."

He sent his eyes around, horrified. "But how can you survive here?"

"A cold shower. A hand wash of my clothes when needed. Some bread. Some cheese. Some wine. That's all I require."

"Tens of millions on the come and he expends nickels for overhead!" Cesar Avoyelles gave his eyes a weary roll. "Are you insane? If you don't like Mme. Flaubert's, I will find you a more suitable place."

"Everything is as I want it, Cesar. I cook. I eat. I work."

The gallery owner averted his gaze, thinking, considering. Then he looked over and said, "I don't want to alarm you…" He made a worried face. "But I feel I must warn you. There are rumors being bandied. Françoise Chiappe has offered two million for the names of those involved in Baudouin Rousseau's murder. I know you were not involved as does Monet, but…" His gray eyes seemed to glint with warning. "But if Chiappe still suspects you… What I am trying to say is, François is not a reasonable man." He made a pleading gesture. "You might not be safe, here. At least back at Mme. Flaubert's if you cried-out for help someone might hear you."

My stomach knotted. "If Chiappe is looking for me, I won't be safe anywhere and no one can help me."

Avoyelles shrugged, looking at me squarely. "That is a possibility," he said. "But with so much at stake…" He made a beseeching movement. "Perhaps if I moved you to the farm I have outside of Paris? You could shave your beard. He would never find you, there."

"If he really wants me he'll find me."

"Only if someone recognizes you—which they will not. The loft in the barn can be quickly converted to a studio."

"Monet has ordered me to stay in Paris until his investigation is completed. Considering how brain-dead that man is, a solution could take years."

"I will speak to him. I'm certain I can get him to make allowances, considering your life could be in danger."

I wagged my head. "For the first time in my artistic career, I feel alive. I cannot explain it, Cesar. But I don't want to risk losing this burning ambition - not for an instant. If I move from here, that could happen. If so, I would rather be dead."

He smiled. "I don't want you to lose it, either. But I also don't want you to fall into the hands of François Chiappe." He thrust a finger toward the ceiling as if making an earth-shaking declaration. "I shall have the barn renovated—just in case. It will take only a week, or so. When it is finished, we will talk, again. If nothing else, it will be available for our next project."

"Assuming I'm still alive."

He hesitated, staring down at his shoes. "When will you be going back to Mme. Flaubert's—in case Maryse telephones again?"

"When I have the first Pointillism layer in place over the sketch. Then I'll take a couple of days to let the paint and my soul rest. But I would appreciate it if you did not mention my intentions to her."

He opened his mouth and shut it, then opened it again. "Maryse knows Chiappe is looking for those involved. She was crying with fear for your safety, the last time she telephoned. I cannot deceive her, Stuart. She is—very special to me. And if you give her a chance she will be very special to you, too. I—I think she is in love with you."

"Look at me, Cesar. Do I look like the type of man who would win the heart of a woman like Maryse?" I shook my head. "Even if it was true, there is still her husband's death to consider."

Avoyelles seemed slightly disturbed by my suggestion. "Well, I hope you know what you are doing. Maryse is a rare commodity among women. I would not cast her aside so easily." He looked at his wristwatch. "I'm afraid I must go. Remember… Keep me informed." He started to leave, stopped and looked back. "Maybe a butt lift? What do you think?"

* * * *

It was another two days of little sleep and a lot of painting before I went back to Mme. Flaubert's. On the way there, I stopped at a clinic and had the sutures removed from my cheek. Then I took a long and well-deserved dinner, purposely arriving at my flat late at night. I went to bed as quietly as I could so as not to disclose my presence.

As excited as I was about the Matisse, it felt good to be away from it. A few days of relaxing, and the canvas would be dry enough to begin the next Pointillism layer. Then I would follow through to the painting's completion.

A few moments later I heard quickly striding footsteps and mutterings. Then came the voices of Buji and Bouvier.

"Maryse has disappeared." It was Buji. He sounded frantic.

"Chiappe?" the other man suggested.

"That is what I am thinking," Buji returned, grimly. "She went out last night and never came back."

"What happened?"

"We argued."

"What about?"

"I was trying to get her to admit that it was she who killed Molyneux."

"And did she?"

"Yes."

"Well, at least we know that Chiappe wasn't involved in it. Which means he doesn't know who was with Baudouin, that night."

"Maybe."

"What do you mean, Buji?"

"She said she was going to see Chiappe. To tell him everything—to get back at me."

"You? What about the rest of us? We'll all be killed!"

"I thought Chiappe did not worry you?" taunted Buji.

"That was when there was a chance for sixty million. I was willing to stick my neck out, then. But now… With nothing on the come… We'll have to leave France!"

"And give up everything? You may have given up on that sixty million, but I have not!"

"I tell you, if she talks to Chiappe, staying in Paris will only get us killed, Buji!"

"She'll die first. Then he'll come looking for the rest of us. At least I'll have that satisfaction."

"You're mad! I'm not sitting around waiting to die!"

I sat up sick at heart. Whoever Buji was, he was probably right. Chiappe would kill Maryse. Even if her only transgression was to have done nothing to stop her husband's murder, he would kill her. I was still hurting from her betrayal. But I would not wish her any harm.

I got out of bed and started to dress. I would have to tell Monet what I had overheard—all of it. He would be furious. I would probably be arrested. But I could not sit by and let Chiappe murder Maryse.

I started for the door, stopped and then removed my clothes. Who was I kidding? Why would François Chiappe let her go unharmed simply because Monet came blustering in? A police officer would hardly strike fear into that gangster's heart. Chiappe would kill her, he'd kill Monet and then, because Monet would blab about who told him about Maryse being held by Chiappe, Chiappe would kill me. She got herself into this mess. She would have to get herself out.

I know, I know I am sounding like a craven coward. But that is because I am one.

Then another thought came to mind. Avoyelles! He was known to Chiappe. Perhaps he could convince the gangster to release Maryse for old times sake - having heard an anonymous rumor of her capture? At least he could try. Avoyelles had said she was special to him.

All right, all right! Despite her lies she's still special to me, too!

Again, I pulled on my clothes. Then I hurried outside.

The café was still open so I went in and trotted to the bank of telephones near its rear door. I dialed Avoyelles' cell-phone. After several rings he answered.

"I am sorry to bother you, Cesar," I said. "It is Stuart. I think Maryse is in trouble. François Chiappe is going to kill her. Yes, I know it sounds ridiculous. But I thought you might be able to talk him—in case what I heard is true. As you said, she is very special—parts of her are heavenly. Yes, I know I was rather scathing in my critique of her. But, when it comes right down to it, I think I love her. Okay. Thank you."

After ringing off I returned to my flat, stripped off and crawled back into bed. Cesar Avoyelles said he would telephone Chiappe at once, and discuss the matter. But Cesar had not been very encouraging. His relationship with the Mafia Don was strictly art-related. And art dealers do not garner much power in the world of the Mafioso. Still, he might be able to reason with the mobster.

I reconsidered notifying Monet. But I changed my mind. He would only blunder in and ruin Avoyelles' efforts. No. Maryse's best chance at survival was in the hands of Cesar Avoyelles. I would have to wait and pray for her safety. Failing that, I could try and get a complete body mask before her funeral.

I tossed and turned most of the night. Several times I went out, located a phone booth and rang Avoyelles. I wanted an update on his efforts with Chiappe. But the gallery owner did not answer. Had Chiappe taken such offense to Avoyelles' interest in Maryse that he killed Cesar as well? It was a very grim possibility.

The next morning, I dragged myself out of bed, feeling like a man who had not slept in a month. As I staggered around trying to find my shoes, a knock on my door startled me. I was paid for another two weeks with Mme. Flaubert. So I was certain it was not she seeking my attention. Besides, she always slept until midday, or at least remained in bed. Boarding house gossip suggested her late rising had something to do with the two young, vigorous protégés sharing her flat. Not that I begrudged her amorous dalliances. If I had her money and unsated inclinations, I might have a couple of protégés of my own—female, of course.

The knocking repeated, insistently.

I quickly donned shirt and trousers. Then I took several barefoot steps toward the door, before stopping. If not Mme. Flaubert, then who might want to see me? Chiappe's men would hardly knock. They would simply bust in and shoot me. But with Maryse in the hands of Chiappe, that thinned down the options. My insistent caller must be either Chief Inspector Claude Monet or Cesar Avoyelles.

With one dark possibilities and one bright one in the offing, I crept over to the door and pressed my ear against it. I heard soft sobbing, from the other side. Conceivably, it was Monet being ravaged by guilt over having disgraced me with his interrogations. But I thought that rather unlikely. He was more the gloating sort, when it came to another's misfortune. Perhaps it was Avoyelles, emotional about Maryse murder!

I crouched down, to peek between the floor and the bottom of the door. From my place of observation, I noted a pair of women's high-heel shoes on the other side. What were the odds of Avoyelles having become a transvestite, overnight? Not good. With his shoulders, he would look ridiculous in high heels.

Throwing caution to the wind, I stood up and opened the door a crack. To my surprise, Maryse Rousseau stood there. She looked shaken and pale.

I was instantly relieved. Then my heart became cold, as the anger I had been harboring against her over the lies, consumed my senses. But she offered me a pleading look. And instantly, all of my rage dissipated like fog on a high wind. I backed away opening the door wide.

"Two men jumped out of a car and grabbed me on my way to the Métro station," Maryse declared, between sobs. She glanced behind as if afraid she might have been followed. Then Maryse hurried inside. "I scratched one in the face and got away."

I shut the door, setting the lock. Then I turned to watch her move across the room. She was breathtaking in her pink sweater, skin-tight gray slacks, and pink spike heels. When Maryse passed the window, sunbeams danced above her dark head, like bits of gold trying to link themselves to each long strand.

"I thought they were going to kill me," she whimpered.

As Maryse continued to move, her hands animated about her, the sparkling light catching her gleaming red nails. It was as if she had just bathed, dressed, painted her nails and come over. Which made me wonder how someone so immaculate could have fought her way free of an abduction attempt by two gangsters with murder in mind?

"François Chiappe's men grabbed you?" I suggested.

She stopped and turned to face me, offering a guarded stare. "Why would *he* be after me?"

I started to explain about the overheard conversations but I stopped short. Since I could not trust her, it was foolish to explain.

"Revenge, comes to mind," I replied, vaguely. "Your husband was a pal of his. And I'm told Chiappe intends to take revenge on those who killed Baudouin. How'd you get home?"

"I took a taxi. But when I got back here, my flat had been ransacked."

"How curious. I did not hear anything."

Her eyes fell away from my stare, guiltily.

I pointed at her long, manicured nails. "Those must've dug deep when you clawed your way free. I'm surprised your fingers aren't covered in your abductor's blood."

She glanced at her hands. Then tears streamed down her cheeks. With a cry of anguish, Maryse rushed over and wrapped her arms about my neck, hanging on as if I was her only hope for life.

"I—I didn't know who to turn to, Stuart," she sobbed. "I was hoping... I'm so frightened."

I know what you are thinking. This is just another act. She's trying to sucker me into letting down my guard. I agree. Part of me knows the odds are against her ever being forthright. The other part doesn't care. He's just praying the rumors about her frigidity were grossly exaggerated. I suppose, as Avoyelles suggested, I should give Maryse a chance to explain. And in the meantime I could offer her the benefit of doubt. Yes, I know, that is not the smartest thing I could do. But she is crying and her body feels so very wonderful against mine. And if I turn her away my nightstick will commit suicide.

I folded my arms around her, pulling Maryse close. "I didn't kill your husband."

"I never thought you did," she sniffed against my throat. "I've been so worried about you. I thought you might've gone back to the States and I'd never see you again."

I tried to lean back to look into her face, but she clung to me. It was as if any separation between us would kill her.

"If you knew I hadn't done it, why in hell did you tell René I had?" I demanded.

Her voice was barely above a whisper against my neck. "I didn't. It was he who told me. I told him it was untrue."

"But he said you claimed I was your husband's killer. He said that was why he was firing me."

She tilted back, staring up into my face. "I don't understand."

I released my grip on her. "Somehow I'm not surprised."

I was completely confused, as well. Both she and René had lied. Her about everything and anything. Him about that message and his instructions to meet with Baudouin Rousseau. Was she lying again – hoping I would accept her version of the truth and blame René? Or was it more likely, he had gotten confused by Monet and just assumed the worst about me? That, of course, did not explain his denial concerning the telephone message. But, perhaps, Monet had misunderstood about that as well—or had lied? After all, Monet had lied about Baudouin not knowing Corsican.

She stepped back, her eyes focusing upon my battered face. "Stuart, what happened to you?"

"I held a little get-together that did not work out well."

I turned and went over to the window. There I perched upon the sill, watching Maryse.

Her hands spread in pleading. "You must be so angry with me," she said. "I am so sorry. I told you everything would work out and look what happened. Everything you worried about came true."

She was lying. I knew she was lying. Nevertheless, I still wanted to believe her. I looked into her sad eyes and I my heart ached. I wanted to pull her into my arms and never let her go. But she had misled me so many time times… Then there was her watching her husband die… And what about her sending those men after me?

"I don't know what to believe," I muttered.

"Stuart, I honestly thought…"

I cut her short with, "Skip it!"

"I'll make it up to you, Stuart." She flattened her palms against the air between us. "I promise. In a short time, I will inherit a great deal of money. You won't have to worry about anything, ever again."

"You keep making promises. I keep getting deeper into trouble. Frankly if you give me any more help, I'll wake up dead." Then my anger took hold and I shouted, "Why in hell did you send your pals over here after telling them I had the diamonds?"

Her face paled. "What diamonds?"

I pointed at my mug. "The ones your pals redecorated my face over!"

She shook her head frantically, sending the cloud of long black hair flying. "I don't know what you're talking about, Stuart!" A moment later, the tresses resettled along her back. "I would never let anyone hurt you."

"Maryse, stop lying to me. I heard you and Buji talking. You told him flat out you'd sent those goons to pound me."

"Where did you hear this?"

I thrust a finger at the floor. "Right here!"

Maryse considered my words long enough to glance nervously at her watch. "Stuart, the only other time I've been in your flat before this moment was when I brought over my sculpture. So I could not have discussed anything with anyone, here."

It was hopeless. She uttered one lie after another and always would. "Never mind! How 'bout explaining where you went the night you were supposed to meet me here?"

"I did come here. But you were out," she returned, without hesitation. "When you did not answer my knock, I knew you must've gone to see Baudouin."

I wagged my head. "I mean before that. You told me to wait in my flat. You said you had to go out for a little while. You said you'd come here, afterward. Where did you go?"

She turned away with a shrug. "I had to talk to someone."

"Your husband?"

She twisted back toward me, offering a baleful look. "What difference does it make?"

"Who?"

"Michelle Molyneux!"

"How convenient. He's dead. So there's no way to contradict your story. Why did you visit him?"

"Stuart, I don't want to talk about it."

Evasion. Just another form of lying, as far as I was concerned. "When we were sitting together on the Métro, you telephoned someone. You spoke to that person in Corsican. I asked who it was. You said it was your husband. Who were you really talking to?"

She faced me, offering a beseeching gesture. "It was my husband."

"Are you certain it was not Avoyelles? Or was it Michele Molyneux? I heard you call whoever you were talking to a bastard, Maryse. I heard you mention a fall-guy. I didn't catch all you said. But those two words were clear. Somehow, I don't see you calling your husband a bastard and he sure as hell would never have been anybody's fall-guy."

Her arms flopped to her sides. "All right! I was speaking with Michele. Why are you interrogating me like this?"

I thrust a finger at her. "You spoke to him in Corsican so I would not understand. Why?"

"Because I did not want you to know what was happening."

"Obviously. But, why?"

"Because it was so ugly!" she screamed. Her hands went to her face and she murmured through her fingers, "God, I can't bear it."

"Ugly because it involved killing your husband?" I taunted.

She began sobbing, her entire body shivering.

"Maryse I saw you at your husband's apartment. It was you, Molyneux, Buji and whoever else was involved in the Lucien Falize diamond heist. You all went there. You all wanted your cut."

Through her fingers she begged, "Stuart, please don't do this?"

"Look at me. Damn it, Maryse, look at me!"

Her hands fell away and she looked over at me through red, tearing eyes.

"Look what they did to me," I said. "What did I do to you that deserved this? What in hell did I do?"

She rushed over and tried to put her arms around my neck, but I pushed her away.

"Molyneux said you had the diamonds, Maryse. Where are they?"

Her eyes dipped away from my stare. "I don't know what you're talking about."

"You're lying, again!"

Her tearing eyes came back up to mine. "Why are you treating me this way?"

I moved away from the window, my anger out of control. "I didn't enjoy what those clowns did to me. I want revenge. The problem is they're tougher than I am. So the only way I can get even is to get the diamonds before they do." I stopped and faced her. "You've got them. I want them. The whole sixty million."

She made a pitying expression. "But I don't have them."

"Why would Molyneux lie? The man knew he was dying."

"He was hurt. He must have been confused."

I shook my head. "No. When I asked if you had them, he said you did."

She went over to the bed and sat down, looking very uneasy.

"Do you own a car?" I asked.

"Why would I? I don't know how to drive."

"Odd, isn't it?" I taunted. "Not driving in these modern times?"

Maryse shrugged. "There is no need to drive when I can ride my bike or use the Métro."

"What kind of car did those men use in your alleged abduction?" I interrupted.

Maryse shifted on the bed to stare at me. "Alleged? Why are you suggesting I lied about it?"

"I can't think of one good reason. But you keep doing your best to continue with what has become a tradition of lies, in one form or another. What kind of car, Maryse?"

"A gray Peugeot."

I sneered, "That's the make and color of your car, isn't it?"

She gritted her teeth, her eyes dropping to her hands. "I do not own a gray Peugeot."

"Stop lying to me! I know for a fact you own a new Peugeot."

She looked up. A tremulous little smile formed upon her face. "Monet, I suppose?"

I turned away, completely exasperated. "I keep telling myself you're worth moving heaven and earth, to have. But after what I've been through, I think those ideas deserve being said only in a rubber room."

"Trust me a little longer, Stuart," she urged, confidently. "Just a few more days. I have everything arranged. Then we will have more money than we can spend."

I went back to the window and resumed my perch, facing her. "Maryse, I can't go through any more days like the last few. I'm here to tell you, I'm tapped out."

More tears formed in her eyes. "I would have given my life rather than let them do what they did."

"Really?" I scorned. "That's nice. But here's the big question, Maryse. Would you have handed over the diamonds to keep me in one piece?"

"If I'd had the diamonds, yes!" she snapped.

My toes grabbed at the floor as I jerked upright from my perch. "You have 'em, lady!"

Maryse responded with a curious, halting pause between each word. "I ... don't ... think... Michele... lied to you... about the diamonds."

"Then how can you sit there and deny you have them?"

"What were his exact words?"

I thought back. Then I said, "'*She* has them'."

"Michele did not even mention my name," Maryse admonished.

"You're the only one he could've been talking about. You were there that night!"

"Did you actually see me, Stuart?"

"I saw a woman."

"But did you see her face?"

"Not exactly."

Maryse sighed, wearily. "Well, what did you see... since we are trying to avoid any type of deception?"

"I saw a silhouette—a shadow. But I know it was you."

"It was not me! It was Reese." She crossed her arms. "That night I went to see Michele, after talking to him on the phone. I had to make sure that if you went to my husband's apartment, Michele would make sure nothing happened to you. But he was not at home."

"You expected Molyneux to protect me while he killed your husband?" I scoffed. "Don't be ridiculous!"

She screamed, "Killing Baudouin was not my idea! I wanted nothing to do with it! I begged Baudouin. But he refused. He said he could stand the pain no longer. He said if he didn't do it, the others would kill him anyway. I told him to call Chiappe. I told him to call the police. I told him to give the others the diamonds if that is what they wanted. But he refused. That is why I was not there. I could not watch my husband die."

I jabbed a finger at her. "You had to be there. You were part of the diamond heist."

Her face went white. "Is that what Monet told you?"

I felt my cheeks grow warm with anger. "You admitted as much."

"When?"

"When you were arguing with Buji!"

"You keep talking about, Buji!" she returned, her voice rising shrill and high-pitched with anger. "Who in hell is Buji?"

Again, I jabbed a finger at her. "You know damn well who he is."

With a curse, Maryse made for the door. But as she gripped the knob, my voice to her back stayed her exit. "I think your husband hung onto the diamonds so you could collect the whole bundle. That was the plan. Along with a little bit of assisted-suicide. Molyneux pumped him full of poison, and then the rest of you waited and watched. Of course only you, your husband and Molyneux knew your husband was going to die. The others thought he would start yapping about where the diamonds were hidden."

Maryse released the knob, and turned to face me; her eyes and mouth opened wide in amazement; her complexion as bloodless as marble. "Who told you these things? It wasn't Michele."

"Right or wrong, Maryse?"

"I had nothing to do with any of it," she said, flatly.

The wound in my cheek suddenly burned and I touched the scab. "Sure. Just like you never set me up. Give me one honest answer, huh? Who's Buji?"

Maryse stared straight into the eyes. "I don't know who you are talking about."

How in hell could she not know? She must be lying and yet her unwavering stare told me she is not.

I moved away from the window, across the room; placing the pullout bed between us. "Okay. How did your husband get involved in the heist?"

"Baudouin was approached by a group of people, nearly a year ago," she said with obvious reluctance. "They wanted him to lead a jewel robbery. But François Chiappe, the man my husband worked for, refused to approve the plan. Baudouin was told to pass on the project. Unfortunately, my husband liked the idea—for whatever reason. So Baudouin decided to help in spite of François' objections. This I know, because Baudouin explained it to me, afterward."

"It was Molyneux who approached your husband, wasn't it?"

Maryse made a pleading gesture. "I don't know. My husband did not tell me who were involved."

First she obviously tells the truth, and then she obviously lies even though she looks like she's telling the truth. What was the point of it? Obviously, because she knows I was just stupid enough to want to believe her!

"Okay," I said. "The store was robbed. What happened then?"

Maryse hesitated. "The stones were delivered to my husband." She moved toward the bed.

"And he did what with them?"

"I don't know!" Her voice was sharp and reproachful.

My own rose cholerically. "But you must know!"

Maryse gave her head a determined shake and sat down on the mattress. "Why? I was not his partner in crime. I was his wife. I cooked for him. I cleaned for him. I kept him happy in bed."

"I think if I was married to a guy who'd latched onto sixty million in stolen diamonds, I'd have asked where the booty was buried."

"You are not me," she responded, icily.

"You must have some idea who Buji is."

Maryse rolled her eyes. "Stuart, that is not even a name."

"It's a nickname, isn't it?"

She got up and strode around the bed, over to me; stopping inches away. "Who says I spoke with this Buji?"

I tapped my chest. "I heard you talking with him."

"Here?"

"Yes, here!"

"You're insane!" she ejaculated. Maryse retreated a step, and continued defiantly. "How could I talk to this person if I was not here?"

"You weren't here. You were somewhere else. But I heard you here!"

There was another hesitation. "Stuart, you need a doctor. You're talking crazy!"

I flung an arm toward the ventilator cover. "Are you denying you sat there and argued with Buji about the missing diamonds? Do you deny you agreed to let Buji and his pals kill your husband?"

She lunged forward and slapped my face so hard it spun me away, breaking the scab on the wound.

"Don't you ever accuse me of that!" Her shaking voice rose to a breaking cry. "I loved my husband! I would have died for him!"

I wiped at the trickle of blood on my cheek, stunned into silence by her savage response. After I recovered my composure I looked into her face and taunted, "But would you have given up the diamonds for him?"

Maryse crossed her arms and offered me her back. Then a moment later she turned to face me. "Michele. Buji was his nickname when he worked as a painter, while going through medical school. But that was years ago."

That was not the answer I had hoped for. With Buji still alive, a very dead Molyneux could not be playing his part.

"Did Monet explain about the drugs found in your husband?" I asked.

"No. Just that..." Her voice faltered. The color receded from her face, superseded by a deathly white pallor. "Just that Baudouin had been injected with whatever it was."

"Injected by Molyneux."

Maryse covered her face and broke down into tears, again. "Why do you keep harping on it?"

It was no act she was giving. At least not this time.

"According to Molyneux, those drugs are similar to sleeping tablets —mostly," I told her. "But the coroner thought such a cocktail of drugs might've been injected as a truth serum."

She looked over at me with a start.

"That was the plan, wasn't it?" I asked. "The gang would show up. Your husband would refuse to cooperate. Then Molyneux would inject the magic truth serum to make your husband tell where they could find the diamonds. Only it was Molyneux's job to make sure your husband did not speak—ever again. Right? That was the wrinkle. A mercy killing that would look like an accidental overdose. The rest of the gang would get stiffed on their end of the take, while you pocketed the bundle. Very clever. Greedy. But very clever."

Again, she offered me her back. "I'm not a thief."

"Maryse, I know everything. Why lie about it?"

She turned toward me crying, "If I possessed the diamonds, I would've contacted the insurance company. I would have arranged to collect the recovery fee."

"Reward? What reward?" I asked, half unbelievingly.

She drew herself up sharply, as if fearful of having said too much. For a moment Maryse sat there sniffing and pawing her face, to remove the dampness. Then she said, "Insurers sometimes pay recovery fees, on stolen property. It's a percentage of the property's value."

A sudden and unexpected wave of avarice hit me. "How much would that value be—in the case of these diamonds?"

"Five or six million – maybe more," she responded, somewhat doubtfully.

Millions? For handing back stolen diamonds? Assuming I found the stones and lived after collecting the reward. Assuming Françoise Chiappe did not have me penciled in for his next hit. Assuming… Millions?

Chapter 8
There's a Hole in My Butt

France's contribution to modern criminal procedures comes by way of Eugène François Vidocq. He was a nineteenth century criminal who turned detective and became the first head of the *Surete*, or what is now the *Police Nationalle*. After resigning from the Surete, Vidocq started a private investigation firm—*Le Bureau des Renseignements*—and employed twenty-eight criminals as investigators. Considering this less than sterling paternity for French police practices, I cannot help but wonder if Chief Inspector Claude Monet was not related to Vidcoq.

"So if you and I get our hands on those diamonds…" I began.

Maryse Rousseau stood up and looked at me with renewed interest. "We would become very rich." Her voice deepened portentously. "And, most importantly, it would be legal."

I sidled away thinking. Why not play along? Why not run a game on her? Why not collect half of five or six million Euros? I could afford a villa. I could afford anything I wanted. I looked back at her. Well, almost everything I wanted.

"Sounds like a game-plan to me," I observed.

She almost smiled, but made no remark.

"You told me your husband wanted a divorce to marry someone else. Who is 'the someone else'?"

"Reese," she returned, her eyes lowering away from my stare.

"Reese? The one you say was at your husband's apartment, rather than you?"

Instantly her gaze was reflecting mine, in angry spades. "René's wife, Reese!"

"René D'aubigne?" I gasped.

Her lips trembled. "Why are you so shocked, Stuart? I'm certain you have not lived as a virgin."

"Close enough," I muttered, despairingly. "You mean to tell me your husband dumped you in favor of some woman described to me as frozen doggy doo-doo on a stick? As God's own frigid bitch? As…"

"I would hardly call Reese that," Maryse interposed, impatiently. "Mme. D'aubigne is quite beautiful and very affectionate. She adored Baudouin."

Beautiful? Affectionate? Adored? Then why had René offered such angry and disgusting descriptions of his wife?

"Are you sure?" I asked. "Because I'm here to tell you, René never referred to his wife as anything less than Godzilla's frosty daughter."

"I have never heard Rene say such a thing about Reese."

"Okay, maybe I misunderstood. But I'm clear on one thing because Monet explained it to me. He said the divorce papers your husband filed listed infidelity as the reason—yours. Any comment on that?"

Maryse's cheeks colored profusely and she looked down at her feet. "It is not what you think."

Stop laughing. I admit it sounds like she is hedging, again. But there could be any number of rational explanations for infidelity. Maybe she was abducted by aliens? Maybe her husband forced her into it? Maybe… All right. I agree. There is no rational explanation for having an extramarital affair.

I shrugged. "What am I thinking?"

She looked up, her eyes tearing. "That I'm a whore."

"I'm not the type to judge. But for argument's sake, why else would your husband file papers that make you out to be one?"

"Baudouin was a strict Catholic," she explained. "As you must know, a Catholic getting a divorce could face excommunication. My husband was willing to endure that. But I knew, in time, he would regret it." Maryse made a defeated gesture with one hand. "So I offered a solution. If he got his priest to nullify our marriage based upon my having taken numerous lovers, Baudouin could remarry. I am not Catholic. So one divorce or a hundred, it mattered not to me." She paused to take a ragged breath. "We went to see his priest. I admitted my terrible sins. Baudouin was promised an annulment. And that is why he filed the papers the way he did."

"Well, that's certainly an explanation. But just to satisfy my curiosity, why on earth would you do that for him? The man was dumping you for another woman."

"My husband no longer loved me, yes," she returned. "But I loved him very much. I wanted to do whatever it would take to make Baudouin happy."

"And you called me insane! Maryse, no woman in her right mind does that. It's revenge time when divorce happens. It's bleed the bastard white, time! It's…"

"I was being practical, Stuart," she interjected. "If Baudouin's affair with Reese did not work out, he might come back to me. I didn't care what people thought. I was trying to reclaim my husband's devotion."

I shook my head, completely baffled by her rationalization. "You were even willing to take him back? After he had an affair and humiliated you with lies about you being unfaithful? Maryse, that is sick."

"No, Stuart. That is love."

I turned away, wondering why women like her were not in the United States. Why couldn't American women love in that nonjudgmental fashion? Why did the average divorcing American wife always grab for a stranglehold on her husband's financial jugular? Just because the guy got a little fickle and went after a number like Fabienne...

I looked back at Maryse. "Speaking of Fabienne Prideux..."

She frowned. "I did not realize we were."

"Huh? What I mean is, I heard René on the phone talking to someone he referred to as 'Fabienne'. By any chance, was he speaking with Fabienne Prideux?"

Maryse made a curt wave with one hand. "They have been lovers for over a year."

"René told you that?"

"No. I saw him leave her flat early one morning. I had just finished bathing. When I came out into the hall, I saw René hurrying away from her door."

"You're certain it was him?"

"Absolutely," she asserted.

"Did he see you?"

She considered my question and then shook her head. "I don't think so. Why?"

"My being able to blackmail him comes to mind."

Her voice was firm, but there was the glint of amusement in her eyes. "That would not work in France, Stuart. An extramarital affair is expected of a husband."

"Really?"

Which one of you said, 'Down Boy?' I admit, for just one second, France became my idea of male heaven. But I quickly realized having a little side-action on the romance front is not worth suffering with the other aggravations. Especially for a guy who never gets any action side, front or otherwise.

"Does René plan to marry Fabienne?" I asked.

"I don't think it will come to that. Fabienne is a free spirit."

"Free spirit?" I echoed, in confusion.

Her lips struggled to open as if with indecision. Then she said, "I saw at least one other man leaving her apartment."

"Who was it? Would you recognize him, again?"

"Stuart, what Fabienne does and who she does it with is none of our business."

"I'm not going to point a finger at her. It's just that Monet, the bastard…"

Her features seemed to freeze. "My point is Fabienne is entitled to her privacy."

"Can you at least describe him?"

"The man was short and quite heavy," she returned, with a heave of her shoulders. "I noticed that his shoes creaked when he walked."

"Monet! I've got him by the short hairs, the bastard!"

She smirked. "So now you will try blackmailing him? Ah, that will make you popular with him."

"Blackmail would be too easy for Monet," I returned, with a wag of my head. "After what that bastard's put me through, I have something more painful and permanent in mind—like bribing her to cut off his balls next time they're having a ding-dong." I went over to the davenport and sat down. Then I jumped back up shouting, "Reese?"

She rolled her eyes in grief. "Now what?"

"Is that another nickname?"

"It is short for Maryse, of course."

Realization set in like a truckload of manure being shoved up my nose. "You mean all I heard really wasn't you?"

Maryse lifted her hands in bewilderment. "What have I been trying to tell you for the past twenty minutes?"

I started looking for rock to crawl under. The most beautiful woman in the world had been in love with me and I had blown my one chance at happiness by falsely accusing her. All right, there are still the other lies to consider. But they were minor compared to when I thought she had planned to kill her husband or when I thought she sent those goons to work me over.

"What's wrong, Stuart?" she asked. "Are you not feeling well? You've become very pale."

My chin dipped in shame. "Maryse, I'm sorry. I'm very, very sorry for the way I've treated you. I had no right… I'm very ashamed."

"*Merci.* All is forgiven."

"It's—just that I skipped breakfast. I'm not myself, when I skip breakfast. And I really was a jerk for thinking what I was thinking. It's all Monet's fault. If he hadn't arrested me…" I raised my eyes to her. "I know you weren't the one talking to Buji which explains why you don't know who Buji is or what I was talking about."

"I thought you had lost your marbles."

"Hold the thought, because I think that's next for me. Does René's wife always go by her nickname?"

"That is what he calls her. Cesar—when she was married to him—always called her Maryse. He used to tease me about looking so much like his wife and sharing the same name. He even said, he was sure he would not know the difference if I took her place in his bed."

"That dirty old man! Wait! You mean René's wife was Avoyelles' frigid bitch, too?"

She frowned. "Cesar called her that?"

"I think I'm quoting him," I returned. "But if she was married to René and used to be married to Cesar and she was having an affair with your husband…"

"I did not lie about it, Stuart."

I suddenly grinned. "I know. But don't you see? I finally know who Buji is, the bastard!"

The expression on her face shifted like water buffeted by a vengeful wind. "I'm very glad for you. But if you still think I plotted my husband's murder…"

"No! Absolutely not! It was Maryse! I mean, I think it was Reese. It sort of fits. Maybe. But whether it does or does not, I know it was not you. That's the important bit—so please don't hit me again."

"Stuart, I don't think we are talking about the same Maryse." Two even rows of white teeth drew in her lower lip and clung to it for a moment. "That name is very common in France."

"But it has to be either you or her. I mean, how many Maryse's have been involved with your husband?"

Her head wagged. "Reese would never have done anything to hurt Baudouin."

"Millions in diamonds changes people," I returned. "I know. I'd never had a greedy bone in my body but when I heard about that reward…"

"I still don't believe she would do what you've claimed."

"The woman I listened to knew your husband. She was also involved in the diamond heist."

"That proves nothing. My husband frequently hired women for the jobs he planned. Baudouin probably knew half a dozen Maryse's, who helped him dozens of times."

So much for plan 'B'. Then another thought came to mind. "How big a bag would it take to hold sixty million in diamonds?"

"That depends on the quality. If the stones are extremely large and of excellent quality a bag as big as your two fists, could hold them. But if you're thinking about the ones that were stolen, I suspect the bag would be twice that size—maybe three times."

"So sixty million in diamonds would fit in a safe?"

"I assume you mean a wall safe?"

I nodded.

"Of course," Maryse stepped close enough to lightly kiss my lips. "But there were no diamonds in Baudouin's safe. Monet took me there yesterday. He told me to show him where the safe was, and to open it. I did. But there was nothing inside."

"Just my luck," I grumbled. "Did your husband do anything odd after the diamond heist?"

Her eyes widened. "Not odd. But it was unexpected. Four or five days after the robbery, he and Cesar went to Brazil." Maryse wrapped her arms around my neck and pressed close. "Baudouin said he had business in Sao Paolo. Cesar was going to visit an old friend. I wanted to go along. But my husband said it was too dangerous. So I stayed home. About a week later he returned."

I let go a disappointed sigh. "Well, that's where the diamonds went. On the plus side, that pretty much confirms my belief that Avoyelles is the notorious Buji." Then an idea darted across my brain. "Did your husband bring back anything?"

She pressed her pelvis firmly to mine. "A big painting. Why?"

"How big?"

"Big enough," she said, nuzzling my neck.

"We have to get that painting."

Her head tilted back with a jerk and she stared at me in disbelief. "Stuart, the police are not going to let me have it."

"It's yours by inheritance."

"Not until the Will is probated."

"Maryse, we have to get that painting."

"Why?" she asked, with an amused chuckle.

"Because there's a rumor going around that your husband swapped the diamonds for a painting."

"Impossible! Sixty million for that thing? It is the ugliest painting I've ever seen. It looks like a bunch of two year olds were handed paint and brushes and told to color a pillow-case."

"I don't suppose you still have a key to your husband's apartment?"

She dropped her arms and backed up a step, looking disappointed. "I do. But I'm telling you the painting is worthless."

I smiled, quite pleased with myself. "I'm sure it is. It's what the painting conceals that's worth sixty million."

Her mouth dropped open in surprise. "You think there is another painting hidden within the frame?"

I nodded. "Your husband bought a piece of junk, concealed the valuable painting behind it, and brought both home in one package."

She threw her arms around my neck, again. "It's a clever idea, Stuart. But that does not sound like Baudouin. My husband would never trade diamonds—something with a standard value for a painting—which relies upon the whimsy of bidders."

I was holding her so tightly I could feel her heart beating. "I feel I'm right."

"I feel you're something," she said, nuzzling me.

"We've to get something straight between us," I told her.

Her pelvis ground against mine. "It already is, Stuart."

"I mean, we have to be honest with each other from now on. Agreed?"

Maryse offered me a crooked smile, her pelvis still moving back and forth over mine. "I will do anything you want. Anything."

My body started trembling like Arceneau's. But a second later the window crashed and I felt a sharp burning sensation in my left buttock. I clamped one hand over the sore spot and jerked toward the window. The glass was in shards on the floor. I pulled my hand away from the burning spot and looked at it. The palm was thick with blood.

"I've been shot in the ass!" I screamed.

I grabbed Maryse and forced her to the floor.

"I didn't shoot you!" she protested, trying to struggle from beneath me.

"I'm trying to save your life!"

She stopped trying to get free and frowned. "If that's all you have in mind, why is your hand down the back of my slacks?"

"Sorry," I returned, jerking my hand out. "It was an accidental reaction to having my butt dimpled by a bullet."

Seconds later several more gunshots were fired, the rounds narrowly missing us. I rolled across the floor to the side of the davenport flopping her over and over with me.

"You're making me dizzy!" she complained.

Another series of shots tore through the davenport. I flattened her against the floor. I prayed the pain in my ass would not get any worse.

"Why didn't they believe me when I said I didn't have their damn diamonds?" I shuddered.

"It might not be who you think it is, Stuart."

"Who else can it be? It's not like I work at making enemies."

"The Corsican Mafia," she returned.

"I'd forgotten about them." I sat up moaning, "Christ, why didn't I stay in Minneapolis?"

"Maybe if I get in touch with Françoise, I could set him straight…"

My eyes dipped and I noticed a spreading red blotch in the area of my groin. "My God!" I pointed down at. "I'm hurt worse than I thought!"

With a startled cry, Maryse abruptly pushed me onto my back and grabbed the top of my jeans. Then with one sharp pull, she jerked down the loosely fitting apparel. Quickly she began examining my blood-covered genitilia.

"And you complained about an accidental hand-slip?" I protested, trying to push her hands away.

She batted at my hands. "I have to check for damage."

"Well?"

"Your equipment appears to be in perfect working order."

"Is that how you tell? By squeezing everything?"

She heaved me over onto my belly and inspected my bleeding backside. "Ah, this side is not so good."

"I'm sorry my butt is such a disappointment!"

"Stop complaining," she said, after a few seconds. "I've seen worse."

"Well, at least I'm not on the lowest rung of your perfect-ass ladder."

"You have a deep gouge along the fleshiest part of one cheek," she continued. "You should have stitches. It's bleeding pretty bad. Don't worry. I can take care of it. Do you have a needle and some thread? We'll also need some alcohol to soak them in. Vodka or gin will do. Whatever you prefer to drink. Because without something to kill the pain you are going to be screaming."

"I'm not about to have you stitch my anything!"

"Why not? My husband was shot twice while we were together."

I gaped in shock. "By you?"

"Of course not. But doctors report those injuries to the police. So I had to learn how to deal with bullet wounds."

"If somebody's going to be puncturing my backside with a needle, I want it to be a licensed professional! Someone I can sue; thank you, very much!"

She grabbed my wrist and pressed my palm against the wound. "Then you will have to hold your hand there to slow the bleeding until I call for help."

"Don't tell them I'm an American. They won't come."

"I know that. I'll tell them you're a Russian."

"Russian's get better treatment than Americans, in France?"

"Of course. Russians are usually drug smugglers. So the ambulance team generally gets a big tip when a Russian gets hurt."

"Tip?"

She nodded. "In the way of a nose-candy. They'll be here in less than a minute, mark my words."

Maryse dug her cell-phone from her purse. Then she called the police. After ringing off, she made another call and requested an ambulance.

She put her phone away, then Maryse gave the wound another scrutiny. "The blood is no longer leaking past your hand, so I think that's a positive sign. But keep your palm pressed against it, anyway. Are you in pain?"

"Of course I'm in pain! It's like somebody's holding a lighted blow-torch to my butt."

Maryse peeked over the top of the davenport toward the window. "I don't see anybody."

"Get down before you get your head shot off!"

She settled back on the floor next to me. "Let's say there is a painting hidden behind the one my husband bought in Brazil, do we give it to Monet?"

"And have him take it home to augment his pension fund? Not a chance. We'll sell it ourselves."

"But the diamonds were used to get it."

"I don't think it's illegal to sell something someone else obtained with something stolen."

"Of course it is!"

"For sixty million I'm ready to chance being right, for a change."

"We can't possibly get that much selling a painting, can we?"

"That depends on the painting. If your husband got a Ruben or a Van Gogh, it could be worth twice that much."

She fell silent, thinking. After a few seconds Maryse asked, "What will you do with your half of the money?"

"The money's yours. I'm in this strictly for the revenge."

"Nonsense. Once we get that money, we'll leave Paris and start a new life together."

I looked at her in surprise. "You and me?"

She winked. "Of course. Do you think I would've been worried about just any man's equipment after he was shot?"

"I did notice you gave certain areas more than one squeeze."

She leaned over and kissed my cheek. "I felt it was important that I become familiar with all that is you."

"Not that I'm complaining, but have you really looked at me lately? On my best day I was not male-model material. Right now, I'm more than a tic past ugly."

"You've gone white as a ghost, Stuart," Maryse said, easing away. "You're not going to faint, are you?"

"Probably. Being shot before being propositioned is a new experience for me. I'm not sure how to handle either one."

She bent down and kissed my lips, passionately. "I'll take care of all the handling."

From outside, I heard approaching sirens.

"What did I tell you?" she said, glancing at her watch. "Forty seconds and they are within earshot. Just hang in there."

"If you keep kissing me I won't be hanging anywhere."

She smiled and pressed her mouth against mine, again. This time, Maryse slipped her tongue in and teased me wantonly. Then with a giggle, she tilted me back and grinned down at the reaction from my magic-nightstick.

"Oh, Stuart, he really liked that one!"

"How am I going to explain that to the medics?" I complained, trying to cover my dancing nightstick with my free hand.

There was the sound of running feet out in the hallway. Then the door burst open and Inspector Monet rushed in, followed by two uniformed police officers. All had their guns at the ready. Each was wild eyed and rubbernecking. When they saw the shattered window, all three men crouched down and approached it on their haunches.

"Where is the Russian?" Monet demanded.

"That's me," I returned.

He gave me a disappointed look. "How long is it?"

"Long enough," Maryse declared with a giggle.

"He means how long since the last shots," I told her.

"About five minutes," she said.

"Are either of you hurt?" Monet asked, still looking out the window.

"Nothing serious," said Maryse.

"What do you mean, nothing serious?" I protested. "I've got a hole in my ass!"

She rolled her eyes. "You had one to begin with."

"I mean another one!"

As Monet crawled over to us, Maryse shoved me over onto my stomach and pointed to the bloody smear my palm was still covering.

"I'll drag you out," said the Chief Inspector. "I have the medics standing by, down the hall." Then he waggled a finger at me. "You were damn lucky."

"So was I," she chimed.

His eyebrows curled with concern. "You were hit too?"

"No," she replied, "but another inch to the left and he might've lost something I would have deeply regretted."

While his men kept watch out the window, Monet grabbed hold of my ankles and dragged me face-down toward the door.

"Roll him over," shouted Maryse. "Just in case there are splinters in the floor." She shifted uneasily before adding, "That could get very uncomfortable."

Without a remark, he dumped me onto my back and resumed dragging.

"It's all about you, isn't it?" I complained to her. "Never mind how a splinter in my ass might feel."

"A lot better than a splinter in you coming loose in me, I should think," she quickly returned.

Minutes later we all were in Maryse's flat: Monet, his officers, Maryse, me, and two ambulance attendants. The latter were spraying topical painkiller on the flesh around the bullet-wound in preparation to suturing it. Monet grimly paced the floor. I looked around, marveling how a flat that had been searched was completely in order. The airy room was spotless. Fresh yellow daisies were in a vase resting upon a low table beneath the window. There was not so much as a hint of dust or damage to be seen.

"You're certain you saw no one?" the inspector asked.

"Not a soul," Maryse replied. "It just happened. One second we were talking. The next Stuart had me pinned to the floor."

"That is certainly understandable," said Monet, stopping to look over at me. "I remember the first time I did that to a beautiful woman. I think I was sixteen. She was built like a brick chicken house, and about thirty…"

"Can we forgo your romantic memories?" I complained. "I could've been killed!"

"Is that when you were shot, Monsieur?" Monet asked. "When you had her pinned to the floor?"

"No, I was shot standing up," I snapped.

"Ah," he said, nodding in understanding. "So the first time you assaulted Mme. Rousseau, you had her pinned to the wall."

"I've never assaulted anyone!"

Maryse gave out a disappointed groan. "I can vouch for that. He had his hand down my pants. But after I made one half-hearted complaint, he took it out."

Monet clucked his tongue in sympathy. "These Americans… They have no idea what romance is." Then he took a small notebook from his pocket and paged through it. Finding what he was looking for Monet said to me, "A man fitting your description was with Dr. Molyneux when he was killed. That man left before the police arrived. Was that you?"

"Yes," I said, with great reluctance.

"You were a witness to a homicide!" he shouted. "You should have remained to answer the investigating officer's questions. I could arrest you!"

"If you will take a look at my face, you will see that I have already been answering questions. And after seeing what happened to Molyneux, I was not about to stick around for another quiz."

"Did you see who was driving the Citroën?" he demanded.

"No. It all happened too quickly."

Monet bent down to scrutinize my face. "Who did that to you?"

"Obviously…" Maryse began.

"I don't know," I interposed, impatiently. "But Maryse had a similar experience earlier today."

He looked over at her, frowning. "Somebody beat the crap out of you, too?"

She wagged her head. "Two men tried to kidnap me. But I got away."

"Why?" he asked, looking from her to me.

"Why what?" I returned.

"Why did the two events occur?" he explained, impatiently.

Maryse started to speak but I, again, cut in. "Because there are lunatics out there you should be arresting."

Monet stared over at Maryse. "Did you know your husband was terminally ill?"

Her eyes darted away from his. "Yes."

He gave a heave to his sloping shoulders. "Why didn't you tell me this before?"

"I did not think it was relevant," she replied.

"In a murder inquiry, everything is relevant!" Monet put his notebook away and then set his hands akimbo at his big hips. "If it is any consolation, Mme. Rousseau, your husband was dead before he hit the parking lot. The drugs injected into him, were the actual cause of death. This, of course, changes the direction of our investigation. Did your husband ever discuss assisted suicide with you?"

"Of course he didn't," I interposed.

"Baudouin made no mention of it to me," she whimpered, tears flooding across her cheeks.

Then Monet looked back at me. "Witnesses claimed Dr. Molyneux said something to you just before he died."

"He did," I returned. "But I could not understand what he was saying. It was gibberish."

"You are so stupid you probably forgot to listen when he was talking!" The Chief Inspector jabbed a thumb toward the door. "I will leave a man to keep watch tonight. In the meantime, I would keep your drapes closed and your lights off until we catch who shot you. It is a small chance. But the assassin might come back."

"Stuart will stay with me," Maryse declared. "So you need not leave one of your men. He will not be going anywhere, tonight."

Monet winked at her. "This time, don't complain about the hand. Maybe he'll get the message." Then he looked over at me and wagged his head. "On second thought, you'd better send him the message and pray he understands how to respond."

After the Chief Inspector and the others left, I turned to Maryse. "Are you sure about me—here? I think we should move everything of yours into my flat. I was a real jerk, earlier."

She came over and wrapped her arms around my neck. "Yes you were. And stitches or not, you're going to make it up to me."

Chapter 9
A Little Trip into Big Trouble

Paris is a very compact city. It is less than seven miles across. It actually can be traversed on foot (with only a few unavoidable exceptions whereby a Métro or bus ride must be endured). This, of course, assumes you are not concerned about Parisian muggers, hookers, pickpockets or the occasional Béarnaise Sauce axe-murderer. Even so, in the event you are chased by some of French society's unsavory elements, rest assured that all is not lost. No matter where you are in Paris, you are never more than 400 meters from a Métro station. This means both you and your pursuers will have a nice footrace followed by a convenient ride home on *Le Métro Parisien.*

"Last chance to back out," Maryse Rousseau declared.

"Not a chance," I returned. "After what I've been through, I'm due for a turn of luck."

Maryse rolled her eyes. "What are you saying? You were on your side all afternoon, getting lucky."

"I mean besides you and—us."

She and I were in Mme. Flaubert's 1949 Citroën parked in a secluded spot at the rear of Baudouin Rousseau's apartment building. Our landlady had kindly rented us her ancient vehicle for a mere forty Euros. I was rubbernecking to see if anyone was watching us. Maryse was fumbling through her purse looking for keys to the building and the apartment. It had been more than eight hours since the medics stitched up the wound in my posterior. The sutures were tightening. The painkiller had worn off. This, in turn, caused flashes of eye-watering agony.

"How're we going to get the painting out of there?" she asked, uneasily. "Neighbors are nosy. They'll spot us carrying it and call the cops."

"We'll open the back of the painting's frame, there," I told her. "If we find what I expect, I'll roll it up and shove it down my pants. Then I'll just walk out with it." I glanced around. "Did you notice anybody following as I drove?"

"I was too busy saying prayers. You screamed every time you depressed the clutch. I don't even want to think about the spasms you went through when you finally got this wreck into high gear."

I gave her an impatient look. "I noticed you didn't complain when I screamed about my tearing sutures, when we were in bed."

She pointed a scolding finger at me. "It had been a long time. I got carried away."

Maryse climbed out of the car and looked around, squinting against the fading sunlight. "Well if anybody did follow, it's too late to worry about them. We're here and they know it."

I got out. Gathering rain clouds blocked the setting sun. The whole sky was turning black, leaving the parking lot a mass of dark, impenetrable gloom. From somewhere nearby insects made clicking sounds. Then I heard a soft rustling as something small and probably furry ran beneath fallen leaves.

I looked over at Maryse. Her face seemed to pale as she moved off.

I followed from shadow to shadow, across the lot to the building's rear door.

There, Maryse used her key and went inside. I trailed in after her.

"Must be like old home week, for you," I remarked.

She glanced around as we hurried along the hallway to the elevators. "I never liked it here. I wanted a cottage."

"How come your husband never bought you one? He was rich enough."

"Baudouin was going to. But, then he got sick. After that, Reese came along."

Maryse was silent on the elevator ride up to the tenth floor. It was like she was dreading the visit to her husband's flat.

"If anything goes wrong," I cautioned. "Just run for it. We'll meet up at the car."

She gave me a concerned look. "What could go wrong?"

I shrugged. "Nothing—more or less. But one can never be certain in a burglary."

"This is not a burglary." Maryse waggled the key to the apartment. "It was my decision to move out, not Baudouin's insistence. I have every right to be in there."

"Be sure you mention that to Monet should the worst happen and I'm arrested. And also mention how I was your invited guest. Otherwise he'll charge me with illegal entry and I'll spend the next twenty years in his office chained to a chair, while being badgered."

As expected, when we got to her husband's apartment, a plastic crime-scene tape spanned the door.

Completely undaunted, Maryse put the key in the lock, turned the handle and pushed. Then she ducked under the tape and followed the door into the apartment.

I rubbernecked, checking to see if we were being watched.

Not seeing any prying eyes, I went in after her and shut the door.

The lights were off in the apartment, so we stood in near-darkness. Only the evening light, drifting through the drapes cloaking the balcony door, disrupted the inky atmosphere.

"Which way?" I whispered.

Maryse moved off, a diminutive silhouette for me to follow.

We had only gone a few steps when I heard a sound coming from one of the apartment's other rooms. I grabbed her arm and dragged Maryse back to the door. But before I could touch the knob, it turned. I gave her a push toward the couch and then quickly followed. Just as we ducked behind it, the apartment door opened, sending a wash of light from the hallway, across the living room.

The door closed making only a slight click.

I held my breath, expecting to be murdered at any moment. Maryse nudged me with her elbow. I raised my head slightly and looked in the direction she was pointing.

From the hallway leading to the rest of the apartment, I saw movement. Two silhouettes approached. One short. One very tall. I looked toward the apartment door. Standing within the apartment was another silhouette.

"Police!" shouted a male voice from the direction of the door.

From the hallway, there were flashes of light immediately followed by popping sounds. I looked toward the door and saw the silhouette crumple to the floor.

I tried to swallow. But my throat was as dry as a dust-ball.

The two figures from the hallway raced past.

I shuddered with relief when they opened the door to leave. At that moment, I peaked over the top of the davenport and caught a glimpse of the pair. One of them was holding a gun. The other carried a large, abstract painting. The one with the painting wore black boots. The other had on dirty running shoes. Not only were they the same two men who had pummeled me to near-oblivion, I recognized their faces as that of Bouvier and Chevalier! I also saw the uniformed police officer. He lay on the floor, unmoving.

Maryse tilted toward me. "You check on the cop. I'll look for the painting."

I stood as Maryse hurried off. Then my eyes drifted through the darkness to the fallen man's silhouette. What if they had killed him? The man probably had family; maybe little kids. I did not know what I could have done to prevent it. But I felt I should have done something.

I crept over to where he lay, and squatted down.

He was still breathing, but each breath was irregular and very shallow. He was unconscious, his gun still gripped by one hand. There were two dark blotches on his shirt near his stomach.

I went over to the door and found the switch for the lights. I flicked it on. In the resulting blaze of illumination I looked around the room for a telephone. I spotted it sitting on the floor near the balcony doors, and hurried over.

After telephoning the police, I went back to where the officer lay. He looked to be about my age. His uniform was new. The pistol looked the same. The soles of his shoes were barely worn. It was like he had been handed his trappings, and sent out to get himself killed.

Maryse returned shaking her head. "The painting they took was the one we were after."

"Sounds like my luck has turned, and turned again."

She pointed down at the police officer. "Is he okay?"

"He's alive. But I don't know for how long. Police are on their way."

She gave me a distracted smile. "Then we'd better make tracks."

I grabbed her arm. "Maryse, I think I should stay with him."

"And get arrested in here, again? Not a chance."

"But, if he dies… I don't want him to die alone. Somebody should be here."

A wailing siren sounded in the distance.

"To do what?" She made a pleading gesture. "Stuart, they'll be here in two minutes. Come on!"

Reluctantly, I followed.

We were just getting into the Citroën when the flashing blue lights arrived in the apartment building's lot.

"I know who those men were," I told her.

She nodded. "Bouvier and Chevalier."

"How did you know it was them? It was as black as sin, in there."

"I smelled Chevalier's disgusting cologne. The other one was so big it could not be anyone but Bouvier."

"We'll have to tell Monet."

"And have to explain what we were doing in Baudouin's apartment?" demanded Maryse. "Not a chance!"

I put the key into the ignition and turned it. Then I pressed the starter switch with one foot. Nothing happened.

"What's wrong?" I asked.

"The battery's dead." She jabbed a thumb over one shoulder. "The jack's behind the seats. It doubles as the engine crank." Then she tapped the windshield. "Get out and give it a spin. I'll push down on the accelerator."

"I've never done that before," I protested.

Maryse inclined her dark head. "There's a hole at the front. Just follow your instincts."

I blinked in confusion. "What instincts?"

"Shove it in and pump for all you're worth!"

I got out, felt around behind my seat until I found something cold and steely that weighed about ten pounds. Then I went to the front of the Citroën, and located the hole. I shoved in the crank and started spinning the engine. As I strained with each turn of the crank, the black sky suddenly split open, shattered by a blazing bolt of lightning. A moment later, thunder crashed. Then, rain poured down. The storm that had been threatening all evening had arrived.

I gave the crank another spin. This time the engine fired. I jerked out the steel prod, dropped it behind my seat, and climbed back into the old wreck, soaking wet.

"Do you have any alcohol?" I asked, as I put the car in gear.

She gave a short nod. "Some. Why?"

"When we get back to your place you'll have to stitch up my ass. It feels like I tore all of the sutures starting that damn engine."

I remained silent the entire drive back to Mme. Flaubert's. I kept wondering how I was going to deal with Bouvier and Chevalier. I wanted revenge for the dance-number those two had given me. I wanted it bad enough to take Mme. Flaubert's crank in with me and use it to rearrange their heads.

"Revenge gets you nothing, Stuart," Maryse warned, as I parked the Citroën.

"What are you talking about?"

Her eyes glinted at me. "Now that you know who tumbled you about, you want a piece of them."

I shrugged, trying to act casual. "Maybe."

"Let it go," she returned.

"They deserve any pain they get."

She pursed his lips, contemplating. "Then we'll let someone else do it."

I glanced over at her. "What do you mean?"

"François Chiappe. They were with Baudouin when he died, weren't they? François will be very interested in hearing about that."

I gave her another look, horrified this time. "But he'll kill them."

"Isn't that what revenge is about?"

I shrugged. "I didn't know there were rules to it."

"There are rules for everything, Stuart."

I shook my head. "I don't want them dead."

"Then let it go. If you try something that leaves either of those two bozos alive, one or both of them will come after you. And it won't be to bounce you, this time. *They'll* follow the rules for revenge."

She was right. But I could not forget what they'd done. Each time I look in the mirror for the rest of my life, I would see the scar where Bouvier had sliced my cheek. But at the same time, I could not bring myself to put them in coffins.

"It's the painting I want," I declared.

"Stuart, forget the painting," she sighed, in frustration. "I told you, Baudouin would not have traded diamonds for that hideous canvas or for anything that might be hidden behind it."

"They'll hide it in one of their rooms," I returned, ignoring her words. "I'll pinch it from under their noses. They won't know who took it. But I'll have it. That's my idea of revenge."

"Stuart, what makes you think they haven't just run with it?"

"To where? They'd have to see what's hidden in it first. That'll take time."

"Bouvier and Chevalier didn't go there on their own. Somebody pointed them to that particular painting."

"How can you possibly know that?" I asked.

"My husband has half a dozen paintings worth thousands each. The ugly thing they grabbed couldn't have cost more than a few Euros. So why shoot a cop for something they could not expect get a centime for?"

I thought about that for a moment and then realized she was correct. After they had beaten me, the pair had argued over who else might have the diamonds. So it followed that they had approached that person and he or she had sent them back to Baudouin Rousseau's apartment. Maryse, probably—René's Maryse.

"They wouldn't have driven directly to Buji with it," I countered. "They got stiffed on the diamond gig, remember? They'll look at that ugly rag and wonder why it was worth stealing. Then one of them will get the bright idea of sitting on it until it can be examined by an art expert."

She chuckled. "You're giving those two credit for brains. They don't have one between them."

"It's simple human logic. Bouvier and Chevalier trusted your husband and ended up with nothing. They're not about to lose out again."

"Maybe. But who would they know who's an art expert? Those two eat soup with their fingers—I've seen them."

"Cesar Avoyelles, of course. Assuming I'm right about him being Buji. I saw them together at the Louvre."

She twisted on the car seat to give me a disbelieving look. "The Louvre?"

I nodded. "I saw Bouvier and Chevalier talking with René and Avoyelles just outside the restoration room. In fact it was the day we went for lunch."

"Did you ask Cesar or René about them?"

"Cesar said they were René's friends. He said they'd stopped in to give René a message. Then they left—the same time Avoyelles did." But after a moment of considering my own words I suggested, "That may not be right. If Avoyelles is Buji, then he'd have lied to me about that. As I remember, those two spoke with both René and him for quite some time. It wasn't as if they had just left a message. Avoyelles is Buji, all right."

She glanced over laughing. "You still think Cesar was involved in diamond thievery? Stuart, he's far too honest."

Honest? Well, no more than I was—considering the Matisse I was painting for Cesar Avoyelles.

"I still want to tell Monet about the shooting," I told her, as I crawled from the Citroën.

She sighed, irritated by my insistence. "You're going to put us in jail."

"How else is Monet going to get Bouvier and Chevalier for shooting that cop? It was dark in there. The cop only saw the gun flashes. He won't be able to identify them."

"All right," she sighed. "But make the call from somewhere far away from Mme. Flaubert's and disguise your voice. I don't want Monet coming around, asking questions."

"Disguise my voice?"

She looked over at me and rolled her eyes. "The police track the calling number. They also record the voice of the caller."

I gulped. "You mean when I reported what happened back there…"

"Let's just hope Monet does not recognize your voice, or we've both had it."

Maryse went to her flat. I went up to Mme. Flaubert's to return the Citroën's keys.

One of our landlady's young men answered my knock. He was wrapped in a robe and looked utterly exhausted.

"Rough night on the old bones?" I teased.

He took the keys with a wheezing nod, and then shut the door.

I quickly made my way down to the first floor.

Didier Arceneau was at my flat knocking on the door, when I stepped off the staircase. I called out to him and continued my way over to Maryse's door. He staggered there looking quite pale, as if dreadfully ill. There was a large bandage on his forehead. It showed signs of fresh blood. His eyes were sort of rolling in his head.

"May I have a moment of your time, Monsieur?" he groaned.

I took his arm and opened her door. "Come in, so you can sit down."

"No, Monsieur. This will only take a moment."

"What happened?" I asked.

"I have been *inconscient*," he replied, wearily. "It was only a few minutes ago that I came to myself. Frankly, I am lucky to be alive."

"Someone attacked you?" I asked, my mind darting to the possibility that Bouvier or Chevalier or both had pummeled him because he was acquainted with me.

The elderly man's eyes danced back in his head, as he touched the bandage. "*Exactement!* Fortunately, Mme. Flaubert was awake so I could get medical attention." He paused a moment, his eyes blinking rapidly. "Of course I had to wait my turn."

I winced. "You don't mean she made you—before she'd help?"

He waggled a hand to refute my supposition. "But one of her young men was deeply entrenched, in her usual nightly pursuits. And she would not interrupt his efforts simply because I might be dying."

"I'm surprised Mme. Flaubert has knowledge of first aid."

"She does not, Monsieur," he said, his eyes rolling again. "But the young gentleman in question does—God give him strength. Fortunately, he was already well along when I arrived. Therefore, I fainted only twice before he was able to extricate himself and attend to my medical condition. Had he merely started with her…" Arceneau made a despairing gesture, letting the words hang.

I again urged him into Maryse's flat. "I think you should sit down."

"It is not necessary, Monsieur," he returned. "The reason for this visit relates to a slight complication with respect to the portrait commission."

"I can't blame you if you've elected to go with another artist."

"Not at all, Monsieur. The complication relates to Mademoiselle Fabienne Prideux." He crept close and lowered his voice. "She visited my flat this evening. And after two bottles of Champagne I stealthily broached the subject of her posing. At first she seemed quite eager." A trembling hand went to the bandage. "Then, for reasons I still do not understand, she struck me with one of the Champagne bottles. Fortunately, it was empty. Otherwise…"

"Didn't Fabienne explain herself?"

He shrugged. "I'm completely baffled, Monsieur. I quite tactfully mentioned you would professionally capture her monumentally memorable figure *au naturalle* but in only the best of taste. I then added a few words about the second portrait, making it clear she would be wearing a nightgown of only the finest lace."

"How could Fabienne find your suggestions so offensive she attacked you?"

"At that point, she was still agreeable. Then I expressed my desire to give her the little one so she would always have something to remember me by. Her response, more or less, pointed out that little ones were hardly memorable. Not wanting to disappoint her, I told Fabienne to relax because I was going to slip her the 'Big Kahuna.'" He gulped, swaying on his feet. "At that point she picked up the Champagne bottle and the lights went out."

"Please come in. I think you need a doctor."

His staggered back, making a dismissive gesture. "No need, Monsieur. However, I must cancel our agreement. There will be no paintings."

"I understand. But I don't have enough cash on me to refund your money. I'll go to the bank tomorrow…"

"You may keep the advance for your inconvenience, Monsieur," he interrupted. "Now you will have to excuse me. I have been feeling quite numb below the waist since I regained consciousness. Hopefully it is only a temporary situation." Then he headed up the stairs, staggering slightly. "*Bonne nuit.*"

Maryse's flat was dark and the bed pulled out when I entered. The streetlight shining through the window silhouetted her nude figure, as she slipped beneath the covers. I locked the door, went over to the bed, stripped off my damp clothes and slid in beside her. I tried to convince my magic-nightstick we both needed rest: him in particular, considering his afternoon marathon. But he refused to listen.

"What had happened to M. Arceneau?" Maryse asked. "I heard the two of you talking."

"The path of love is neither straight nor downhill for him. He's decided to give up his romantic pursuit of Fabienne."

"All that grand passion and he gives up without a conquest," she sighed, sliding against me. "Poor man."

Her warm skin against mine set my nightstick to wagging. "Tomorrow morning when Bouvier and Chevalier leave for work, I'll search their apartments. It won't take but a few minutes."

Maryse rolled onto her side, slipping one arm across my waist. "Why not let me do it?"

"It'll be too dangerous."

She squirmed against me. "Mmmm. You're nice and warm."

"Parts of me are on fire."

She sat up. "I forgot to look at your stitches."

"The wound is no longer leaking, so I think they're still holding. Have you ever noticed Cesar Avoyelles's cologne?"

"He wears Paloma Picasso Mon Parfum. Why?"

"What do you know about it?"

"The painter, Picasso—actually his daughter—lent her name to it. It is quite popular among Parisian men—the wealthy ones, that is. Why?"

"I smelled it, tonight."

"What is so unusual about that?"

"At your husband's apartment."

She kissed my chest. "That was Bouvier. But he was not wearing Paloma Picasso Mon Parfum. I think he stepped in dog pooh."

"I don't mean his stench. I mean the citrusy odor after he and Chevalier left. Didn't you notice it?"

"I don't remember it. Why?"

"I think we missed someone."

She again rose up and gave me a curious stare. "Stuart, what are you talking about?"

"I think someone else was in your husband's apartment."

"Of course. The cop."

"No," I returned. "Someone *else*."

She sank back on the bed and half crawled on top of me. "I didn't see anyone."

"Well, he's seen us. Otherwise he would've left when Bouvier and Chevalier legged it."

"I think you're imagining."

"I don't agree. I also think whoever it was is going to let Bouvier and Chevalier know we saw them shoot that cop. Then what?"

"They would kill us, of course," she said grimly. "But, I think you're worrying too much. I'm certain no one else was there."

"I think it was Cesar Avoyelles—Buji."

"Don't be ridiculous. Even if he is your Buji, what would Cesar be doing there if he sent Bouvier and Chevalier for the painting?"

"To make sure they came back with it, of course."

"Stuart, Cesar is one of the wealthiest men in Paris. He is not going to risk a long prison sentence for a few diamonds."

"I happen to know that Cesar is financially overextended, and being pressed for money. Remember when you said your husband went to Brazil with Cesar? Well, I think your husband told him about the Van Gogh."

"Stuart, there was no swap."

"Did your husband wear Paloma Picasso Mon Parfum?"

"Of course. And that is probably why you smelled it, in Baudouin's apartment."

I fell silent, thinking. "I don't recall Molyneux wearing it."

"Michele was not one to squander money on scent." She settled back to the mattress rolling away from me. "Leave it alone, Stuart. Do that for me? Let's forget about paintings, diamonds—all of it. Please?"

"If I'm right about a painting, the reward from the insurer might double what you thought we'd get for the diamonds."

She rolled next to me and nuzzled my neck, pressing her pelvis against my hip. "They're not going to pay for a painting. It's the diamonds they insured."

"But the diamonds were used to get the painting. Of course they'll pay."

"Let's worry about it tomorrow."

"Did your husband meet with Cesar shortly before the jewel robbery?"

"Not that I recall." She paused a moment before saying, "No, I lie. They did get together at the apartment one night. Baudouin sent me shopping—it was getting close to Christmas and he knew how much I enjoyed the holidays. Michele and Cesar were there. They joked about how my husband had better rent a truck to carry back all I would buy."

"That must've been when those two put the idea of the robbery to your husband. What about René? Did he ever visit there?"

She slid over half on top of me, her lips against mine, her hand reaching down and grasping my nightstick. "I have other things on my mind."

Despite further risk of damage to my sutures, I made no argument when she directed my nightstick's course. Neither did he.

Chapter 10
A Hat-Trick on the Corpse Front

France is probably most remembered for its use of the Guillotine as the preferred form of execution. It is often a misconception that French physician Joseph-Ignace Guillotin invented this infamous beheading device. Actually, it was Dr. Antoine Louis who fathered it. Monsieur Guillotin's only connection to the device was humanitarian. He tried to convince the French National Assembly to use a more humane method of capital punishment—that being the guillotine—as opposed to other methods of execution such as the garrote or being drawn-and-quartered or being burned at the stake. Monsieur Guillotin was successful in his efforts and beheading became the form of capital punishment for France until 1981. The only reason it is not being used today is that capital punishment was outlawed.

Early the next morning, I got out of Maryse's bed, pulled on my clothes and went over to the window. It offered a better view of Paris than the one in my flat. This overlooked the street in front of the Mme. Flaubert's Boarding House. Despite the relatively early hour, people were already out. Some were rushing to work or to the shops. Others moved along the sidewalk, strolling with linked arms. Still more filled the chairs around tables in front of *Cafe de Flore*. Most of those were smiling and sipping espresso. Others were chatting over raised cups.

"I'm afraid to go to work," Maryse Rousseau announced.

I turned and stared as she climbed naked from the bed. Instantly, my magic-nightstick went into high gear trying to motion her back onto the mattress.

"I'll walk you to the Métro, if you like," I told her, enjoying the reverse striptease of her slipping into her clothes.

"And if I'm abducted from it?" she asked, ignoring my stare.

"Okay. Then I'll ride with you going and coming."

Her head wagged as she stepped into her jeans. "I'm going to leave Paris."

I was stunned and rushed over to her. "To where?"

"Nice." She straightened her shoulders. "My mother lives there. I'll be safe with her. Why don't you come with me?"

"I can't. Not today. I'll meet you there, tomorrow, if you like."

Maryse went over to the Chef Rack and picked up a hairbrush. "Stuart, forget the painting," she declared, rapidly dragging the brush through her long, shiny hair. "Even if Baudouin did swap the diamonds, even if he had hidden another painting behind that ugly abstract, he would've removed it once it was safely home."

I shook my head. "Not something that valuable."

She dropped the brush back onto the rack. "You think you know my husband better than me?"

"No, it's just…"

"Look, if you're absolutely certain it is there, let me look for it. You wait at the Métro station. If I find something I will take it from the frame and bring it along. If not, we will enjoy a few weeks in Nice with my mother before looking for a place of our own."

"And how will we live? I've got a few thousand tucked away, but that won't last long."

"Like I told you, in a short time I will have plenty of money. We will never have to work, again." Then she frowned. "Where did you get a few thousand?"

I started to explain my relationship with Avoyelles. But I caught myself in time and claimed the money came from Uncle Stuart.

"That will be enough to get us a nice flat while we look for a cottage."

I was tempted to go with her. But eventually I shook my head. "I have to go through with this, Maryse."

"Why? I tell you there is nothing valuable concerning that painting."

Again I shook my head. "There has to be."

Her head tilted back, sending shimmering hair into a delightful dance down her back. "Okay. Then telephone Monet. Tell him about the shooting. Let him arrest those two before you go nosing around. Once they are in jail there will be no risk in searching their flats."

"And have Monet find the panting? The first thing he'll do is search their flats. We'll never see it again."

"He's not going to steal that ugly thing," she scolded. "And even if he does find it, I can always claim it is mine."

"But it could take months to get it back. Months during which it would conveniently disappear." I returned to the window and slid it open. A cool breeze blew in, making the red curtains billow. "I know I'm right, Maryse."

She came over and put her arms about my waist. "Is it worth getting caught over? What those two did to you before will be nothing to what will happen if you're caught in one of their flats. Come with me to Nice.

We'll leave Monet an anonymous telephone message about the cop and the stolen painting. He will arrest them and secure the painting. Once my husband's will is probated, it will be returned to me. Then you can prove your theory."

I backed out of her embrace. "Maryse, I have to know if I'm right."

"Why?" she asked, puzzled by my lack of patience.

I checked my watch. "Do you know which flats Bouvier and Chevalier live in?"

Her dark eyes rolled with frustration. "They have the two on either side of Molyneux's. Michele's is number three. Bouvier's is the one closest to the stairs." Maryse returned to the Chef's rack and turned on the espresso maker. "There will be no way for me to warn you if they come back. Between us we have one cell-phone. There are no phones in their rooms. I can't very well stand out in the hallway and shriek or they will figure something is wrong. Then we will both be in it up to our tails. Please do not do this?"

"As soon as I see them leave for work, I'll go up. They won't be back until the end of the day. It'll take two minutes in each room. Then I'll go with you to Nice."

"Stuart, my husband was a very smart man."

"He was a killer!" I scoffed.

Maryse blanched. "Yes, he was," she said, her voice quaking. "But that didn't make Baudouin stupid. So why would a smart man trade a pile of diamonds for a painting that might be discovered when he smuggled it into this country?" Sorrow seemed to wash over her. "It is far more likely he bought an ugly piece of art to hang in his office and kept the diamonds."

"Kept them where?"

Her hands became fists of frustration and she waved them overhead. Then her arms dropped and she said, "What does it matter? The diamonds are not ours."

"I'm not letting those goons get away with that painting after what they did to me!"

Her expression grew solemn. "Believe me. They will not get away with anything once Monet is told."

"But they could sell it before Monet arrests them!"

"Stuart, if you believe nothing else I say then believe this: I knew Baudouin. I knew him better than his mother, better than his father, better than his priest. I knew him better than anyone because I was married to him. I knew all his secrets. I knew all his needs, wants and fantasies." Then she added in a tired voice, "Trust me when I tell you he would not swap diamonds for art."

Disappointed because of her rational logic, I returned to the window. From behind one side of the drapes, I peered out. At that moment, Bouvier and Chevalier hurried onto the sidewalk and trotted down the block as if they were late for an appointment.

"They just left," I said, more to reassure myself that what I was about to do was safe, than to inform her.

She crossed her arms and glared at me. "If you do this, we're through."

"All I'm going to do…"

Two red spots of anger appeared on Maryse's cheeks. "Stuart, if you leave this is goodbye!"

I went over to my trunk and opened it. From within I took out the largest palette knife I owned. After sticking it into my pocket, I went to the door and pulled it open.

"I'll be as quick as I can."

Maryse's face remained furious. "Don't worry about me," she snapped. "I won't be here when you get back."

She meant it. But I was determined.

"Then, I wish you the best," I said, and closed the door on my way out.

When I reached the third floor, I tiptoed down the hallway to Bouvier's flat. Just beyond his door I could see a police tape tacked across Molyneux's door. That surprised me. Everyone, including Monet, knew Molyneux had been killed miles away. So why was his flat treated as a crime scene? Perhaps that was how it was done in the real world? Or perhaps it was the only way Monet could keep Mme. Flaubert from renting it until the investigation into Molyneux's death was completed? Not being able to rent that space must be preying heavily upon the old girl's mercenary heart.

I used the palette knife to jimmy-open Bouvier's door. Seconds later, I was inside his flat, with the rest of the world locked out.

His accommodations were considerably smaller than mine, but the flat was furnished in the same fashion and it smelled a great deal better. Its simple furnishings limited the number of places where a large painting could be concealed. So I quickly set to searching.

After looking under the davenport and rummaging through a pile of dirty clothes, I decided Chevalier must have it. Then another idea came to mind. I pulled open the foldaway bed. There, under the blanket, was the painting. I picked it up and noted, with a great deal of surprise, that the canvas had been painted in thick layers of tempera. In fact it was clumped with the water based paint. The subject-matter was a reclining female, nude. It was done in cubist fashion. Bits of her were here. Other bits were there. She looked like a crossword puzzle with a number of pieces in the wrong place, and several completely wrong, in terms of gender.

I turned the painting over and examined its back. As expected the usual wood cover was attached to the frame. Like a kid expecting to discover buried treasure, I put the palette knife to work, removing the back-'s mounting screws.

Two minutes later, I lifted off the wood cover. But to my shock, there was nothing tucked between it, and the canvas. Either those goons had already disposed of the hidden painting, or the sixty-million Euro masterpiece I was expecting never existed. Disappointed and embarrassed, I dropped the painting back to the mattress. I did not relish the idea of eating crow. But it would be on tonight's menu when I went to Nice.

I started for the door, hoping to catch Maryse before she left, when a bolt of inspiration hit me. I strode back to the bed, grabbed up the painting and turned it canvas up. Then I pressed my thumbnail against one corner digging my nail into the tempera. Slowly, I scraped the paint away.

As the thick layer of color curled beneath my nail, I saw a heavily lacquered underlayment. The horrid tempera artwork had been done in deliberate bad taste. This diminished its value and made importing the painting easier. The real work of art lay painted beneath the tempera.

"Who's the smart one now, Maryse?" I gloated.

Using the palette knife, I spent the next seven minutes carefully prying off the staples mounting the canvas to its frame. Then I flatted the canvas on the bed, paint down. This was no coffee-stained fake. The fibers were genuinely yellowed, stiff and festered with age. From the coarse weave, I estimated the canvas to be about a hundred years old. That, of course, fit with what I had overheard concerning Baudouin Rousseau's swapping of the diamonds for a Van Gogh.

I rolled up the canvas and stuffed it beneath my shirt. Then I closed up the bed and took the empty frame with me, when I left the apartment.

The frame had no value. But I was still in revenge-mode. Now that I had the painting, I was going to create a little misinformation to shake the bond between Bouvier, and Chevalier. By placing the empty frame in Chevalier's flat, I would point Bouvier's initial suspicions concerning the loss of the painting at his chum. With a little luck, the pair would pummel each other senseless, trying to get one or the other to own up to the theft. Framing Chevalier for the painting's disappearance would be a childish effort. But revenge is a childish act. Still, I could not resist it.

I entered the flat on the other side of Molyneux's using the palette knife to jimmy the lock. There, I dropped the frame onto the davenport, making no effort to conceal it. I wanted the 'evidence' out in the open to maximize its shock-value. I was smiling when I made my exit.

Halfway down the hall I heard footfalls on the stairs and arguing male voices. I did not know who was climbing up the steps. But if Bouvier and Chevalier were returning, I could not chance them catching me in the hallway. If they saw me, the pair would quickly assume I was the thief —and rightly so. My chances of making it out of the building alive with that painting stuffed down my pants would not be good.

Quickly I hurried over to Molyneux's door and put the palette knife to work. Just as I saw the top of two heads bobbing into view, I slipped under the crime-scene tape, and stepped into the dead man's flat. Then I closed the door and locked it. Had they seen me? I could only pray they had not. A flimsy door would not stop those two from entering.

I turned away from the door, and looked around. To my surprise, the deceased doctor had lived in comparative luxury. His flat was twice as large as mine. He had a table and several chairs. There was an expensive leather davenport and hassock. On the right was a doorway leading to a bedroom fitted out with the usual sleeping accommodations. Through an arch on my left was a kitchenette replete with sink, refrigerator and stove. That explained why he did not endure Mme. Flaubert's cooking. He could do his own and thank God for the privilege. Then my eyes fell upon something of great value—a telephone.

I hurried over to it and picked up the handset. A dial tone droned in my ear. Quickly I rang Maryse's cell-phone. A few seconds later, I heard her breathing on the other end of the connection.

"Maryse, this is Stuart," I whispered. "Get the hell out. Bouvier and Chevalier are back."

"I know," she said, sounding frightened. "I saw them come in with three of Chiappe's men. Where are you?"

"I'm in Molyneux's apartment."

"What in hell are you doing there?"

"Hiding from them, what else?"

"Did you find the painting?"

"I've got it. Now get going. I'll meet you at the Métro."

The connection abruptly went dead.

I returned the handset to its cradle. Then I took the canvas over to the sink and turned on the tap so just a trickle of water ran. I did not intend to remove the tempera coating entirely. But my curiosity was such I wanted to know what Baudouin Rousseau had received for sixty million in diamonds. And since I would be trapped where I was for an indeterminate period while Bouvier and Chevalier pummeled each other over the missing painting, my time would not be wasted.

I began at the center of the canvas, gently rubbing my thumb against the dissolving Tempera. Little by little more and more of the lacquered sub-painting appeared. It was a work in oil. The paint was thickly daubed with bold, heavy brushstrokes. The colors were dark and limited, mostly shades of blue and brown. I had not found the signature. But I was convinced it was a Van Gogh!

Suddenly, I heard a Bouvier's frantic voice through the wall, trying to explain away the missing painting. This was followed by a different voice, threatening murder. Another man cursed. Yet, another shouted more threats. Then I heard Chevalier pleading for their lives. A door slammed. Then several sets of moving feet scrambled down the hall to Chevalier's flat. There the voices rose again. This time with respect to the empty frame. Both Bouvier and Chevalier begged for mercy. Both denied knowing what had happened to the canvas. Unfortunately, the other men were not impressed.

I shut off the water and looked down at the painting. A Van Gogh would bring a hundred million in today's market. I could give it to Maryse. Or I could hand the painting to the five men in the adjacent flat. One result would cause great astonishment and possibly lifelong adoration – not to mention a world of luxury amidst unbridled sex. The other would likely save two men's lives—with the probable forfeit of my own. Why in hell had I not listened to Maryse?

As terrified as I was of what would be my fate, I could not allow murder to take place when it could be prevented. On wobbling legs and heavily dragging feet, I started for the apartment door.

Just as I reached it, I heard a quick series of popping sounds. This was followed by thumps, as if a pair of heavy suitcases had been dropped to the floor.

I stopped in my tracks, sick with fear.

Moments later, I heard a door quietly close and three sets of shoes tread away from Chevalier's flat past Molyneux's door, going toward the stairs. It was easy to take revenge. The tough part was controlling the outcome and accepting accountability for it.

I turned the knob and opened the door a crack. Looking out, I saw the backs of three men in dark suits beginning their descent of the stairs. There was no doubt in my mind about the popping noises or the thumps. It was the same sounds I had heard at Baudouin's apartment, when the police officer was shot.

Maybe they were still alive? Maybe if I called for help someone could get here in time to save them? I hurried back to the telephone and dialed the police. I reported what I had heard and then rang off. They would arrive in a few minutes.

I pulled the door open and crept out. I held my breath, waiting until I no longer heard the departing men's footfalls treading the steps. Then I tiptoed over to Chevalier's flat.

The door was not locked. I turned the knob and nudged it open, slightly. On the floor, lay both men. There were red dots on their shirts. Their eyes were wide open. But they were not breathing.

I felt dizzy. Not so much from the sight of two corpses; particularly, those two corpses. I still suffered from the beating they had given me. But, I was wobbly with guilt over my foolish vindictiveness. Had I left well enough alone, neither Bouvier nor Chevalier would be dead. Not only that, they would not have profited from the painting. Instead it would have gone to François Chiappe.

I crept back to Molyneux's flat, went inside and shut the door. I would be questioned by Monet, at some point. Everyone who lived at Mme. Flaubert's would be. There was also the possibility of my flat being searched. I did not know why. But a search always seemed to be the outcome of every police questioning, at least in the movies. So why would that not be the case in real life? If so, I could not hide the painting in my flat, or Maryse's. I had to secure it somewhere the police would not search. A place like this. A place where they had already searched. But where could I put it? It would have to be somewhere I could reclaim it easily. It would have to be hidden so it would not be discovered should Mme. Flaubert rent the flat before I could get back here.

I looked around, going into the bedroom and the kitchenette. But neither room offered a solution. Then I recalled the ventilation system. It was still several months before heat would be needed. So I hurried over to the vent-cover and quickly removed it, using the palette knife as a screwdriver.

I intended to hide the painting just behind the vent. There it would not easily be spotted and it could be quickly reclaimed, when the time came. But when I pulled off the metal grid, I not only saw the gaping heat-duct, but the other end of the speaking tube. It made no difference as far as concealing the painting. But the speaking tube terminating at this flat explained where the plotters had been when I overheard their conversations.

Quickly, I stuffed the canvas inside the duct with both ends pointing out toward the room. Then I reattached the vent-cover. Afterward, I stood up and backed away to study my work. The scroll of canvas was not visible. So assuming no one decided to remove the cover in order to give it a cleaning, the Van Gogh would remain safely concealed.

After returning to the hall, I put the palette knife to use one last time to set the lock on Molyneux's door. Then I looked around. No one was in sight. No one, apparently, had heard the pops or the killers' departure. Confident that I, too, would not be noticed I tiptoed down the hallway, and quickly descended the stairs.

Assuming Maryse had gone to the Métro station, I strode out the front door of the boarding house, and hurried away along the sidewalk.

In the distance, I could hear approaching sirens. Maryse would not be pleased with the news about Bouvier and Chevalier. But she should be thrilled about the Van Gogh. What woman would not want a painting worth a hundred million or so? It would certainly lure her back to Mme. Flaubert's. Then, after she and I had satisfied Monet's questions, we would wait until he and his men departed for the day. Afterwards, I would sneak back up to the third floor and retrieve the painting. After that, Maryse and I would head for Nice—bag and baggage. There we would flog the Van Gogh, and buy a villa at *Cote d'Azur*. Monet would posture about me leaving Paris. But with my newfound wealth and a home where he could easily reach me, the not so clever Chief Inspector would not quarrel too long about the move to Nice.

Ten minutes later I was making my way through the crowd on the Métro Station's concrete landing. But Maryse was nowhere to be seen. Had she been so angry about me finding the painting that she had not waited for me? Or was she still back at her flat? After seeing Chiappe's men with Bouvier and Chevalier, I could not imagine her remaining there. But she had mentioned being fearful of abduction on the Métro. So she might have remained there, assuming her flat would be my first stop. Quickly, I headed back to Mme. Flaubert's.

By the time I arrived at the front door the police were controlling access, in and out. The officer guarding the entrance refused to let me pass, saying no one was allowed in. I turned and went across the street not sure what I should do. If Maryse was in her flat, I felt it was important that I warn her to remain quiet about the Van Gogh. I did not want her to blurt it out when Monet became offensive in his questions.

I trotted down to the corner and went into a *cabine téléphonique*. After sliding my *Télécartes* through the reader, I dialed her cell-phone number. This time, however, she did not answer. That meant she was either in one of the Métro cars and could not receive a signal, or she was in her flat and Monet was questioning her. I rang off and went back out onto the sidewalk. There, I shuffled around with hands in pockets, offering all who passed the disappointed look upon my face.

"Get a grip, Stuart," I told myself. "Even if she mentioned the painting, you could tell Monet it was a miscommunication. He would search your flat and hers, and then not finding it, assume I had told the truth and move on."

Then I remembered the studio and my obligation to Cesar Avoyelles. Selling the Van Gogh would mean I would no longer be under Cesar's thumb. I could refund his money and refuse to complete the Matisse. But it might take weeks or months to flog the Van Gogh. Until then, I still had my commitment to Avoyelles.

Twenty minutes later, I was standing in front of the blue door adjacent to the *Tabac Shop*. I took out the key, unlocked it, followed the door in, and hurried up the steps.

At the top, I unlocked the door to the studio and pushed it open. Then I strode in, trying to decide whether I should enjoy coffee with coffee for breakfast, or coffee with a tin of condensed soup. I was just about to settle on cocoa with a bit of cheese on the side when I saw it. The body of a woman.

Her corpse was hanging by the neck from a rope attached to a hook in one of the rafters. Her arms dangled limply by her sides, the fingernails were dark with drying blood. She had long dark hair. She was dressed in a leather jacket and a leather skirt. Her figure looked horrifyingly familiar.

"Maryse!" I cried, hurrying over to the lifeless figure.

It was only when I looked into the bloated face that I realized the dead woman was not Maryse Rousseau. I did not know who she had been. But that did not ease the pounding of my heart. No matter how I tried to explain this, I would be suspected in the woman's murder. The doors had been locked. I had the only key. She was in here—hanged.

I backed over to the door, still shaking. I might be able to drag her body out, after dark. I could leave it in the gutter on the next block. But what if someone saw me carry out her body? My efforts to move the corpse would only prove my guilt. There was no other way around this. I would have to notify Monet.

I went downstairs to the tobacco shop and told the manager to ring the police.

Chapter 11
The Truth and Mostly the Truth

The Eiffel Tower is one of the world's best known monuments. It was built for the 1889 World's Fair by, Alexandre Gustave Eiffel. He submitted its design as part of a competition. The structure stands 984 feet high. It has 1710 steps to the top platform. 18,038 pieces of steel are used in its construction. These are joined by 2,500,000 rivets. It weighs about 7,000 tons. Every few years it gets a paint-job in shades of brown —50 tons of it. The tower has two restaurants, an observing desk, a post office, and elevators. It is also one of the top ten most popular places from which to commit suicide.

Nearly 400 people have done so, to date. Only two of the attempts were unsuccessful. In one case, high winds blew the leaper into the girders where he clung for life. The other case was a woman who landed on the top of a car. Curiously, she later married the owner of that car. So, whether leaping for faith or loss-of-life or love, this is the place from which to do it.

"I think you're cursed!" ranted Chief Inspector Claude Monet.

I was in his office. It was after midnight. He was sitting behind his desk dressed in the same suit he had worn during my previous grilling. The same ratty tie was coiled upon the desktop. I was shackled hand and foot, sitting in a straight-back chair. He was lounging in a swivel, with his big feet propped upon the desktop. It could have been an instant replay of my first interrogation except for two differences. First, I had been stripped of my clothing and dumped into a prison jumpsuit. Second, I had been forced to put my hands into a plastic bag containing a mild acidic solution. Both of these strange occurrences were necessary, according to Monet. Each would establish whether or not I had recently fired a gun.

"I've never owned a gun," I declared.

"I did not ask you that," he snapped in return. "I asked you to explain your situation in the context of probability."

"I can't."

His feet hit the floor and he splayed his hands. "Neither can I. And yet the circumstance exists." He held up a hand and began ticking off points on the fingers. "Two people were murdered today, at Mme. Flaubert's—where you live. A woman you claim not to know was hanged in your art studio—also today. Before these very disturbing occurrences, someone tried to kill you. Before that, you were present when Dr. Michele Molyneux was run down on a sidewalk. Before that, you were present when Baudouin Rousseau was murdered—in his own home." He rested his forearms upon the desk and tilted toward me. "You are like a magnet for death."

"I am merely a victim of circumstance."

He eased back in his chair and rubbed his eyes with the heels of his hands. "Why can't you be a victim somewhere other than in France?"

"Does that mean you're not going to charge me?"

His brows arched in mock shock, as his hands dropped. "Do you think I am doing this for the pleasure of it?"

"Frankly, I think persecution is your favorite hobby."

Monet crossed his arms. For many seconds he remained silent. Then he asked, "Where is Mme. Rousseau? When I went to her flat to question her, she was gone."

"Surely you can't blame Maryse for those murders?"

He snorted, "You have been blinded by her beauty, M. Stuart. Make no mistake. She killed her husband. And although I cannot prove it I think she is involved in the other murders."

"Bouvier and Chevalier were shot by François Chiappe's men."

Monet rolled his eyes. "You saw these men actually kill Bouvier and Chevalier?"

I wagged my head. "Of course not. But I saw them leave."

"Then you can identify them?"

"No. All I saw were their backs as they went down the steps."

He frowned. "Then how can you be certain Françoise Chiappe's people were involved?"

"Maryse said she saw Bouvier and Chevalier return to Mme. Flaubert's, in the company of three men. She said those three men worked for Françoise Chiappe. Considering who her husband was I think Maryse should know what she's talking about—at least when it comes to gangsters."

"You are assuming she is not lying," he quickly returned. "If Mme. Rousseau is telling the truth, what makes you think she did not hire those three men?"

I gave him a confused look. "Why would she?"

Monet's chin rose confidently and he waggled a finger above his head. "To stop the blackmail, of course."

"What blackmail?"

"For murdering her husband, what else? Have you no understanding of human nature?"

"And was the hanged woman also blackmailing her?"

"No. But her motive there is just as good if not better." Chief Inspector Monet stood up and adjusted his belt, so it did not dig into his big belly. Then he resumed his seat, again looking at me. "Bouvier and Chevalier were unflinching, when it came to blackmail. Both had been convicted of it no less than four times." He paused a moment his eyes going dreamy. "You should have seen the photos they took of our Prime Minister and that curvaceous…" Then the glare I had become accustomed to returned. "Never mind! I intend to question Mme. Rousseau. You will tell me where she is or you will spend the rest of your days behind bars!"

"I want a lawyer."

"You're not getting one until I am finished with you. So unless you want me to dump you back in the cells, tell me where she is."

"Maryse said she was going to Nice to stay with her mother. I assume she did so."

His lower lip curled, slightly. "I don't suppose you know her mother's name and address?"

I shook my head. "It was only this morning that Maryse suggested the trip. Had I been smart, I would've gone with her."

"The prospect of you doing anything intelligent, M. Stuart, would stun the world," he sighed. Then one of Monet's hands formed into a fist and it struck the desktop with a resounding thump. "Was this suggested trip before or after Bouvier and Chevalier were murdered?"

"Obviously it was before," I replied, more than slightly irritated at his dig about my intelligence. "I have not seen her since."

He tilted forward, shaking that fist at me. "I know for a fact that you have not told me everything you know about the murders of Bouvier and Chevalier!" Then he raised the threatening hand, uncoiled its fingers and dramatically and pointed the index digit at the ceiling. "An indisputable fact!"

"Well here's a fact for you, Chief Inspector. I don't know anything else. Therefore I cannot tell you anything else. End of fact!"

"You think by keeping quiet, you are protecting yourself?" he scoffed. "I tell you, I—Chief Inspector Claude Monet—have already cracked this case!"

"With me as the killer?"

"The evidence is clear!"

"Let me get this straight," I said. "Your theory is, I went up to Chevalier's flat and shot both him and Bouvier, even though I have never fired a gun in my whole life? Two men you have described as hardened criminals."

He scowled. "You see a flaw in that?"

I nodded. "For starters, why would I shoot them?"

"For the pleasure of it, of course," he returned, with a self-satisfied smirk.

"And where would I get a gun in Paris?"

"For your information, I already know where you got the gun."

"Really?" I asked, giving my eyes taunting roll. "Did I pull it out of thin air like a magician?"

"You got the weapon from Mme. Rousseau."

"Maryse does not own a gun!"

"She does own a gun—one that is the same caliber as that used on Bouvier and Chevalier. She also has a permit to carry it—concealed."

I blinked, completely surprised by this revelation. If Maryse carried a gun, why had she been afraid to go to work? Why was fear forcing her to give up all she had in Paris, and move to Nice? Why, when she could protect herself, was Maryse running away? Or did she have a gun? Was it not more likely Monet was baiting me with a lie? He had done so regarding Baudouin Rousseau's knowledge of the Corsican language.

"I've never seen her gun," I told him, cagily.

He snorted. "You are lying."

"Look, I'm tired of this. Book me or turn me loose."

"Very well, you are charged with murder—three times. Your trial will occur sometime during the next ten to twenty years. We are backed up a bit, in the courtroom arena. But don't worry. You will be fed every day—more or less."

"You'll never make those charges stick!" I squealed.

He half-rose to his feet and thrust a finger at me. "Make no mistake, M. Stuart. I have gotten convictions on less evidence."

"What evidence? All I've heard so far are wild allegations. I have no motive for killing anyone. I have no desire to kill anyone. I would not know how to shoot a gun, even if I had one. I…"

"My men searched Bouvier's and Chevalier's apartments," he interrupted; smugly, resuming his seat. "They found an empty painting frame in Chevalier's flat."

Monet's specific mention of the frame in the context of his accusation, gave me chills. Obviously, he had linked me to the frame and thereby linked me to the shootings. But for the life of me I could not fathom how he had done it. Both the frame and the painting came from Baudouin Rousseau's apartment.

"A painting frame?" I jeered. "You call that evidence? Paris is awash with painting frames."

"The evidence is not the frame, as such," he said, making a vague movement with one hand. "But it was, as well as the doorknob to Chevalier's flat, afflicted with your fingerprints." He offered me a toothy smile. "That, M. Stuart, is undeniable evidence of your involvement in those murders."

You are probably asking yourself, how could I be so stupid as to leave that frame in Chevalier's flat, without first wiping away my fingerprints? Further how could I have not done the same to the knob, after opening Chevalier's door and seeing two corpses? The answer is, of course, quite simple. I am that stupid.

"My fingerprints?" I choked, failing to sound casual.

He clucked his tongue. "Surely, you do not find that difficult to believe?"

My stomach attempted to turn itself inside out, and my left eye began to twitch. "I—I—possibly left my fingerprints on the doorknob when I tripped coming out of the bath. I distinctly recall grabbing onto it, to stop my fall."

"How amazing. You fell all away across the hallway and somehow managed to grab hold of that particular doorknob, in order to stabilize yourself. Is that also how the painting frame acquired those same fingerprints, M. Stuart? Perhaps, the door opened as you grabbed the knob? And then, you stumbled across the two corpses only to successfully grab the painting frame in order to stop your fall? And then, making a more discreet departure, you left Chevalier's flat without seeing his body or that of Bouvier's?"

His words sounded logical to me. "Would you believe me if I said, 'yes'?"

"No."

Adolph Hitler once remarked, 'Make the lie big, make it simple, keep saying it, and eventually they will believe it.' Unfortunately, I was not a Nazis with a funny moustache. And even if I was, nothing I could say would sway Monet's opinion—truth or otherwise.

I fell silent, thinking. Somehow I had to come up with a rational explanation for my fingerprints being on that frame. Then a brilliant idea came to mind. I would do what any other rational person would do, under the circumstances. I would lie.

"Actually I think I can explain the painting frame," I told him.

"That is very encouraging," he said with a nod. "But first, can you describe it to me?"

My mind went blank. I was pretty sure the frame was wooden. Most are. And I was almost certain it was brown. But beyond that, I could not say.

"In case you are having trouble recalling it," he said, "the frame is big, brown, heavy, ugly, ornately carved, and made of wood."

"That was exactly how I remember it, Chief Inspector. And I know exactly how my fingerprints got on that frame. In fact, just a few days ago I purchased it."

"Where?"

I blinked. "Where, what?"

Monet took his dirty pipe from his pocket and brought out a black, leather tobacco pouch. "From where did you purchase it?"

"I—I—I think it was from a second-hand shop – I don't recall the name. I'm pretty sure it was over on..."

"The shopkeeper did not give you a receipt?" he casually interjected, scooping the tobacco into the pipe's bowl from the pouch, with his thumb.

I wagged my head. "It was a cash arrangement. In any event, the frame was stolen yesterday or the day before. Therefore the site of its discovery and my fingerprints on it are logically explained."

"Chevalier stole it?"

"I think that's self-evident."

The Chief Inspector carefully tamped the tobacco into his pipe with his thumb. Then he put the pouch away and took a lighter from his trousers. Afterward, he flicked the lighter to life and put fire to the pipe-bowl. He puffed. He tamped. He put more fire to the bowl. Then he puffed again, repeating the tamping and lighting process until clouds of smoke half-hid his face.

"Have you learned nothing since your last interrogation, M. Stuart?" After batting some of the smoke away, he looked over at me. "Do you not realize that I, Chief Inspector Claude Monet, cannot be fooled by your adolescent lies?"

Monet had an accusatory way with words that made me shudder. "If I killed them, why would I put a frame containing my fingerprints in Chevalier's flat? If I killed them, would I be stupid enough to forget to wipe off the doorknob as I left Chevalier's flat?"

"That is exactly the sort of thing I would expect you to do, M. Stuart," he returned, taking the pipe from his mouth. He crossed his legs, bouncing one big shoe against the desk, impatiently. "You are completely inept at everything. Now, are you going to continue with these false-hoods? Or may we proceed?"

"I am not lying."

His thick brows curled into a sharp vie. "Have you heard of *La Sante Prison?*"

Again my stomach inverted. *La Sante* is regarded as one of the ten worst prisons in the world—not just in France. One of the ten worst in the *entire* world—bar none!

"I may have heard mention of it," I choked.

"It is a not-so-nice little getaway just a few miles from here," he explained, meditatively. "In there men of your age spend their days and nights fending off sexual deviants. And during the lulls in-between they are preoccupied with rats the size of small dogs. Those not so nice fur-balls like to gnaw off noses, fingers and toes.

"But on the plus side, *La Sante* offers a casual atmosphere for all who are incarcerated. In fact, the entire prison population sleeps naked—even on the coldest nights in winter. They do this so they can stuff their clothes into the cracks the rats sneak through." He made a mocking gesture of pity. "Unfortunately, that leaves their entire bodies exposed to the icy air, lice and other mattress-infecting vermin. I am told one young man went to sleep and woke up to discover that one of his testicles was missing—chewed off by bedbugs the size of my thumb." He paused a moment to take a breath. "From experience, a month in there is the perfect cure for the habitual liar. Shall we test that premise on you, M. Stuart?"

After a minor hesitation and major panic I told him, "All right. You've made your point. I admit it. I did put the frame in Chevalier's flat. But I did it before they were killed. It was intended as a joke."

His voice rose, sharply. "You're lying, again! Your fingerprints on the doorknob were the only ones we found. That means you opened the door. Therefore, you went into that flat and you killed them." Monet paused to smirk with supreme satisfaction. "Proof positive of your un-mitigated guilt."

Why had I gone to see if Bouvier or Chevalier were still alive, after hearing them being gunned down? Why didn't I just assume there were dead? It's not like they were people I would grieve over.

"On your feet. I'm taking you to *La Sante*," Monet ordered, standing up.

"Wait! Please? I'll tell you whatever you want to know."

He thrust the pipe at me, like it was a sword. "If you think I am bluffing, think again!"

"I am not delusional, Chief Inspector. I am taking you at your word."

Monet made a sound of satisfaction deep in his throat. "Start talking."

"Bouvier and Chevalier stole a painting from Maryse Rousseau. I went looking for it in their flats. I know it was wrong..."

"It was illegal!" he bellowed.

"All right, it was illegal. Be that as it may, I searched Bouvier's flat for the painting. In there I found the frame. I thought if I moved the frame from his flat to Chevalier's, it might shake them up a little."

He slumped back into his chair. "You would have needed an earthquake to shake-up those two!" he snorted. "They had violent criminal records going back to when they were children. When was Mme. Rousseau's flat broken into?"

"I guess I didn't make myself clear. The painting was actually taken from Baudouin Rousseau's apartment. I said it was taken from her because I assume Maryse will inherit everything."

"You hope she does, you mean." He smiled, making an airy arc of smoke with the pipe. "I am curious. How do you know from where the painting was taken? She does not reside in Baudouin Rousseau's apartment. I have not given permission for anyone to enter there."

I tried to swallow my tongue. But it was too busy trying to strangle my vocal cords for admitting the painting came from Baudouin's apartment when Monet had assumed it was stolen from Maryse's flat.

"I was planning to call you..." I began.

"Really? About anything in particular?" he said, whimsically.

"Actually, it has to do with a police officer being shot."

He leaned his forearms upon the desk and grinned. "How very interesting. Do continue."

"You see, I saw Bouvier and Chevalier shoot a police officer in Baudouin Rousseau's apartment."

"I know you were at Rousseau's!" he thundered. He jutted toward me, his face intense. "I know it was Bouvier and Chevalier who shot my officer. I know you saw what happened. I know everything!"

"Now who's lying?" I blurted.

He jabbed a fat finger at me. "I know it was you because your voice was recorded when you reported the shooting. For helping that officer, I am grateful to you. In consideration of that, I have extended patience I would not have otherwise done. Had you not telephoned, that young officer would have died." He set down the pipe and crossed his arms. "But, that will not distract me from seeing you prosecuted for these murders."

I frowned. "How could you possibly know Bouvier and Chevalier were the shooters? It was pitch-dark in that apartment. The police officer entered in the dark and was shot almost immediately. He was unconscious when they fled."

Chief Inspector Monet grinned, evilly. "Their fingerprints were found on Baudouin Rousseau's desk." He spread his arms in mock grandeur. "As you can imagine, their deaths were a great personal disappointment."

"I'm not the one who caused that disappointment."

"No?" Monet threw a frown at me. "Are you suggesting Mme. Rousseau killed Bouvier and Chevalier?"

"I told you! It was François Chiappe's men!"

"Then convince me! Or I shall take you to *La Sante*, anyway."

I did as instructed—mostly. In hopes of keeping the Van Gogh, I told Monet the painting had already been removed from the frame when I found it. There was, however, no way to explain my having heard the voices and popping-sounds without admitting where I had taken refuge. That, of course, would mean his men would search Molyneux's flat. But I was confident the Van Gogh's hiding place would not be discovered.

He fumbled with his lower lip in silence for several minutes, after I finished talking. I watched, waited and prayed that my mostly-true story had been convincing.

"To whom would the painting have been given?" he said, thoughtfully. "Why would they part with it—considering the outcome of the theft? Why would they have stolen it, in the first place? It was hideous!"

"I'm sure they sold it," I lamely offered, hoping to close the issue.

"Don't be ridiculous. That painting was a blight upon artistic expression." He knocked the ash from the pipe's bowl into one palm, returned the pipe to his coat and the dusted the ash into the trashcan beside his desk. "I saw it when I investigated Baudouin Rousseau's murder. Who in his right mind would buy such a vile painting?"

I could not help but taunt him with, "Baudouin Rousseau, for one."

He batted the air. "He did not purchase that painting. M. Rousseau bought what was beneath it. But Bouvier and Chevalier would not have known that—unless they had been told."

My heart sank. I thought I had been absolutely brilliant figuring out the visible painting actually concealed another. "I don't understand what you mean?" I lied.

"It is simple logic, M. Stuart. First ask yourself why Bouvier and Chevalier took that particular painting? M. Rousseau had several others worth a few thousand each." He paused, as if thinking about his previous words. "Why not grab one of those? Why? Because they had been told to steal a particular painting. But why shoot a police officer in doing so, to avoid arrest? Simple illegal entry would amount to only a few months in jail or perhaps a fine. They attempted to kill that officer because it was the only way they could get away with a painting they were convinced was priceless. But anyone who has seen that painting knows it has no value." There was a faint hesitation. "So, therefore, what is worthless and visible must conceal something of value that is invisible. Clear?"

"Assuming your theory is correct—and I am certain you are wrong—who hired them to take that painting?"

"Mme. Rousseau, of course."

A male uniformed officer entered. "No nitrates were found on M. Stuart's clothing or his hands, Chief Inspector."

Monet made a disgusted face. He dismissed the officer with a finger-wave. Then he resumed his interest in me.

"Let us assume you did not shoot Bouvier and Chevalier…"

"Obviously I didn't or your stupid tests would've proved I did!"

He snorted, "Do not take me for a fool, Monsieur. A pair of gloves and a change of clothing would easily defeat those tests. As far as I am concerned, you are still the prime suspect. But…" He dramatically thrust a finger toward the ceiling. "For the time being, let's assume you did not shoot them. Would you recognize the voices of the men you claimed did shoot Bouvier and Chevalier?"

I wagged my head. "They were just angry voices; their words came through the walls twisted with rage. They could've been anybody."

"I guess it makes no difference, anyway," he muttered. "If they were hired by Chiappe, they are no longer in France." Then his eyes brightened. "But the painting might be. You would recognize the painting if you saw it again, yes?"

"Of course."

I silently cursed myself. Monet had deliberately suckered me into a telltale admission. The only way I could recognize the painting was if I had seen it. But in my own words, I had been unconscious until shortly before being arrested, during my first visit to Baudouin Rousseau's apartment. Therefore I could not have seen the painting, then. The wounded police officer would have told Monet the apartment had been dark, when the shooting occurred. Moments earlier I had told him the same thing. So how I could have gotten a recognizable view of the painting in the dark? I could not have, and he knew it, unless I had removed the painting from its frame.

He laughed softly, quite pleased with himself. "Excellent." Then he frowned. "Why did you not immediately come forward with what you knew about the shooting at M. Rousseau's?"

"I was afraid I'd be arrested for being there."

He gave a noncommittal nod. "I guess at this juncture it might be a moot point."

"Does that mean I'm free to go?"

"Of course not!" He took a comb from his pocket and swept it through his hair, eying me askance. Then he put it away and said, "When my men searched Bouvier's flat, they discovered a note. It was written in his own handwriting. That, of itself, is not very interesting. But what was written upon the paper is irresistibly intriguing."

He paused hoping my curiosity would prompt me to ask for an explanation. But I remained silent, fearing what was to come.

"That note bore your name," he eventually declared.

I scoffed, "You find my name written on a note irresistibly intriguing?"

He nodded. "Even more intriguing was what was written beneath your name."

Again, he fell silent baiting me to ask for an explanation. But, again, I kept quiet.

"It was a currency entry," he explained. "Sixty million Euros. Now, why would Bouvier have such a note, M. Stuart? Obviously, he felt there was a link between you and that huge amount of money. But what would that link be?"

Monet was becoming my worst nightmare. He knew about the stolen diamonds. He also suspected me of participating in their theft.

"I have no idea," I lied.

He laughed, softly. "How unconvincing." Then he placed his arms back upon the desktop, leaning toward me. "Here's what I think… I think you were assaulted by Bouvier and Chevalier. I think you intended revenge for that beating. You saw Chevalier and Bouvier leave M. Rousseau's apartment, with a painting. I believe you thought if you found that painting and took it, but left the painting frame in Chevalier's flat, they would suspect one another in its disappearance. That, or so you hoped, would cause one of them to kill the other." His hand reached out in an expression of sympathy. "Am I not correct?"

It was like Monet could read my mind! "More or less."

"A great deal more than less, I think," he smirked. Chief Inspector Monet stood up and began to pace. After a few moments he stopped and faced me. "They were after the diamonds, weren't they?"

I nodded. "I had no idea what they were talking about. At the time, I did not even know who they were. They wore dark clothes and masks. It was only when they left Baudouin's apartment that I saw their faces— and their shoes."

He frowned. "Shoes?"

"When you're on the floor trying to avoid being kicked, you take a healthy interest in your attackers' feet. The light from the hallway outside Baudouin's apartment hit their shoes, and their faces. It was then I realized who had assaulted me."

He pursed his lips studying me as if I were a deceitful child. "Did they mention any names during the attack?"

"Buji."

"Buji?" he frowned.

"I think they thought he had the diamonds. That's when they left."

Again Monet fell silent, thinking. "Who is Buji?"

I teased him with, "I don't know if you don't."

"Regardless of who Buji is, why would they assume there was a link between you and the diamonds? Look at you! Who in his right mind would think you had sixty million in diamonds?"

"Someone with bad eyesight?"

"Did they tell you where the diamonds came from?"

I shook my head.

"Then I will explain." He returned to his chair and got comfortable. "A few months ago there was diamond heist. The Lucien Falize Jewelry store was relieved of sixty million in cut stones."

"I know what you're thinking. But I wasn't involved in it."

"I know you were not. No one in their right mind would bring you in on such a daring robbery." Monet stuck a forefinger into an ear and rapidly rotated it. Then he took a deep breath and exhaled. "But the issue is not your involvement. It is why Bouvier and Chevalier thought you had the diamonds." He tilted back in his chair, folding his hands together across his big belly. "After reading that note I knew the reference to sixty million meant the Lucien Falize robbery." His hands became animated as he continued pontificating. "There was no other explanation. So I reviewed the investigation into the theft—thoroughly. In fact, while you were in the cells waiting to be brought to my office, I examined the security camera video of the robbery.

"Four people dressed in black, their faces concealed by baklavas, entered the store." His lower lip curled disdainfully. "We, of course, assumed a fifth person was outside in the getaway car. But that individual was never seen. The theft was well-planned. The theft was well-orchestrated. The thieves knew exactly what diamonds to take. They knew exactly where those diamonds would be stored.

"One of the thieves was a very large man. Another was a woman. Those two held the people in the store at bay, using pistols. Another thief stood by the door counting off the seconds. The fourth collected the diamonds and dumped them into a bag." His eyebrows rose. "Within three minutes the thieves, and sixty million in diamonds, were gone." He pointed a finger at me. "The robbery was what you Americans would call an inside job. We suspected this from the beginning. Why? Because the thieves took a specific group of stones from a location known only to the store's employees.

"As such, this should have been an easy case to solve. Making it even easier, or so I thought at the investigation's onset, was an absent female employee. She had worked at the jewelry store for only a few months. Nevertheless, she was considered trustworthy. But I had to ask myself, why was she not there on that particular day? Coincidence?" He studied me with a critical eye. "I did not think so. But the manager of Lucien Falize told me the woman had arranged the time-off in advance—to see her physician. We, of course, visited her doctor. And much to my disappointment, he verified her appointment. Not only that, but he told me she was being examined by him at the exact moment of the robbery. Why should he lie? The woman returned to work. When I interrogated her, she was completely unflustered and answered all my questions without hesitation. So, I reluctantly removed that woman from my suspect list." Monet twisted his head to smile at me. "Then, you came along and changed everything."

"Me?" I tried to force a laugh. But it came out like a sheep's bray. "Are you saying my brilliant insight solved that case for you?"

Chief Inspector Monet wagged his head. "In my opinion, you do not have the brains God gave baby geese." He took a thick file folder from one of the drawers in his desk, and set it down on the desk. From within the file he removed an eight by ten photograph. The Chief Inspector studied it a few seconds and then held it up for me to see. "Recognize her?"

I nodded without hesitation. "It's the woman who was hanged in my studio."

"Very good. This is an enlargement of her employment photograph from Lucien Falize. She worked there under the name of Beatrice Lafayette. But after checking her fingerprints, today, we discovered that her legal name was actually Maryse D'aubigne."

I blinked, momentarily stunned. Not by the fact that Maryse D'aubigne had participated in the robbery. I already knew that. But I was taken aback by her beauty.

"Are you sure she was René's wife?" I asked. "His description of her —something I heard frequently—really falls short of that woman."

Monet put the photograph back into the file with a nod, and returned the folder to his desk. Then he interlaced his fingers on the desktop, and continued. "Although, she continued to work at the jewelry store after the theft, the fact that she concealed her true identity convinced me that Mme. D'aubigne helped in the robbery. Physically, she was the right size as the woman in the security tape. But if that was true, then it follows her physician – Michele Molyneux—was also involved. Otherwise, he would not have lied for her. But if those theories are both true, why did they take such a risk as staging a medical exam as her alibi? Because by doing so, each of them supplied an unbreakable alibi for the other!

"Where does this leave us?" continued Monet, he spoke almost eagerly, as if off his guard. "Because of your assault over the stolen diamonds we were able to identify two of the five thieves: Bouvier and Chevalier. Because of the hanged woman in your studio, we identified her as the woman in the robbery. Because Dr. Michele Molyneux had lied to protect her, we knew he must be involved. Considering his physical characteristics, I believe he was number four—the one counting off the seconds. However, we still did not know the name of the fifth person— the one in the getaway car. Or, for that matter, the one who planned the robbery."

I knew from the overheard conversations that Molyneux was somehow involved in the robbery. But never in my wildest imagination did I think Molyneux had been an active participant or that Monet could link Molyneux to the theft. In any event, that meant the getaway driver must have been Buji. A little tidbit I would keep to myself.

"Why would they not be one in the same?" I asked.

"I will come to that. As I told you earlier, Bouvier and Chevalier had lengthy criminal records. But, neither could have been considered brain-trust material. So after watching the swiftly elegant execution of the robbery, it was easy to conclude that they had not planned it. Those two were the smash-the-windows-and-grab, types." He chuckled softly, clearly enjoying himself. "Mme. D'aubigne and Dr. Michele Molyneux had a great deal more intelligence. But neither of them had a criminal record. Therefore they had no experience at planning thievery and, it turned out, they had even less experience at driving a getaway car. Thus, they could not have planned so smooth an operation or have been the getaway car driver. So who else was involved?"

"A Chief Inspector of police nicknamed Buji, might qualify," I quipped.

He growled, "Don't get cute!" Then he resumed his blasé attitude and said, "Think back. You know the answer. It is as clear as the big nose on your face."

Again, from the conversations overheard, I knew Baudouin Rousseau had been the brains behind the diamond gambit. I also knew he ended up with the diamonds. But not wanting to give away any more than I had, already—which would incriminate me even deeper—I meekly shrugged.

Monet's arms rose and fell with exasperation. "The four we have identified are all dead. Who else was murdered? Baudouin Rousseau, of course!"

Again, Monet had come to the correct conclusion using simple surmise and speculation. I hated to admit it. But he had far more intelligence than I was attributing him.

"Why did I link M. Rousseau to the theft, you may ask?" The Chief Inspector raised hand and extended fingers to count off significant points as he continued. "One, we knew Baudouin was having an affair with Mme. D'aubigne. Two, Michele Molyneux had been a close friend of Baudouin Rousseau. Three, we knew Baudouin Rousseau withdrew approximately one hundred thousand Euros from his personal bank account a few days before the jewel robbery. Four, the getaway cars—there were three used in the course of the thieves' escape—cost a total of ninety thousand Euros. The last point is not a perfect match to the withdrawn amount. However, it is close enough for discussion purposes. Five, M. Rousseau had been an expert at planning high-profile robberies. His success at it had carried him through the ranks of the Corsican Mafia quicker than any other man in its history. Therefore, he planned that robbery." Then Monet gave me a Cheshire grin. "Which leaves only the getaway driver to identify."

"Why couldn't it have been Baudouin Rousseau?"

"Because he was too ill. Remember, M. Rousseau was dying of cancer." Monet chuckled softly under his breath. "Would you care to take a guess as to the driver's identity?"

I wagged my head, again fearing what was to come.

He rubbed his hands together, gleefully. "At first I could think of no reason for Bouvier and Chevalier to suspect you of having the diamonds, other than you had been involved in the diamond theft as the getaway car driver. So I checked with your country's immigration department. They confirmed that you had not been to France for over a year, prior to this visit. I also checked with the state where you lived concerning your driving record. Considering your general ineptitude behind the steering wheel, illustrated by the numerous accidents on your driving record, I quickly decided you could not possibly be the getaway car driver." His voice became calm, calculating. "But that did not answer the original question. Why did Bouvier and Chevalier think you had the diamonds? Answer? Bouvier and Chevalier were told you had the diamonds. But who would have done that? Answer? The driver of the getaway car."

"That being?"

"Have you not been listening to me? It can be no one except Maryse Rousseau!"

"Maryse? How could she qualify? A job like getaway car driver means somebody experienced at high-speed driving in heavy traffic!"

166

"She has that experience. Mme. Rousseau drove an Alfa Romeo 147 in *The European Touring Cup*, three years running. She might well have continued to do so, except she married Baudouin Rousseau. In fact, her racing ability was what attracted him."

Again, I was stunned by what Maryse had kept concealed. "I can think of a few other attractions to her credit that he might have noticed."

"As may be. But we are discussing the diamond theft," Monet quickly returned. "Now, let's see… Where was I? Baudouin Rousseau had invested a small fortune backing that robbery. But how could he protect his investment? He was too ill to actively participate in the theft. Yes, he had Molyneux involved to make sure things went as planned during the actual robbery. But who did Baudouin have to make certain the gang did not run off with the diamonds or get caught trying to flee the robbery? His trustworthy wife, Maryse Rousseau." He made a vague movement of one hand. "As you can see, my deductive reasoning is flawless."

"Then explain how Maryse would benefit from telling Bouvier and Chevalier that I had the diamonds?"

"Bouvier and Chevalier were on a rampage after Baudouin's death. You will recall Mme. Rousseau's claim about being abducted by two men? She even said she clawed one of them in the face, and then leaped from their automobile. But was that true?" Monet let go a mirthless chuckle. "Not entirely. When I saw her there was no indication of having endured physical violence or having meted it out. Her nails are long and as sharp as bat-teeth. Had she clawed anyone, at least one of those nails would have been broken and all would have been encrusted with blood. But neither Bouvier nor Chevalier had evidence of being clawed anywhere on their bodies. So if she had been abducted, how had she escaped? Instead of heroically fighting for her freedom, Mme. Rousseau had bargained for it. She told Bouvier and Chevalier that you had the diamonds."

As much as I wanted to think the best of Maryse, Monet had made a very solid surmise. Still…

"But there's no reason they would've believed her story about me," I returned.

"Why shouldn't they? First, she told them you were her lover. Pillow-talk often discloses never-before-told secrets. I, myself, have been lured into that trap. Secondly, you were at Baudouin Rousseau's apartment, the night he died. They knew you were left there alone, to face the police. See? Theoretically, you being there after the others left gave you an opportunity to search the flat and, conceivably, find the hidden diamonds. But even if they decided you did not have enough time to search out the diamonds, there was still the possibility you already knew where the diamonds were hidden. In fact, they may have assumed that getting the diamonds had been your reason for visiting Baudouin Rousseau that night. And if you did know where the diamonds had been hidden, it would not have taken long for you to recover the stones and toss the bundle over the balcony to the person who had told you the where the diamonds could be found—Mme. Rousseau."

"But the people on the ground would have seen me do that."

"We are talking about what Bouvier and Chevalier might have assumed, not what you actually did. The point being that they would be convinced. And that is why they did what they did to you." He waggled a finger overhead. "Remember, a very clever woman was telling this tale to men who were not God's gift to intelligence. Further, those two idiots desperately wanted to believe her. Millions were at stake! She not only twisted you to her will, but she did the same with them."

Resignedly, I sank lower in my chair. I had assumed, once I realized Maryse D'aubigne was probably the female participant in the overheard conversations, that Maryse Rousseau was not involved in any of it. But Monet's facts and surmises made it very clear that Maryse had been part of the diamond heist. That, of course, logically meant she had been at her husband's apartment the night he died, and so on and so on.

"You do not look well, M. Stuart," he taunted. "Is the truth too tough to swallow?"

"Hard to digest, anyway."

He stood up and began to pace, again. "Since we know who the thieves were, we also know who killed Baudouin Rousseau. The night he was murdered, there was a gathering at his apartment—including you. The four members of the robbery team, plus Mme. Rousseau, descended upon Baudouin Rousseau. Why? In the case of Bouvier, Chevalier and Mme. D'aubigne, they expected to be paid for their part in the diamond theft. Only Mme. Rousseau, Baudouin Rousseau and Dr. Molyneux were privy to what was really going to occur."

"Mercy killing, you mean."

He stopped short and stared as if I had more brains than I should. "Exactly. How did you come by that?"

"A dying man. A bunch of stolen diamonds. Just a guess based upon things that had happened in the past."

"Yes," he murmured, seemingly surprised by my apparent intuition. "But before we address those issues, let us consider why Baudouin Rousseau had the diamonds in the first place?"

"To dispose of them, of course."

"Wrong!" he shouted, triumphantly. "That is not why he had them. That is why the stones were given to him." His arms flailed the air in exasperation. "You do not see the difference?"

I wagged my head. "Not really."

"Of course you do not. I forgot your limited mental capacity. Instead, concentrate on why Bouvier and Chevalier thought you had the diamonds."

"Because Maryse convinced them I did—at least according to your theory."

His eyes rolled back in his head and he looked up at the ceiling, both his arms raise overhead as if praying. "Sweet mother of God, it is like talking to a brick wall!" Then his arms flopped back to his sides and he stared at me as if I might be the stupidest thing breathing. "Yes she convinced them. But why would they think the diamonds still existed? Have you not been listening to me?"

"Because they were stupid—as you said. And, as you said, she…"

"Yes, yes," he cut me off. "But you are still missing the point. Why did they think the diamonds existed at all after being in the hands of Baudouin Rousseau for several months during a time when he was to dispose of the stones?"

Monet frowned. After a few seconds of my not making a response, he shook his head in despair. "Are you a complete dunce? Rousseau was supposed to have disposed of the diamonds. And yet Bouvier and Chevalier told you they had searched his apartment for the diamonds! So what does that tell us?"

I knew what he was getting at because I knew Baudouin Rousseau had told his cohorts he had not disposed of the diamonds, according to the overheard conversations. But I feigned ignorance in order to see how far Monet could carry his deductions.

"You're making my head hurt," I complained, as if his brilliance was too difficult to follow.

Chief Inspector Monet chuckled with genuine delight. "Because Baudouin Rousseau told them he had not disposed of the diamonds. Now is it clear?"

"Yes. But not long ago you said Bouvier and Chevalier stole the painting because there was another of great value underneath. If so, how did Baudouin Rousseau acquire that valuable painting and still hang onto the diamonds?"

"He didn't. Try to concentrate. The night Baudouin died everyone—except Molyneux and Mme. Rousseau—assumed Baudouin had told the truth when he claimed he had not disposed of the diamonds. It was not until later, after Mme. Rousseau pointed Bouvier and Chevalier to the painting, that it became a target for theft. Otherwise it would have been taken away the night M. Rousseau was killed."

Again, he stopped and waited for me to ask questions. When I did not he blurted, "Aren't you curious as to why Baudouin Rousseau would risk violent retaliation from his gang by lying about the diamonds?"

"I'm more interested to know why Maryse sent Bouvier and Chevalier to steal the painting? By doing so, she put them onto what had happened thus revitalizing their interest in collecting their end of the robbery. Why wouldn't she simply wait for her husband's will to be probated, take possession of all property and then flog the lot?"

Monet returned to his desk and settled back into his chair. "Originally, that was the plan. But things went wrong. She was abducted by Bouvier and Chevalier, as we previously discussed. Unfortunately for her plans to fool them, you survived their visit. You see, she thought Bouvier and Chevalier would lose their tempers and beat you to death trying to get you to tell them about the diamonds. You being dead would mean the loss of their last hope to locate the diamonds. As such, they would stop searching. But you convinced them that someone else must have the diamonds. When that happened, they returned to her."

Based upon what I had overheard in the conversations, Monet was correct about Bouvier and Chevalier returning to Maryse but it was not Maryse Rousseau they had approached. It had been Maryse D'aubigne. I kept that to myself, as well.

"At that point Mme. Rousseau was facing two furious animals who would stop at nothing to get what they wanted," he continued. "So, she told them she and you had talked—since she last talked to them. And because you were terrified by Bouvier and Chevalier, you finally told her where you had hidden the diamonds. Based upon this disclosure, which I am certain they extracted using painful force, Bouvier and Chevalier believed her story. They went after the painting, which was supposed to contain the diamonds. But when they brought it back to Bouvier's flat they discovered that nothing was hidden behind the canvas. As you can imagine, they were at a loss as to what to do. Had you lied to Maryse? They had scared you thoroughly, so that was not likely. Had she lied to them? They had made certain she had told the truth. So if neither you nor her had lied, where were the diamonds? Obviously, someone else had known about the stones being hidden in the painting and had gotten to the diamonds before them. But who could that be? The most likely person to have been entrusted with that knowledge was Mme. D'aubigne— M. Rousseau's lover."

"But if Maryse sent those goons to get the painting, why when they confronted her afterward, did she not tell them about the hidden painting?"

"Because of greed," he returned. "She assumed that something so ugly and worthless they would not quarrel over if she asked to have it as a memento of her husband. Remember, they were after diamonds not art."

"They might've burned it."

"But they didn't. It was a great risk, I agree. But she was in great peril at the time." He hesitated, thinking back over what he had said. Then he began again. "Bouvier and Chevalier were convinced they had not been lied to. That meant they must've been deceived by someone else. Who could that be? Well, who was still alive and who had been the lover and presumably the one to receive all of Baudouin Rousseau's property now that he was dead? Mme. D'aubigne! So they went looking for her."

"You think Mme. D'aubigne knew the diamonds had been traded for a painting?"

"I think she suspected it. Or perhaps, M. Rousseau actually told her during a period when the pain killing drugs he used had put him into foolish spirits. In any event, she realized that it would only take time before Bouvier and Chevalier got around to her. So she telephoned François Chiappe. Mme. D'aubigne told Chiappe all that had transpired at Baudouin's Rousseau's apartment the night of M. Rousseau's death. She knew Chiappe would kill all involved. So, I expect she misled him as to her own involvement. Perhaps she claimed to have learned of the events, afterward. In any event, Chiappe reacted to her information and killed both Bouvier and Chevalier."

"So Chiappe killed her, anyway?"

"Exactly. Her having knowledge of all that had transpired at Baudouin Rousseau's apartment meant, despite her denials, that she had been there. He would not have allowed her to escape his retribution."

"So Baudouin Rousseau scammed Bouvier, Chevalier and Mme. D'aubigne about the diamonds to keep them thinking the diamonds still existed, when in fact they had been sold?"

"Exactly," he returned. "Why was that imperative? To ensure Baudouin Rousseau's plan would succeed. What plan, you may ask? The plan to make certain Mme. Rousseau ended up with the painting traded for the diamonds so she could live out her life in the luxury he so badly wanted for her." Monet fell silent for several seconds to gloat at me. "Now you see why it is a fool's folly to toy with me? My brilliance is unsurpassed."

The egotistical bastard!

"Then tell me what painting is hidden—assuming your brilliant theory holds water?" I goaded.

He made a vague movement with one hand. "I do not know that yet. But I expect to before this night is over. Then…" Monet stopped abruptly, as if an arresting finger had been pressed against his lips. After a thoughtful moment he said, "Do you see how this is all coming together?"

"More or less."

Monet glanced towards the heavens. "I think less more than more," he muttered. "It means Maryse Rousseau—who, as I told you, hired Bouvier and Chevalier to steal the painting—also knew, at the time of her husband's death, that the diamonds had been swapped for that painting."

"But if you knew that Chiappe's men had killed Bouvier and Chevalier, why am I here?"

"I did not know that. I still do not *know* that. I cannot prove any of what I have said. Everything is pure surmise based upon the current evidence and what you have just told me." He tapped the side of his nose. "But I know I am correct. I am never wrong."

"If you're never wrong, how is it I've been arrested twice and forced to endure…"

"But I have not finished my theory," he interposed. "When I received the initial Forensic Report on Baudouin Rousseau, you were present. Therefore you heard he was drugged via syringe injections. Since we now know that Molyneux was part of the robbery, we must also assume he was in Baudouin Rousseau's apartment when M. Rousseau died, therefore it was he who made those fatal injections."

"But if Molyneux did it, how can you accuse Maryse Rousseau?"

Monet studied me from under narrowed brows. "Her being there, when her husband died, means she shared culpability for the mercy killing. A wife might know about an assisted suicide. She might even refrain from reporting what was planned because of her husband's suffering. Knowing about a mercy killing and doing nothing to prevent it is mute action to murder. But, I—being a warm hearted humanitarian with a compassionate nature—would never consider arresting such a woman as long as she was not a witness to the act."

I wagged my head. "I don't believe it."

"That does not surprise me. But I tell you they were all there. Baudouin, Mme. Rousseau and Molyneux."

"I mean you regarding yourself as a warm-hearted humanitarian!"

"I am also a bulldog when it comes to prosecuting those who are guilty, or who interrupt me!" he roared.

His gloating had gotten the best of me. So I tossed out a red herring for him to chase. "What if I told you that Baudouin's death was caused by a self-inflicted overdose?"

"I would call you a liar."

"But it was."

His head wagged. "Nonsense! Baudouin Rousseau knew he had to die as he did in order to protect his wife's future."

"Why would Molyneux help? What was in it for him if Maryse was to get the painting?"

"Do you have no experience with women?"

"Not as much as I would like, I admit. But..."

"Michele Molyneux intended to marry Mme. Rousseau after her husband died. I suspect the idea was supported by M. Rousseau. Regardless, by marrying Mme. Rousseau, Molyneux would share equally in her fortunes."

"So Molyneux also knew the diamonds do not exist?"

"No. Like the other three, he believed the diamonds were still somewhere to be found. Unlike the other three, he had been told by M. Rousseau that Mme. Rousseau had possession of those diamonds. You see, until there was a marriage between Molyneux and Mme. Rousseau, there was always the chance that Molyneux might take the painting and dispose of it on his own. Therefore, the secret had to remain between Mme. Rousseau and her husband."

"Why would Molyneux not attempt to take his share of the diamonds to sell on his own?"

"I will come to that."

"Then explain Baudouin's and Maryse's divorce," I said. "Why would Baudouin want Maryse to benefit when he was having a love affair with Mme. D'aubigne? Isn't it more likely he would want his current lover to have the painting?"

The Chief Inspector chuckled softly. "The divorce was a sham."

"It can't be. You, yourself, told me about the public record filing."

"There was a filing just as I described," Monet responded impatiently. "It was genuine to the extent that divorce proceedings had legally been started. But in actuality, the divorce was a blind to separate Mme. Rousseau from the painting in the eyes of the others. Remember, the plan was to make everyone—except Mme. Rousseau—think M. Rousseau had taken the secret of the diamonds with him to his grave. If that premise is not true, why had the divorce been delayed for months?"

"Delayed? Maryse told me she and her husband were waiting for a court date."

"For over three months? Nonsense! They could've gotten a divorce hearing within a few weeks. The delay was purposeful so Mme. Rousseau would be able to inherit her husband's estate as his wife when he died. And thereby inherit the painting which she would later, discretely, sell."

Again, what he said made sense. The initial court appearance should not have taken months. Especially when the parties involved had agreed on everything.

"Okay," I said. "Maybe I buy that. But if I stole sixty million in diamonds, why would I risk handing the whole bundle over to Baudouin Rousseau? Why wouldn't I demand my share of the stones and sell the goods on my own?"

"You would have, because you are an idiot. But this brings us back to your question concerning Dr. Molyneux selling the diamonds. You see, each diamond is laser-etched with its own serial number. Getting rid of such easily identifiable stones would require special contacts. Baudouin Rousseau was the only one of the thieves who had those connections."

It all made sense except the delay. "But why wait three months after the diamond theft to gather for the split?"

"Ah, there you have finally asked an intelligent question," replied Monet. "Baudouin told the others it would take him three months to dispose of the stones." The Chief Inspector's lips twitched. "Conceivably, it could have taken that long. But the real reason Baudouin selected that timeframe was because he had three months to live. His physician had told him as much. How do I know this? I spoke to his doctor. Why did M. Rousseau wait that amount of time? Because, like all of us, he wanted to live as long as possible. At whatever point he could no longer endure the pain, he intended to summon his followers and what happened would happen."

"Then it follows that Chiappe killed Molyneux after M. D'aubigne told Chiappe about Baudouin's death."

"I do not think so. The method of death was such that I suspect it is far more likely Mme. Rousseau ran him down."

"But if she was going to marry him…"

"Initially, I think she intended to. But, for whatever absurd reason, she changed her mind and set her cap for you—or at least pretended to." He waggled a finger at me. "I find her interest in you very suspicious as well as being in questionable taste."

Whether Maryse actually intended marrying me or not—and from personal experience that idea did sound absurd—there was undeniable plausibility in what Monet had claimed about Molyneux's death. The car had struck and charged back into traffic as if the tactic was routine. Maryse, as a former race-car driver would have accomplished such a feat easily.

"You are probably wondering why Molyneux was able to inject M. Rousseau with that fatal cocktail of drugs without the others objecting," suggested Monet.

"Molyneux and Baudouin scammed the others into thinking the drugs were a truth serum."

Again his eyebrows shot up. "You came by that deduction, how?"

"Your officer said the coroner had suggested it, when she brought you the autopsy report."

"Ah, yes," he murmured, again looking at me as if I had grown brains. "Very clever of you to formulate that theory based upon so little information."

I shrugged. "It's a gift."

One of his thick eyebrows drooped slightly, at my brag. "Then explain why you were necessary at the apartment, that night?"

"As you suggested, I was the fall-guy."

"Yes, but who made you the fall-guy?"

"Molyneux, I suppose."

He made an assenting gesture with one hand. "Perhaps I have been underestimating you." Then he smirked, "But let us test that premise. How did Molyneux get M. Rousseau's body over the balcony railing? Bearing in mind that M. Rousseau was a tall man who still was—despite his illness—quite heavy."

"He must've gotten help from the others."

"He did. But who helped him?"

"Bouvier or Chevalier, I suppose. They're quite strong."

His head wagged. "Why would they help after Molyneux killed their golden goose?"

That meant it was either Maryse or Mme. D'aubigne who had helped. I shuddered thinking how cold-blooded such an act would be, considering each woman's relationship with Rousseau.

"Then I guess that only leaves the women," I returned.

He shrugged. "One woman. Remember, Mme. D'aubigne had also been cheated by Baudouin Rousseau. So why would she assist? Obviously, she would not. Therefore it was Mme. Rousseau. There can be no other conclusion."

I knew from Monet's statements to Maryse in her flat that Baudouin Rousseau had been killed by the drugs. So it was not like she was helping push her husband to his death. But, I still found it sickening that a woman would help dump her husband's body over a railing and watch it fall ten stories.

"If Molyneux and Baudouin had planned for Baudouin to die that night, a fall guy would have been essential to protect the survivors—that makes sense," I said. "Molyneux would've understood that. But nobody but Maryse and René knew about René ordering me to go to Baudouin Rousseau's apartment. Only they knew about the phone message."

"But Molyneux did know. It was he who left the message."

"How can you possibly know that?"

He shrugged. "Simple reasoning. Mme. Rousseau lured you to lunch —so you would be convinced her husband had witnessed the event. Then, as she and Molyneux planned, Molyneux telephoned René D'aubigne and left the message—not as M. Rousseau but as himself on behalf of M. Rousseau."

"But René denied there was a message."

"Because M. D'aubigne was told to do so."

"But…"

"Remember," said Monet, "René was not part of this dangerous affair. So, to gain his cooperation Molyneux used subterfuge. He told René you were Mme. D'aubigne's lover. Upon hearing that, René was eager to help. Molyneux promised you would be put into the merciless hands of a killer—Baudouin Rousseau—for trifling with Mme. Rousseau, and you would never be heard from again if M. D'aubigne followed Molyneux's instructions."

I wagged my head. "René hated his wife. Why would he care who was bedding her?"

"M. D'aubigne hated his wife because she was unfaithful and cold to him—but for no other reason. So getting even with her lover suited him perfectly. Molyneux told M. D'aubigne to pressure you into going and later, should the police call, to deny all of it. This, so no one involved in your death would be compromised. Naturally, René readily agreed to it."

"But if you knew he had done that…"

"As I told you this is nothing but surmise. I, indeed, suspected many things. I created dozens of scenarios. I investigated each of those possibilities thoroughly, in relation to M. Rousseau's murder. But until today—when Mme. D'aubigne's body was found—I did not have the necessary proof to determine which scenario was the correct one. Once I recognized her from the diamond heist, it all fell into place—including the subsequent killings."

"I don't understand why Molyneux treated me after Bouvier and Chevalier beat me up."

"Why would he not?" returned Monet. "Molyneux had nothing against you, personally. Yes, he envied your relationship with Mme. Rousseau. But he was also a physician. I think he felt tremendous pity for you." The Chief Inspector got up and came around the desk. Then he sat on its edge, grinning at me. "There is one thing yet to resolve. Where did you hide the canvas after you removed it from the frame?"

You are probably thinking, why doesn't the idiot just own up and tell the truth? It's not like Maryse deserved any consideration. Not after listening to Monet. And I cannot argue with your reasoning. But once you start lying it is extremely hard to stop. Particularly, when the liar does not like the intended recipient of the falsehood.

"I guess there's no sense holding out on you," I told him.

He licked his lips, greedily. "I will get a promotion for this."

"I don't know where the painting is."

Monet jumped up roaring, "But you have to know! I know you took it from the frame!"

"I did. But I heard Bouvier and Chevalier coming back as I was dumping the frame in Chevalier's apartment. So I hid in Molyneux's flat —and later heard what I heard. I did not come out until I knew the killers were gone."

"And?"

"I'd left the canvas in Bouvier's flat. When I went back in there, it was gone."

His expression became miserable. "You idiot! How could you do such a stupid thing?"

"It wasn't planned, I swear."

He stalked back behind his desk. "Of all the ridiculous, inept…"

A uniformed officer entered. "Sir?"

Monet pointed at me. "Turn that idiot loose and then take him to his clothes. I can't stand the sight of him!"

"The feeling is mutual, Chief Inspector," I chimed.

My words brought crimson to Monet's cheeks. "Then we shall not say goodbye when I have you deported."

Chapter 12
Stewing with the Corsican Mafia

The legal age of consent in France is eighteen. That, of course, assumes the consenters are both of sound mind. However, girls between the ages of fifteen and seventeen can marry with the consent of at least one parent. The theory behind limiting parental approval for marriage to just one parent is, indeed, necessary in France. Nearly eight million French citizens live without a partner. Of those, over one million are divorcees, and the number is growing. Considering my 'relationship' with Maryse Rousseau, and Monet's latest revelations concerning her, I can understand the French divorce rate. No man in his right mind would even consider marrying a French woman.

As I was hurrying away from 11 rue des Saussaies and the irascible Chief Inspector Claude Monet, a gray Peugeot screeched to a stop at the curb. Two men I had never seen before—each in dark suits—got out of its rear compartment, and blocked my path. The murky stains on their ties and the garlic emanating from their bodies indicated both men were not strangers to linguini with clam sauce. And because they were nearly as wide as they were tall, I assumed the pair ate it often, and in liberal quantities. Curiously, one had a face livid with deep, fresh scratches. It was as if some terrified woman had clawed him to escape whatever plans he had made for her.

"I donated at the office," I told them.

Unfortunately, this feeble attempt at humor resulted in both men casually pulling aside their coats to reveal holstered pistols.

"On the other hand, a few Euros shouldn't break me," I muttered. "Is this a mugging? Or are you police officers collecting for Chief Inspector Monet's pension fund? Either way, I'm the cooperative type."

"M. Chiappe wants words wit' you," one of the men said.

My knees buckled. If one of them had not grabbed me by my hair and held me up like a marionette, my chin would have hit the sidewalk.

There were only two reasons the leader of the Corsican Mafia would want 'words' with me. One, because he intended to kill me for Baudouin Rousseau's death and thereby remedy the stitched-up-hole-in-my-ass mistake. Or, two, he was upset over the forgeries his wife purchased from Avoyelles, and Avoyelles—hoping to save his own skin—had named me as the artist. Either way, I was a dead man!

"I swear to God," I whimpered, trying to stiffen legs and spine. "I had nothing to do with what happened to Baudouin Rousseau."

"In the car," one of them growled.

"If it's the paintings, I had no idea they were to be sold," I begged.

The other man grabbed my arm like a vice. "M. Chiappe don't like waitin'."

"Killing me won't solve anything!" I protested.

"Car!" the first shouted, shoving me toward the vehicle.

There was no escape. So when they literally tossed me into the rear seat of the Peugeot, I made no attempt to escape. Where could I go that bullets could not follow?

Sitting behind the vehicle's steering wheel was a thickset, dark-complected fellow. He glanced back and grinned, as my abductors settled on either side of me.

"I don't suppose there's time to find a priest?" I asked. "I'd like to make a quick confession before—you know."

"No priest can help you," the driver returned, grimly.

The Peugeot pulled away from the curb and quickly melded into traffic. The guy on my left was sucking food residue from between his teeth, and wheezing wine vapors. The one on my right was belching garlic and whistling through his nose.

"Where are we going?" I asked.

"L'Ondine Café," slurped the one on my left.

"M. Chiappe don't like his lunch late," chimed the driver.

"No," said the one on my right, with a grim wag of his dark head. "Don't like it late, at all."

"So that's it," I said, to the vaporous pair. I let go a loud laugh of relief. "Food. I don't know how M. Chiappe found out about my meager culinary repertoire. But I'm willing to weigh in on behalf of his palate. Would he enjoy Brochettes de Boeuf? I find a glass of Malbec is heavenly with that. Or, if he prefers fish, I create a mean Flounder Roulades Florentine. I prefer that with a bottle of Viognier. If there's a market along the way, I don't mind spending a few minutes shopping."

"Shuttup!" shouted the driver.

So much for light chatter on the culinary front.

Several minutes later there was an explosive noise from the front seat. This was immediately followed by a groaning sigh of relief from the same vicinity. Instantly, the men on either side of me rolled down their respective windows, and frantically tilted toward the incoming breeze.

For a split second I did not realize my danger. Then it hit me, face on. In fact, if I had been smoking, the car would have exploded. As it was being trapped between the tooth-sucker and the nose whistler, I caught the full force of the driver's thoroughly revolting outpouring of methane.

For a moment time seemed to stand still. Then my life quickly passed before my eyes. A moment later my vision blurred. Then everything went black.

By the time I recovered, we were headed east on Rue des Saussaies. At Rue Montalivet the car drifted right for a block and then turned onto Rue de Duras. When we reached Rue du Faubourg Saint-Honoré the vehicle got into the right lane and took a right at Rue Royale. Two blocks later, we hung a right at Place de la Concorde. From there we continued on until we reached Quai d'Orsay. After turning onto it we did a slight right at Voie sur Berge Rive Gauche. Whereupon we caught Quai Branly and followed it to Boulevard de Grenélle. Once on it we quickly slid into the right lane until we reached Rue de la Croix Nivert. The car hung a right there and two blocks along took a sharp left onto Rue de l'Amiral Roussin. Minutes after that, the Peugeot rolled to a stop in front of L'Ondine Café; a blonde stone building with a large neon sign just above its double-doors.

A nudge in the ribs later and I was being escorted into the restaurant.

I walked across a large dining room furnished with white-cloth covered mahogany tables, and red leather upholstered booths. There was only one customer in the place. He was a white-haired, elegantly-dressed gentleman. He sat at a table near the rear of the restaurant, not far from the swinging doors to the kitchen.

The customer wore a blue suit with a red carnation in the lapel. Based upon his hair color and sallow complexion, he looked to be about seventy years of age. He was slightly built and wore thick glasses. As my escorts and I drew near to him, I recognized the elderly man from his photos in various news magazines. He was François Chiappe.

Standing in a semi-circle beyond Chiappe were half a dozen men in suits cut from the same black cloth. Each of them watched me as if I might be a venomous snake, crawling from a lunchbox.

"Your guest, M. Chiappe," announced one of my escorts.

The white haired man did not respond. His chin was resting upon his breast and his eyes were closed. From the steady drone coming through his nasal passages, the elderly fellow was asleep.

"Your guest, M. Chiappe," repeated my escort.

The Mafia Don raised his head with a jerk. Then his dark eyes fluttered open. Upon seeing my scratch-faced escort, he twisted in his chair to look over at me.

"Do you know who I am?" he asked, in thickly accented English.

I nodded. "But I'm not the grudge-holding type, M. Chiappe."

François Chiappe blinked as if my French was incomprehensible. Then he thrust a bony, wrinkled finger at me. "You got somethin' against me?"

I gave my head a fervent wag. "The stitches in my ass barely pull."

He glared at the pair who had escorted me in. "Did I tell you to stitch up his ass, for Christ's sake?"

"No, M. Chiappe!" both men chimed.

"Then what in hell did you do it for?" The Mafia Don demanded.

"We didn't do nothin' to him, M. Chiappe!" my escorts vowed, in unison.

The mobster glowered back at me. "What in hell are you playing at?"

"Please let me explain about Cesar Avoyelles," I begged. "I had no idea he was selling paintings to your wife. As God is my witness, M. Chiappe, I would've cut my own throat rather than disappoint her."

This time the gangster got to his feet, again staring accusingly at the pair who had escorted me in, and pointing an accusing finger at me. "When was he with my wife? Is he the one who's been screwing her?"

"M. Chiappe, I swear on my mother's eyes it never happened!" pleaded the escort on my left.

"On my son's life, M. Chiappe, she's never been near him," enjoined the scratched escort.

Again, Chiappe glared at me. "What in hell's wrong with you?"

"Nothing!" I blurted. "The ass thing came about when your people shot me. That caused my hand to slide inside the back of Maryse's pants. It was just an impulse. I apologized for doing it. But then, she said she hadn't really meant to complain…."

François Chiappe blinked and again glared at my escorts. "You let him cop a feel from my wife?"

"It couldn't have happened, M. Chiappe!" protested my escorts.

Chiappe turned to look at the men behind him. "Whichever one of you shot this idiot in the ass when he was groping my wife, is going to get his ears boxed!"

There was a frantic denial from all addressed.

François Chiappe slowly turned back to me. "I know my wife gets a little flirtatious after a couple glasses of wine, but no way does that give you the right to paw."

I felt an immediate pain in the center of my chest, and my hand gripped my shirt. "I wouldn't! Not if somebody put a gun to my head, I swear! I was talking about Maryse."

"That's who I'm talking about!" shouted the gangster.

I pointed a finger at him. "You're married to Maryse Rousseau, too?"

"No!" Chiappe roared. "I'm married to Maryse Chiappe!" He rubber-necked from man to man, demanding of his people. "What in hell did you do to this idiot? It's like his brains are scrambled."

After another round of apologies and denials, the elderly man tilted toward me and asked, "You are Stuart S. Stuart, aren't you?"

I nodded. "Unless you're thinking I'm my uncle, M. Chiappe."

His arms rose and fell, with exasperation. "How in hell can you be your own uncle?"

"I'm not. But my name is the same as his. Only he's in Siberia with some blonde bimbo with plastic boobs. But believe me when I say, after what I've been through, I have no qualms about delivering his thieving ass to you on a platter."

"Again, with the ass!" The mobster spread his arms in a beseeching gesture. "Get it through your head! I had nothing to do with your ass!"

At first I wanted to disbelieve François Chiappe. But why would he lie about his people shooting me? He was the head of the Corsican Mafia. He was accountable to no one. But if his people had not shot me, who had?

"Anything you say!" I told him, desperately fanning my hands as if to erase everything I had said. "And you certainly had no part in what caused me to pass out on the drive over here."

Once more he looked at my escorts. "I told you to bring him to me, not beat the hell out of him!"

"We never laid a glove on him, M. Chiappe!" one escort protested.

"Not a finger, M. Chiappe," pleaded the other. "He looked like that when we grabbed him."

The mobster glared back at me. "I politely ask you here for a little discussion and you run me up a wall? You do that again and I'm gonna' put you in a box and bury you so deep that nobody but nobody will ever find you!"

"It was the driver," I explained. "He cut one that must've been mother of all flatulent-outbreaks."

François Chiappe pointed to the chair across the table. "Put the lunatic there. And keep an eye on the bastard," he ordered. "He's not right in the head."

A nudge from behind pushed me over to the chair. Another dropped me into it.

"Do you know why I wanted to speak with you?" demanded the Mafia Don, as he resumed his seat.

I wagged my head. "But I'm praying I won't become a subterranean fixture."

A waiter appeared on silent feet and put a place-setting in front of me. He carefully positioned plates and goblets before hurrying off. As he departed another waiter appeared with a bottle of wine. He partially filled my host's glass and waited. The elderly fellow tasted the vintage and then nodded his approval. Then, the waiter filled the Mafia Don's glass before scurrying around the table to do the same for me. I tasted the red wine and was surprised at its unique flavors of fruits and vanilla.

"Is okay?" the waiter asked, in broken English.

"As long as it isn't poisoned," I whispered back.

The fellow set the bottle near my host, and then hurried off.

"Patrimonio," the gangster declared, indicating the bottle with a tilt of his head. "From my vineyard. Do you know Patrimonio?"

I wagged my head. "I've never gotten anybody pregnant."

"I'm talking about the wine, for Christ's sake!" He reached over and tapped the side of the bottle. "This one aged four years in my cellar after coming from my winery."

"Exotic flavor," I returned, setting down the glass. Considering his latest outburst and his previous threat to bury me, I could not help but ask, "Am I going to spend any time in your cellar?"

François Chiappe frowned. "What for?"

I fanned the air with both hands, again. "No special reason."

He tilted across the table, impatiently. "This isn't the ass thing, again, is it?"

"No," I said giving my head a determined shake. "Absolutely not!"

"What do you know about me?" he asked, making a vague gesture as he eased back in his chair.

"Just that you're a—a businessman."

"A businessman?" he chuckled, glancing around at his men. "He says I'm a businessman."

"More or less," I added, as his guards chuckled.

The elderly gangster adjusted the lay of his expensive suit and repeated my 'businessman' comment softly beneath his breath as if it amused him no end. "Well, we'll have a business lunch. Then we'll talk some business. How's that sound?"

"I hope it's not linguini in clam sauce," I muttered. "I've experienced about all I can take of that."

"No," the mobster returned, signaling my escorts to back away. *"U Tianu d'Agnellu Incu u Castagne."*

Lamb stew was not my favorite meal. But it was better than bad-smelling Béarnaise sauce from a dumpster deposit, or body expulsions in closed cars. I quickly nodded my appreciation.

I looked around wondering if what I was seeing might follow me to my grave. The walls were shining mahogany. The ceiling was a collection of copper panels, embossed with images of grapes on vines. The floor was carpeted in a blood hue but without pattern. When my eyes returned to François Chiappe, his chin was again on his breast. He was snoring.

"Very elegant restaurant," I told the men watching me. "Very comfortable. Under any other circumstance, I'd love being here. In fact, if I live through dessert I'm sure I'll be back."

They found no humor in my nervous remark.

My nose caught the enticing scent of lamb, chestnuts, onion, garlic, tomatoes and olive oil. Instantly, my salivary glands went into high gear. Not only was I ready to eat, but I had a sudden urge to marry the chef.

I gave another try for laughs with, "In fact, if the ambrosia coming from the kitchen is an example of what is usually served, I'm ready to move in."

The men watching me were not amused by that, either.

One of the waiters reappeared. This time he was carrying a porcelain tureen. From this vessel, he ladled large portions of thick, steaming stew onto our plates. Then he set the tureen on the table, and departed.

François Chiappe jerked awake. Seeing the food, he placed the cloth napkin adjacent to his plate upon his lap.

"Eat," he growled.

I dug in, immediately—not worrying about what I might spill or where. Each bite passing my lips was heavenly! If this was going to be my last meal, so be it! For the first time in weeks, I was eating food worthy of France.

"I was born in Porto-Vecchio," Chiappe declared, between bites. "My father was a fisherman. He was a hard worker. But, then, it was a hard life. He wanted me to follow in his path. But I chose another one." The Mafia Don paused a moment as if weighing issues. "He cursed my decision 'til the day he died."

"My father wanted me to be a Podiatrist," I enjoined.

The gangster looked over at me in confusion. "A what?"

"Foot doctor," I returned. "But I've never been big on feet. How about you?"

He gave me a bewildered stare. "I just got two, like everybody else."

"Do you miss your home island?" I asked, hoping to shift the topic to something he would enjoy discussing.

He nodded. "But it ain't there no more."

"Corsica?" I scoffed.

"Damn tourists. They've taken over everything." He set down his fork and then looked at me steadily. "You're giving me indigestion. So, it's time we get to the point. Where in hell's the Van Gogh?"

My stomach knotted. Was Françoise Chiappe cutting in on Avoyelles' action, intending me to mass-produce Van Gogh's? As much as I had enjoyed the stew it took me several tries to swallow what was in my mouth.

"I'm not sure I understand," I croaked. "I have a Matisse in the works. No Van Gogh."

His upper lip twisted slightly into a bone-chilling snarl. "Don't test my patience, M. Stuart. Baudouin Rousseau traded the Falize diamonds for a Van Gogh. Where is it?"

So much for enjoying lunch.

You are probably thinking the worst about Maryse Rousseau. And I could not agree more. Only she knew I had the painting that Bouvier and Chevalier had stolen. Only she knew that beneath its tempura covering was a Van Gogh. Only she could have shared the fact that I possessed a Van Gogh with François Chiappe. The scratched face on one of my escorts proved that either she had been taken hostage by them, or Mme. D'aubigne had met her fate at their hands. So why had Maryse been so dead against me recovering the painting? Simple. Reverse psychology.

"I am not an expert on Van Gogh's, M. Chiappe," I told him. "It looked like a Van Gogh – based upon the small amount of canvas I exposed. But it might be something else."

The impatience in his tone was clear. "I didn't ask your opinion. I asked where it was!"

I tried to give him a smile. But, the right side of my lips failed to move. "I don't have it with me."

François Chiappe glanced at one of the men nearby. The fellow calmly walked over and, with a backhanded swing, struck my face.

Instantly, I tasted blood. Just as quickly I had an urge to vomit—among other things. But I feigned calm by crossing my legs and arms, and leaning back in my chair. So far, the whiter than white test was holding up. But its future looked pretty grim from where I was sitting.

"I hid it," I told Chiappe, wiping the blood from my mouth on my shirt sleeve.

"Where?" he gritted.

At this moment you, no doubt, would have turned over the painting to this murderer-of-murderers and settled for life as a failed artist, rather than being a failed artist who was also rich but very dead—roughly speaking. Considering the circumstances, again I must agree with you. After all, the only reason for hiding the Van Gogh was to please Maryse Rousseau.

"It's in Michele Molyneux's flat," I replied. "Behind the ventilator grill."

François Chiappe made a remark in Corsican to a man near him. That fellow, in turn, jerked out a cellular phone and quickly moved off.

"Do you want dessert?" the Mafia Don asked. "The chef prepared *Mendiant au Chocolat Blanc.*"

As much as I loved white chocolate with walnuts, dates, and orange-zest I decided any more pressure from my stomach might cause an uncontrollable reaction—particularly if there was another bout of violence.

"No thanks," I returned. "I don't like to overstay my welcome."

He took out a large, engraved, silver cigarette case and opened it. The expensive container's gold-plated interior was empty. One of the men behind him withdrew a crumpled pack from his suit and sloughed a cigarette up so Chiappe could grab it. Then another man came forward with a lighter in flame and lit the cigarette, as its filter reached the mobster's mouth. The Mafia Don filled his lungs, and then coughed out a cloud of smoke.

"I'm trying to quit," François Chiappe declared, giving the cigarette a disgusted look. "But after I eat, it's tough not to want one." Then he looked over at me. "I'm told you're an artist."

"Not everyone agrees." I shifted in the chair. But the movement of my backside on wood caused me to groan, as the stitches in my wounded backside stretched.

"What's wrong?" he asked. "The stew did not agree with you?"

"It's the stitches," I explained.

He glowered, "Christ, what did I tell you about that ass?"

"Sorry. Could I ask you something?"

He shrugged. "I can kill you only once."

"How did you know about the Van Gogh?"

He winked. "A little bird told me."

"Maryse?" I asked.

He nodded.

Well, if there was any doubt that settled it. "Frankly, I'm surprised Baudouin found a Van Gogh."

"Baudouin was a smart man," returned the gangster.

"I take it you will be placing it in your collection?"

"My wife likes Van Gogh. Personally, I don't see it. The guy was a nutcase—like you." He took another drag on the cigarette. The smoke ebbed and flowed without a cough, this time. "How is Maryse taking her husband's death?"

"Not as good as I think she was expecting," I replied. "And recent news is going to dampen her spirits even further. But I'm sure she'll get over the financial disappointment, in time."

"*Femme rit quand elle peut et pleure quand elle veut.*"

If any other person had said that, and I might've taken the remark about women crying when it suited them as a general slap against the female sex. But after what I now knew about Maryse, I accepted the Mafia Don's words as gospel—at least about her.

"I've arranged Baudouin's funeral," declared François Chiappe. "It was the least I could do. He was a good boy." He tilted across the table, confidentially. "I understand that you and Baudouin's wife are an item."

"Not in the sense of anything permanent or disgusting."

He waggled a finger. "Beautiful women aren't easy to come by—especially for a guy like you."

I said, "She wants me dead. But I'm reluctant to give in."

He made a vague movement with one hand. "Broads are like that. I've had three try to kill me. Stop taking it so seriously." He filled his lungs with smoke again, and then snuffed out the cigarette on his plate.

"Baudouin was going to be my successor. Consequently, I am very unhappy about his death. Things must be done."

I nodded, trying to look sympathetic, "Good help is so hard to bury."

He eased back folding his hands in prayer fashion. "You were arrested, after he was whacked. How'd that happen?"

"I had nothing to do with it, I swear. I went there under false pretenses and somebody hit me on the head. By the time I came to, he was dead and the cops were arresting me."

He gave one of my escorts a nod. A moment later I felt a hand at the back on my skull.

"It's still as big as a goose egg," the man behind me said.

Chiappe pointed a finger at me. "That bump on the head is probably causing your other problems. You should see a doctor before it gets any worse. What's Monet's take on Baudouin's hit?"

"You know him?" I asked, in surprise.

Chiappe smiled. "I know every cop in Paris. What's he say?"

"Monet's certain I didn't do it. I mean, I don't have a murderous bone in my body."

The Mafia Don frowned. "Are you saying I do?"

"Of course not!" I groaned, as the chest-pains returned. I grabbed at my shirt, let go a loud moan. "I'm certain you'd never hurt a fly."

Chiappe tilted toward the man nearest his right and said out of the side of his mouth, "Get your gun out—just in case. I think he's trying to tear off his clothes."

A moment later a very large and deadly pistol was pointed in my direction. Involuntarily, my digestive tract made room for dessert.

"Monet thinks it was Maryse Rousseau, doesn't he?" François Chiappe said.

"I, uh, actually several names were mentioned. But I think Monet favors Molyneux. It's a needle thing."

He thrust a warning finger at me. "One more time about your ass, and there won't even be memories of you!"

"I'm sorry, M. Chiappe," I returned. "What I meant to say is, syringe. I get a little excited, sometimes."

He eased back suddenly wrinkling his nose. "I can smell it."

"I suffer from hypoglycemia. But once my digestion gets to work on the stew, I'll be fine."

He pushed himself a bit farther away. "I think it already has."

Chiappe tilted toward the man holding the gun on me. "I want the safety off and your finger on the trigger, understand? Don't pull it unless he grabs for me. But be on your guard. I think this guy is about to go off his rocker."

The man who had hurried off with the cell-phone, returned. Again there was a brief conversation in Corsican between him, and Chiappe. Then the Mafia Don got to his feet looking more displeased than I thought possible.

"There was no painting!" he growled.

I jumped up in a panic. Immediately, I had a pistol against the end of my nose. "It has to be there!" I nasally exclaimed. "That's where I put it. Please believe me when I say I'm not lying."

"Dump his body in the Seine," hissed the François Chiappe.

"Wait!" I shouted. "Are you certain your man was at the right flat? You can always kill me. Let me go back there and look for it?"

"There was no mistake," snapped Chiappe. "Cesar Avoyelles was visiting Maryse Rousseau when my man got him on the phone. Between the two of them, they would've known which apartment to search."

"Avoyelles?" I croaked. Had the two of them taken it? He was no Mother Theresa and needed money, badly. Why chance a forged Matisse when a genuine Van Gogh could bring him twice as much with no risk. As for Maryse... "Maybe Avoyelles took it?" I suggested. "Did you think of that? A hundred million in painting is a terrible temptation for a man the banks are pushing for repayment. You could be killing me for nothing."

He made a disgusted face. "As bad as you stink, you're overdue for burial." Then it was like a light came on in the old gangsters eyes. He said something in Corsican to a couple of his men and they hurried away. Then François Chiappe's cold eyes returned to me. "There is no worse sin than to malign a friend."

"What friend?" I asked.

"Cesar Avoyelles."

"With respect, M. Chiappe he is neither my friend nor yours. Let me prove it to you. Let me go to Molyneux's flat and get the canvas. I promise I'll deliver it right back here."

"I didn't get to where I am by being stupid," the Mafia Don growled.

"Look at me?" I pleaded. "Do you honestly believe I'm stupid enough to think I could escape from you?"

"You couldn't find your ass with both hands—unless you used your nose." Chiappe hesitated a moment, then said to one of the men who had brought me there, "On second thought, take him back to Molyneux's flat—just to be certain. If it isn't there—put a round in his eye."

"You're going to kill me even if Avoyelles took it?" I whimpered. "The man is a crook. All those paintings he sold your wife are fakes. You don't have to believe me. Bring in an expert—besides Avoyelles. Have the paintings examined."

"They were examined!" growled François Chiappe.

"Why would I lie when I know it's going to upset you?" I countered. "Look, M. Chiappe… I know the paintings are fakes. I know because I painted the ones he sold your wife."

His face went white. Instantly, I realized the fatal mistake of making that last disclosure.

"You painted 'em?" he bellowed. "You know what I laid out for 'em?"

"It wasn't done on purpose," I begged. "My uncle made me do it. Not that he planned to defraud you. He didn't know who Avoyelles' customers were. I was just a kid at the time, wearing a red Speedo—with a built-in, never-used accessory."

The gangster nodded to the two thugs nearest him. They hurried off. Then Françoise Chiappe came over to me and slapped my face. "If what you say is true, painting those forgeries is the biggest mistake of your life —and the last. Take him back to Molyneux's flat. Make him show you where he put the Van Gogh."

"And if it is there, M. Chiappe?" asked the thug to whom the Mafia Don had given instructions.

"I don't wish to see M. Stuart again," returned the mobster. Then he shook a finger at me. "And don't think my wife isn't going to answer questions about you groping her ass!"

My two escorts came around and nudged me back the way we had come.

On the ride to Mme. Flaubert's Boarding house I pondered possibilities. I could try and escape as the car sped along. Or, I could leap out of Molyneux's third floor window once we got there. Or, I could just let them shoot me, afterward. Somehow the last option seemed the most practical and the least painful.

When the car stopped on the street in front of Mme. Flaubert's, the driver and the scratched-face escort went into the café to wait. The other escort propelled me into the boarding house, up three flights of stairs, and down the hall to Molyneux's flat.

When we arrived, the door was slightly ajar. I went in and looked around. The vent cover had been removed. The empty ventilator gaped like the maw of a feeding cod. Someone had, indeed, taken the Van Gogh.

On rubbery legs I went over and dropped to my knees in front of the vent. Then I stuck my head inside and peered down. Only empty blackness reflected back. Slowly, I pulled my head out and stood up.

"Is it there?" the thug asked.

I nodded. "But we'll need something like string and a hook to latch onto it," I lied. "It's slipped down the chute." Then I pointed to Molyneux's Gladstone bag. "There's probably something in his medical bag. Unless, of course, you can reach down far enough to grab it."

You might be wondering why I was stalling. After all, the situation was hopeless. He had a gun. Two of his armed consorts were in the café, and it would not take them long to hunt me down—should I manage to escape from this goon. But I was a desperate man. Never in my life had I expected to receive a bullet in an eye. Consequently, I was not looking forward to the one promised by François Chiappe.

As the thug picked at his teeth, I went over to the Gladstone bag. "I might be able to bend one of the suture needles into a hook," I said, opening it. "Then it's just a matter of going fishing."

"How much is that rag worth?" he asked, his curiosity growing.

"At least a hundred million—maybe more."

Thinking I would be preoccupied searching the bag for some time, he bent over to peer into the vent.

I grabbed up the Gladstone by its handles, and lunged at him. As his head came out of the vent, I banged the bag down upon his skull as hard as I could.

With a grunt the thug collapsed to the floor, unconscious.

With my heart thumping like there was no tomorrow—and in all likelihood there wasn't, for me—I dropped the bag and rushed out of the room.

If I changed clothes—something I definitely needed to do—I might be able to sneak out of Mme. Flaubert's through the fire exit, at the back. Then, if I could catch a taxi… Then, if I could get to the airport… Then, if I could buy a plane-ticket… Then if I could get on the plane… Then —I might be safe. But before I could hope for that, I had to get my passport and money.

When I got to Maryse's flat, I stormed inside. To my surprise, she was standing at the Chef's Rack putting a cover on one of several coffee-tins.

"So Avoyelles didn't lie about having a little meeting with his talkative bird, huh?" I shouted. "You're supposed to be in Nice, remember?"

She sniffed the air and made a face. "What did you step in?"

Curiously, I noticed a Plumber's Pot on the floor beside the Chef's Rack. Within its cast-iron pot was molten lead. Even more curiously, I noticed the sculpture she had asked me to store, lying upon the davenport, its massive lead base with resident sparklies removed—and gone.

"Your pal Chiappe ordered a hit on me because of the Van Gogh," I snapped.

Maryse frowned. "What Van Gogh?"

"The one I told you I found when I called you from Molyneux's."

A little embarrassed flush spread over her face. "You never told me about a Van Gogh."

"Right. I just stood up there babbling," I returned, rushing over to my suitcase. "I've got about five seconds to get the hell out of here with money and passport before that gangster comes down and shoots me in the eye. First my ass. Then my eye. If I get out of this alive, I am going home and I'm never coming back to France."

"What gangster?" she demanded.

I pointed at the ceiling. "The one upstairs in Molyneux's flat! How could you do that to me?"

She fanned the air in front of her face. "Stuart, I didn't do that to you."

I found my passport and the remainder of the cash from my last bank withdrawal. Then I stuffed everything into a pocket and headed for the door. "Don't write. Don't phone. Don't visit. As far as I'm concerned, we never met."

"What have I done?"

"There are too many things to list! But one in particular stands out. You never told me you used to be a race car driver! In fact, you told me you didn't know how to drive."

"I told you I didn't have a driving license. You just assumed I did not know how to drive."

"How can you be a race car driver and not have a driving license?"

"I had a license then. I don't now."

"Keeping half of a secret is the same as lying, Maryse!"

"Stuart you're not thinking straight because you are frightened."

"For your information, after what I've been through these past few days, nothing scares me!"

As I started out into the hallway, René D'aubigne blocked my path. He was holding a pistol with one hand. His other gripped a huge blood-spot covering the front of his shirt. There were deep, fresh claw-marks across his face.

"Except a pissed-off guy with a gun and blood running out of his belly-button," I added.

"Where is it?" he growled, backing me into the room.

"Where's what?" Maryse asked, one of her hands going protectively to the coffee cans.

"The Van Gogh," he gurgled.

I looked over at Maryse in disbelief. "Who in hell haven't you told?"

"I didn't tell anyone because I didn't know about it!" she shouted back, her voice pained with resentment.

"Give me the Van Gogh!" René gritted.

"Cesar Avoyelles has it," I told him. "But you'd better be quick. Françoise Chiappe sent a few men after your pal."

René blinked, dully. "When?"

"Cesar doesn't have it," enjoined Maryse. "He said someone had gotten to the heating duct before him."

"He's lying!" I declared.

Maryse crept toward René cooing, "Let me get you a doctor, René. If you don't do something soon, you'll die."

"We're all going to die!" he shouted at her. Then he looked over at me cackling softly, as bits of bloody phlegm collected at the corners of his mouth. "You couldn't stop sniffing around after Maryse, could you?"

"I wouldn't put it that way," I returned.

"You still don't get it do you?" he coughed. "She set you up. She and her husband set us all up. Played us for suckers."

"Don't listen to him, Stuart," she pleaded.

"We pulled the Falize job," continued René. "Then Baudouin took the diamonds to sell. Only he never sold them. He traded them for that damn Van Gogh—Maryse told me all about it."

I pointed at René and said to her, "Never told him, huh?"

"He's talking about Reese, Stuart."

"But Maryse knew different," René gurgled on. "She sent Bouvier and Chevalier to Baudouin's apartment to get the abstract." He coughed, sending a mist of blood from his mouth. His eyes dropped down to his bloody belly. "Bouvier and Chevalier were supposed to meet up with us this afternoon. Only she ran out on me, last night—to fink to Chiappe about Baudouin's death. We were going to sell the Van Gogh in Nice. That's when Chiappe's men started shooting. I got even with her for that." He looked up at me and forced a bloody grin. "I'll be okay. All I have to do is get the Van Gogh."

I could see René was dying. Dying men usually don't tell lies. At least that's how the film-scripts read. So I asked, "Are you Buji? You drove the getaway car?"

He gave a wobbly nod.

"You were upstairs in Molyneux's flat discussing what to do about Baudouin Rousseau?" I pressed.

Another nod. "Maryse was right. She said I was as good as dead."

"Let me call an ambulance before it's too late, René," Maryse urged.

"Him you offer doctors. But when I was shot in the ass… 'Oh, that was nothing'!" I snapped.

He pointed at Maryse. "She arrived at Baudouin's flat just before we left. Did she tell you she helped Molyneux toss Baudouin over the railing?"

Despite Monet's previously accurate surmise of the event, I could not help but give Maryse a horrified look.

"My husband was already dead, Stuart," she murmured. "Michele said we had to do it otherwise you would be arrested. Try to understand. I did what I did to protect you."

I scoffed, "What you really mean is, Molyneux had you help him toss your dead husband's body over the railing to make it look like murder so I would be blamed! Then you and your joy-toy left me lying on the floor, holding the bag."

"When we were leaving, Michele told me we had to abandon you otherwise we would all be killed by Chiappe," she returned. "When I insisted we take you with, he began shouting. Then everything went black.

When I awoke, I was here in my flat. My head hurt. I had a terrible lump on it. Michele was with me. I don't remember anything about what happened."

"You could have told Monet I was innocent," I shouted at her.

"Tell him what?" she returned. "You were questioned and released before I even knew you'd been arrested. After that, what difference did it make?"

"It might've kept me from being number one on Chiappe's hit-list!" I snapped. "He says he didn't order me shot, but the way everybody's lied to me I'm thinking he took his cue from you."

René coughed up a clot of blood. "That was me who shot you, I am pleased to say. I was trying to blow your balls off. Both Mme. Cossette Fortescue and Dr. Molyneux told me you were making love to my wife. I could tolerate Maryse being involved with another Frenchman. But an American? Never!"

"I've never met your wife—not alive," I protested.

He smirked at me. "Since you no longer have the Van Gogh, it's dying time."

"René, can't we talk about this?" I pleaded.

Heavy footsteps clattered in the hallway. René jerked toward the sound. A moment later, Rene fired. Then there were two shots from the hallway. René collapsed to the floor. Then the gangster I had hit with Molyneux's bag staggered into her flat, a huge blood-spot forming at the center of his chest, where René had shot him. He fired another round into René's head and then pointed the gun at me. But as the weapon discharged, he toppled forward.

The round burned my shoulder and I spun away in pain. When I turned back, Maryse was squatting beside both men.

"They're dead," she declared, standing up.

"Get used to seeing bodies," I told her. "The way my luck's been going my funeral is next on your to-do list."

She rushed over to me. "Stuart, we'll get away before Monet arrives. My car is just a few blocks away."

"Now you admit to owning a car? Somehow, I don't think I can trust you."

She flung her arms around my neck. "I'm sorry I lied to you."

I shoved her away from me. "Did your husband actually find a genuine Van Gogh?"

"Of course not. It was a forgery Avoyelles arranged it as insurance—in case Chiappe demanded a cut of the diamonds. I would claim Baudouin had traded them for it and give it to him."

"But it's gone. Why did Avoyelles take it from where I'd hidden it if it was a phony?"

"I told you, he didn't. I heard him tell someone who called that he would go up and look for it. When he came back down, he was again on the phone telling that same person the vent cover had been removed and the painting was gone."

"Then you must have it!"

Maryse pointed to the debased sculpture. "I have the diamonds. They were cast into the lead base." Then she pointed to the coffee tins. "I melted the lead and scooped them out with a strainer. The diamonds are in the tins, now."

"Bouvier and Chevalier were beating the crap out of me and I had those damn diamonds all the time?"

"You weren't supposed to get hurt."

"I could have been killed!"

"We'll leave Paris and start over. I made a deal with the insurer. I give them the diamonds and they give me five million as a recovery fee. Five million, Stuart. Everything legal. We'll be able to do whatever we want."

"You keep the money, Maryse. It's what you deserve."

She tried to put her arms around my neck, but I pushed her away. Maryse turned and rushed back to the chef's rack. There she took the cover from one of the cans. It was nearly overflowing with glinting stones.

"It's all here, Stuart. Sixty million. If you want, we'll keep everything."

"I would've done anything for you. Anything. But not any more. All I want from you is gone!"

I rushed out of her flat.

Unfortunately, Chief Inspector Claude Monet had other plans for me. I met him and his men coming into Mme. Flaubert's rear door, as I was charging out.

"Shots were reported," he declared.

"In her flat," I returned, and tried to push past.

One of his officers grabbed me, and pointed at the bloody hole in my shirt. Monet ripped open the sleeve and smiled as he eyed the wound.

"A bullet-graze, I think," he said. "She tried to kill you, didn't she?"

"Of course not," I snapped.

"Did you kill her?" he demanded.

"Don't be an ass, Monet!"

"Then why are you in such a hurry?" the Chief Inspector shouted.

"Because two of Chiappe's men are in the café with orders to kill me!"

"Tell me the truth for once!" he shouted back. "Admit it. You confronted her with what you knew and she tried to kill you!"

"I'm not protecting her. And for what it's worth, she had no idea what was going to happen to her husband. Remember when you asked me what Molyneux said? I lied. It wasn't gibberish. It was a confession. He told me Baudouin and he had planned it all. That Maryse had nothing to do with it. That it was Reese D'aubigne I saw in Rousseau's apartment. How's that for the truth?"

"You're lying!" he gritted.

"Prove it, Monet. I'll stand up in any court and repeat that until I'm blue in the face."

Chief Inspector Monet ordered his men to take me to Maryse's flat. He followed along, with all the ferocity his rotund figure could express amidst a myriad of curses against my paternity.

When we reached Maryse's door, I pushed it open and stepped inside. The corpses were still there. But Maryse and the diamonds were gone.

"Two more bodies!" Monet bellowed.

I was pushed up against a wall and frisked. When they were satisfied I was not armed, they handcuffed me. As I slumped down on the davenport Monet glared at me.

"Are you Azreael? Are you the Angel of Death?" he demanded, pointing down at the corpses.

"Right. But I've misplaced my wings. Look, Monet. I'm too damn tired to carry the fight any further. Lock me up anywhere you want and toss the key. I've had it."

"What happened here?" he shouted.

"I killed them both," I returned. "My real name is Cock Robin. And I shot Blackbird and Sparrow with my little bow and arrow. Can we go, now? I'm late for my funeral. Françoise Chiappe plans to dump me in the Seine after shooting me in the eye, and he does not like to be kept waiting."

The Chief Inspector frowned. "Why is he going to kill you?"

"He suspects me of groping his wife and painting a bunch of forgeries, among other things."

"You were having an affair with his wife, too?" Monet gasped.

I shrugged. "When in Paris and all that…"

Monet threw his hands up and let go a long, exasperated sigh. "Six murders and you're humping a Mafia Don's wife! Do you know what that is going to look like in my monthly report?"

"Is that all you care about?" I demanded. "Yourself?"

Monet looked around and then slowly shook his head. "Listen, you stupid bastard! Do you know why I did not consider you a suspect in Baudouin Rousseau's murder?"

"You sure as hell did! Your men arrested me!"

He waggled a finger. "But you were no longer a suspect after you told me what you recalled about the bump on your head."

"I didn't recall *anything*."

"Exactly! Had you been lying, you would have told me how painful the blow was that knocked you out. But you told me you did not know what had happened. One moment you were standing. The next you were getting up off the floor. When someone is rendered unconscious by a blow, they never remember it; they never feel it. Never. It is a medical fact. They recall up until the instant before the blow. They can remember everything that occurs after regaining consciousness. But nothing about the injury, itself. Therefore I knew you were telling the truth." His hands went to his big hips and he snorted, "Well, M. Stuart, which of you killed these two? You or her?"

Suddenly I felt like I had stabbed my best friend. Maryse had told me a similar story. One moment she had been trying to convince Dr. Molyneux to take me with them when they left her husband's apartment. The next, she was at her flat with a bump on her head. He had knocked her out. In so doing, she had been unable to help me get out of there. She had told me the truth. About why she had helped with her husband's body. About trying to make Molyneux take me along when they left—all of it. But during that one important time I had failed to believe her.

"Maryse wasn't even here when those two shot it out," I muttered. "I'll swear to that. They were both after me. And I'll swear that Maryse wasn't the getaway car driver in the diamond heist, either. The fifth thief, for your information, was René D'aubigne."

"You fool!" shouted Monet. "Don't you realize Maryse Rousseau lied to you? Admit she did it and I will have her arrested."

"Of course, she lied to me. But that's not a crime. Where I come from it's a preoccupation—at least with the women in my life."

"It looks like they killed each other, Buji," one of this men said. "The guns are in their hands. Both guns were recently fired. All we need is a match on the bullets."

"Get him to a doctor and then lock him up!" ordered Monet, pointing to me. "If they did shoot each other, then I want him and his luggage personally delivered to the airport and put aboard the next flight back to the United States. And if he so much as makes one squawk about it, shoot the bastard!"

"What about Mme. Rousseau?" asked one of the police officers. "Should we bring her in for questioning?"

"What for?" Monet shook a finger at me. "With him lying through his teeth, what chance would I have getting that woman convicted?"

Chapter 13
Finis

In Paris, even the sewers are a tourist trap. In fact, Paris opened its sewers to the public for tourism in 1867. Since then, millions have enjoyed its not-so-sublime atmosphere of unusual sights and familiar smells. There is even a museum dedicated to Parisian sewers. It is called *Musée des égouts de Paris*. It is located in the sewer directly beneath *Quai d'Orsay*. Where else would one expect to find it?

But enough of Parisian life...

It has been six months since I returned home to Minneapolis, Minnesota. You may well ask, did I find inspiration in the city of lights? I did, actually. And since returning to the City of Lakes I cannot create my paintings fast enough for my new following. Why? I would like to claim my talent improved in Paris. But I think the truth is closer to having loved and lost Maryse Rousseau.

I still think about her. I cannot help it. You see I paint her portrait over and over, in a variety of poses—all nude, of course. Well, not all of them. There is one in my flat that offers just her beautiful face. It hangs above the fireplace. As for the nudes—I have painted more than a dozen of her. Each offers all her loveliness, tastefully done of course. Each of them sold for a small fortune—well, several thousand dollars each, anyway. But that is a small fortune for me.

Minneapolis's largest art gallery now offers my paintings. I find that quite interesting. You see, before I went to Paris I approached them with what I had created. They laughed. Then a new owner took over and it is I who is laughing, as the saying goes—all the way to the bank. Should you visit my home city, stop in at *Galleria de Parisian* and take a look. You will not be disappointed. Especially if a painting of Maryse is available. But be prepared to dig deep. The new gallery owner has suggested raising prices because of the great demand for my paintings.

Monetary success, of course, allows me to paint full time. I am not rich. I think in time I shall be. But that is not important. Being able to create my art and have it appreciated, is the real reward.

You are clucking your tongue and calling me a liar. But I swear those words are true. Money is always appreciated, of course. No one likes to work without pay. But I would still paint even if no one was willing to purchase my creations. That is the artist in me.

I had a dream about Maryse, last night. When I awoke from it, I sat on the edge of my bed and cried. I cannot help but wonder if I had gone with her to Nice, when she begged me to, if I would be sharing my life with her?

Many times I have been tempted to write Maryse. To apologize for not believing what she had told me in those last minutes together. Not that I have forgotten her lies. My heart still aches over them because they were unnecessary. I would have done anything she asked. But lies or not, it is a moot point. We are a thousand miles apart and I have no idea what her address is, so we will never see each other again.

Even my magic-nightstick is heartsick. He refuses to consider another woman. He just hangs there, limp. No waving. No jumping up and down. No winking. He is just limp, like he is waiting to be choked. I purchased a couple of naughty magazines last night, hoping they might bring him to life. No such luck.

You are probably wondering about what happened to some of the others, after I left Paris…

My uncle is still in Siberia. He says he is going to change his name to Popovitch and build a villa on the Black Sea. He hates it in Siberia. The winters are far too cold. But he will have to remain there for some time to come. You see, a certain Corsican Mafioso who shall remain nameless —François Chiappe—has taken residence in my uncle's Sao Paolo villa. Since it was my uncle who supplied Cesar Avoyelles with the forgeries sold to Mme. Chiappe, the Mafia Don thinks my uncle's villa is fair compensation for his loss. My uncle does not agree, of course. But he prefers to lose the villa to Chiappe rather than his head.

Cesar Avoyelles left Paris. Rumor has it he went to Germany. But— and you must promise to keep this a secret—he is alive and well not too many miles from where you are standing. Yes, if you guessed that he owns *Galleria de Parisian*, you would be quite right. He, of course, had to change his name. Unfortunately, he has not completely changed his habits. So if you hear of a newly discovered Matisse done in Pointillism being offered at auction, do not bid on it.

Chief Inspector Monet has written to me several times. It is not out of friendship. Each letter seeks reassurance. He wants to be certain I shall never darken his door again. Each time, I reply to the effect that nothing would get me back to Paris as long as he is alive.

M. Arceneau is married. He and Mme. Jenay Simon tied the knot a few weeks ago. Unfortunately, they honeymooned on the *Isle du Levante*.

Between his marital duties to a woman who has not enjoyed sex for nearly twenty years, and the island's nudist lifestyle, M. Arceneau was hospitalized for exhaustion after only a few days. He assures me there is no permanent damage—at least to his heart. He is not as optimistic concerning other areas of his body. But I suspect he will recover completely once he gets back to his vineyard.

Mme. Flaubert continues her pursuit of life, love and being France's only culinary Quasimodo. I do not miss her cooking. But I have other good memories concerning her establishment. The latest gossip there, as you might imagine, continues to be about her. Apparently she now has three young men sharing her expansive quarters. Yes, I said three.

Did you get that the first time around? If not, think about it some more. It will come to you.

You have probably noticed the craft show on the sidewalk. I, as an artist of small but growing repute, felt an obligation to attend the annual West Lake Street Art Fair. No. That is not me. Not the bearded bumpkin sitting in front of a sketchpad drawing naughty cartoons. No. You're turning your head in the wrong direction! I am over here. No the other over here. Well, you are getting warmer. Try to focus. I am the one wearing the black Beret, the striped t-shirt, the black slacks and the black sandals—no socks. No, not the Mime! He's an idiot. I'm the other idiot. Yes. That's me. The thin one with the big nose, shaggy hair, scruffy beard and no grease-paint. You looked right past me! Not him, either. He sells used cars. There! See? I am waving at you. Yes. That's me, in front of the Eiffel Tower kiosk. Come over and take a look at my creations.

I don't expect to sell any paintings at this exhibit. My prices are far too high. But I hope the latest one of Maryse Rousseau—the reclining nude you are drooling over—will expose my qualities as an artist to those who stop to admire. It certainly exposes her.

"You don't think that's obscene?"

Those words were uttered in French by a young woman with a Parisian accent. Excuse me. I have to deal with yet another critic. Doubtlessly some foreign religious fanatic with connections to the Pope, or so she will claim.

"I don't deal in obscenities, Madam," I declared, as I approached her. "I'm certain if you brought over your husband he would explain that to you."

The complainer is about five foot four. She is wearing a short leather skirt, a silk blouse thin enough to serve as a window screen with nothing underneath, and knee-high, black leather boots. Over her long dark hair is a gold scarf. Concealing much of her finely chiseled face is a pair of wraparound sunglasses.

"I am a widow," she said, still moving her eyes from painting to painting.

"Many condolences, Madam," I returned.

She is obviously a blue nose type. You will find them everywhere—particularly in the Midwest and South. They go around pointing fingers and complaining, when they should be home with their family—making those lives miserable. Well, maybe she did that already considering her husband is dead.

"Might I suggest you move on to the next artist?" I told her. "She offers disgustingly sweet portraits of puppies being cuddled by babies. I am sure you will find those far more in line with your anal-retentive views."

Her hands went akimbo at her hips. "It is more than obscene," she declared. "It is pornographic! Have you no shame?"

Despite her infantile and myopic views on art, I did enjoy listening to her deliciously sultry voice uttering perfect Parisian French. "I also do not deal in pornography, Madam. But if you are searching for some, the fellow doing the cartoons will happily oblige. Just raise your skirt and let him emblazon what God gave you on paper. In your case, he will probably do it for free."

"You should be arrested."

I rolled my eyes despairingly. Why are some women so prissy? Does she really think she will have any impact upon me? I admit she is having a strangely revitalizing effect on my magic-nightstick. It is as if he has come into contact with her before. But I chalk that up to a lack of sexual activity coupled with a profile view of her dairy-sized bust-line and blissfully contoured backside. Once she moves on, nightstick and I will revert to our morose, monkish personalities. My God, look! She's bending over. I swear to God it is a religious experience!

"Most of what I see here is the work of someone quite gifted," she remarked. "All but that one painting. It was clearly done by a sexual degenerate."

"Is the offending painting the Eiffel tower Suicide, Madam?" I choked, as my eyes studied her taunting derriere. She did not seem to look at any painting in particular, but the pose was hypnotizing. "The Moline Rouge Pickpocket? Or the menu from Mme. Flaubert's Boarding

House? From personal experience, the Menu is definitely pornographic to the palate. But it hardly qualifies otherwise."

"The reclining nude, of course," she returned, straightening upright.

I offered her my most patronizing albeit lusting smile and bowed slightly. "That, Madam, is not for sale to you—at any price."

"Then why is it here?" she asked, again bending over to examine my paintings.

My God! It's déjà vu! I'm back in Maryse's flat watching her bend over to pick up her clothes after crawling out of bed! Everything that woman has is so round, so firm, so fully packed! My magic-nightstick is not only waving and bobbing, it is screaming to be set free! Christ, if she does not leave at once I'll be arrested for doing something I will remember and cherish the rest of my life in prison!

"I'm afraid I must ask you to leave, Madam," I whimpered, trying to cross my legs. "You are having an unwelcome affect on—on something very dear to my heart."

She made a slightly disgusted sound. "The least you could have done is used a beautiful woman as your model, for the nude."

"Are you blind?" I shouted, pointing at the portrait. "She is the most beautiful woman in the world! Look at her perfectly formed breasts. They're—they're almost as perfect as yours. And look at her delicately chiseled face. Then there's her figure. How can you claim it is not flawless? Well, maybe not as perfect as yours. But if you are still unconvinced, take a gander at her derriere! Isn't it the most magnificent thing ever sent from heaven—yours excluded, of course? Madam, if you had any appreciation for true art you would realize that any man would die smiling for the love of Maryse Rousseau!"

The woman pulled off her scarf and sunglasses. Then she turned and smiled at me. "Would you really die for me, Stuart?"

My hand went to my chest as a gripping pain started. "Dear God!"

My breathing started rasping and then my knees buckled. If I had not been near the kiosk and grabbed hold of it for support, I would have landed on the sidewalk face down - doing irreparable harm to my magic-nightstick.

"Maryse?" I choked.

She shrugged. "Who else?"

"What—what in hell are you doing here?" I stammered.

"Why would I come all this way, if not for you? " She made a disgusted face. "Certainly not the food. American cuisine is revolting."

I shook my head, still convinced I was hallucinating. But my magic-nightstick was now trying to batter his way past my zipper.

"I—I—I…" I stammered.

She came over to me, stretched up and lightly kissed my lips. "You've had six months to consider your future. I think it's time you made a decision. Don't you?"

"Monet told you where I was?"

"Of course. But only on the condition that I never bring you back to Paris. For some reason he claims you're cursed. It's ridiculous, I know. But he actually thinks if you return to France the murder rate will quadruple."

"I, uh… You… He's…"

"Stuart, no matter what you say I'm not going back without the man I love. So if you will not return to France with me, I shall be forced to remain here and haunt you day—and night."

"Night?" I gulped.

Maryse wrapped her arms around my waist and pressed her pelvis firmly against me. "Especially at night, Stuart; all night; every night. I promise, you won't get any sleep."

"I'm pretty sure something's going to keep me up tonight."

She smiled and ground against me. "I guarantee it."

"Maryse, you don't love me. You can have any man you want. Why torture me?"

"What do you mean I don't love you? Because of what René said? I've done things for you I would not have done for my husband."

I shook a finger at her. "That kinky stuff was your idea—not that I didn't enjoy it."

"I meant when I helped Michele with Baudouin's body. I thought it was the only way I could protect you."

"I believe you about that. But…"

"I've loved you from the first time I saw you, Stuart."

"That was just my red Speedo—with its mind-controlled distender."

She winked. "I admit, that helped. But it wasn't the only reason. We are soul mates, you and I. There is no escaping our destiny."

I gulped, "I don't have a red Speedo, anymore."

"Of course you do," Maryse returned. "I bought one for you before driving over here. I packed it in your suitcase."

"This… You… It doesn't matter," I stammered. "I'm—I'm over you, sort of, maybe, sometimes—at least I was."

Her hands drift down to squeeze my buttocks. "But I am not over you."

"Maryse, I can't go through that pain again. I don't think my heart can take another two weeks with you. I know my ass can't. You should see the scar."

"I intend to." She slipped her arms about my neck. "I promise to take very good care of everything you've got. Front. Back. Everything in between. Especially your heart." Then her mouth went to mine and her tongue slipped between my lips. After a moment she tilted back and looked down. "From the stiff way you are standing, this is going to be easier than I thought."

"I can't think when you do that," I protested. "My brain goes to sleep. My magic-nightstick takes over. He's already asking for an aisle seat on the plane."

She frowned. "Magic nightstick?"

I made an embarrassed movement, with one hand. "It's that guy thing."

She laughed. "I'll take very good care of him, too."

I flinched, backing from her embrace. "I'm settled, now. I have a following for my art."

"Then we will build upon that," she returned. "In Paris. We have a beautiful cottage on the outskirts. It has a lovely garden of yellow and pink roses. There is a huge studio behind our house where you and I will create our art. We have enough money to satisfy our needs and caprices. What else could you want from life—besides what I am offering?"

I tried to say no. But my magic-nightstick had batted the word from my vocabulary. "If I do this, we have to get something straight between us."

She wrapped her arms about my waist and pressed her pelvis against mine, again. "Trust me, Stuart. Everyone can see it already is."

"No. I mean… You and me… You see…"

"Has there been another woman since me?" She tilted her head back and gave me a pouting look.

"Of course not. Neither he nor I have had any inclinations—until now."

Maryse pulled me tighter, her body molding against mine. "Then what are we waiting for?"

I nodded, knowing I would capitulate no matter what. "Can I ask you something before I—we—you—passport—Paris?"

"There has been no one since you, Stuart."

"I'm pleased to hear that—more than you'll ever know. But I have some other questions. One, in particular, regarding Mme. Cossette Fortescue."

She frowned. "You can't mean you've been fantasizing about that disgusting creature?"

"Dear God, no! But it's been driving me crazy. The woman hated me right from the beginning. Do you have any idea why?"

"Of course. She was Michele's Molyneux's stepsister. He'd told her his concerns over you winning my heart. She, being very greedy, was worried you might put an end to her financial dreams. That, of course, made her very upset and she tried to get you out of the way."

"Ah, I remember her mentioning a brother who was a physician. But how could I ruin her financial dreams?"

"She was to share in what Michele realized from the sale of the diamonds. He and I were to split the bundle. It was she who stole the Van Gogh. She saw you leave Michele's flat and went in to search it. She was arrested when she tried to sell the painting."

"I suppose that's some satisfaction."

"Any other questions?"

"Why did Chiappe hang René's wife—Reese—in my studio?"

"He didn't. It was René. He knew she had betrayed him and the other to Chiappe. He also knew that you had taken the studio he used to rent from Cesar. So when he caught up with Reese, he dragged her to the studio. He still had a key for the doors. And he killed her there thinking you would be blamed."

"But I heard René confirm that you had told Chiappe about the Van Gogh?"

"No. He said Maryse had told Chiappe—Maryse his wife."

"I'm sorry. I should have known better than to think you who have told Chiappe about the Van Gogh."

"Stuart, how could I? Think back carefully. All you told me was you had the painting and I was to skedaddle; remember?"

I replayed the scene in my head. She was absolutely correct. I had not mentioned my expectations concerning what lay beneath the tempera, at all.

"You did lie to me about the diamonds. And you lied to me about your divorce and your driving. If your husband had not been dying, he would never have wanted free of you, would he?"

She slowly shook her head. "But he was dying. And he knew if he did not protect my future no one would. I am very sorry about misleading you. But I had taken vows with my husband. I had to honor his name and his wishes."

I hesitated, as my nightstick pounded away trying to get free. "I don't suppose your offer includes making an honest man of me?"

"Honest? I hope not. You would stand out like a sore thumb in France. But I think we should marry as soon as we get home." She checked her watch. "Come. Let's take your paintings and go. I think they will sell very well in Paris. Well, all but the nude. We will keep that in our bedroom for when I get old and you need reminding about what you are supposed to do, on Saturday nights." She grabbed up the nude and then looked over at me. "I saw the painting of me in your flat. It was excellent. I shipped it to my mother. You have not painted any other nudes of me, have you?"

"Of—of—of course not."

I do not care what you say about honesty in a relationship, after what I've been through, I am entitled to another little lie.

"Our flight to Paris leaves in less than one hour," she said, snatching up several more paintings. "You grab the rest. Your passport is in my purse. I've purchased our tickets and given notice to your landlord. I also packed your bags and sent them on ahead—all except the disgusting magazines you had under your bed. You won't need those, any more."

I frowned, amazed at how quickly she had taken control of my life. "Weren't you taking a lot for granted?"

Her head wagged. "I knew all I had to do was bend over, and you would do anything I asked. Don't you remember me doing that when you were painting on your uncle's patio? I quickly noticed how that always put your Speedo into expansion mode."

"That's because you always wore a short skirt and little lace panties."

"You'd never talked to me. How else I was I going to get you interested?"

"Of course I didn't talk. I didn't know what to say. I was transfixed after the first time you bent down."

"I think we should honeymoon on *Isle du Levante*. What do you think?"

"I'd better see if there are any hospital-room vacancies, first."

"Why?"

"A recommendation by M. Arceneau."

She laughed. "I heard he'd gotten married."

You are probably thinking Maryse is the biggest mistake I could make. I admit she can easily sway my judgment—and everything else. I admit a man like me is forever going to be asked how I latched onto someone who looks as beautiful as her. But I cannot help myself. When it comes to Maryse Rousseau, I am weak. You see, she is and always will be my fantasy.

"Uh, Maryse… You did return the diamonds, didn't you?"

She winked. "Of course I did."

Stop saying that. Maryse and I both agreed to start fresh. I know I made a small lie. But that does not mean she just lied to me about the diamonds. Besides, what could she possibly do with sixty million Euros worth of them? Never mind. What a stupid question!

The End

www.ingramcontent.com/pod-product-compliance
Lightning Source LLC
Chambersburg PA
CBHW070121260626
47160CB00004B/1567